The Sugar Rebellion

Lyle Garford

The Sugar Rebellion

Except where actual historical events and characters are being described for the storyline of this novel, all situations in this publication are fictitious and any resemblance to living persons is purely coincidental.

Copyright © 2018 by Lyle Garford

All rights reserved. No part of this book may be reproduced or transmitted in any form or by any means, electronic or mechanical, including photocopying, recording, or by an information storage and retrieval system, without permission in writing from the publisher.

Published by:
Lyle Garford
Vancouver, Canada
Contact: lyle@lylegarford.com

ISBN 978-0-9952078-4-4

Cover photo by PHB.cz (Richard Semik)/Shutterstock.com

Book Design by Lyle Garford
www.lylegarford.com

First Edition 2018
Printed by Createspace, an Amazon.com Company.
Available on Kindle and other devices.

The Sugar Rebellion

Dedication

This one is for
Graham and Kellee

The Sugar Rebellion

Chapter One
March 1795
Grenada

The tension and energy in the air was tangible, a physical presence he felt he could reach out and grasp with his hand. Fedon sensed it as he came in, walking to the front of the room and stopping to face the waiting crowd. Two white men followed him in, but they turned away to stand off to the side with their backs to the wall in a deliberate effort to gain distance from the others. The waiting people ignored them and all eyes turned to Fedon in anticipation. The buzz of conversation filling the air dwindled to silence as he held up a hand and they waited for him to speak.

As the growing anger and frustration of the people slowly turned from mere talk to active thoughts and plans to act, everyone knew Julien Fedon was the man to lead them in the coming rebellion. The son of a white French father and a black, former slave mother, Julien was a well-built, handsome man with dark, curly hair flowing to his shoulders and light coffee colored skin. This made him part of a large and growing population throughout the Caribbean of mixed race people known as mulattos. Now in his early thirties, he already had the leadership experience of running his own coffee plantation with over one hundred slaves to work it. His natural charm and respectful manner in dealing with people combined to give him a presence people deferred to whenever he came into a room. Fedon radiated strength and could dominate any conversation if he chose to.

For many years now those conversations were about rebellion and the desire to gain a share of the enormous wealth to be had from the plantations of the Caribbean. The vast majority were sugar plantations, but several owners like Fedon were growing other crops such as coffee. The plantation owners and people with French roots on the island of Grenada began to seethe with slow, growing unrest from the moment the island was restored to British rule. The signing of the 1783 Treaty of Versailles returned it to the British when hostilities finally ended in the American War of Independence. Although safeguards to the rights of the French settlers remaining on the island were built into the Treaty, in practice they were worth little.

Roughly half of the plantation and business owners on the island were of French origin and a large proportion of these were mulattos like Fedon. Efforts to have their interests and concerns addressed by British politicians on the island were rebuffed at every turn. Many mulattos also retained their belief and ties to the Catholic faith. Ninian Home, the current Governor of the island, was a tyrant as far as the mulatto population was concerned. On taking office he shifted official policy of the British administration from one of passive acceptance of Catholics on the island to active disapproval and periodic, outright persecution.

The Governor also owned the largest number of

The Sugar Rebellion

slaves on Grenada and was well known for his paternalistic, strict treatment of slaves as little better than simple children. The entire slave population of the island knew who he was and loathed him. Grenada was a seething, bubbling pot of anger and frustration ready to boil over.

The real spur to action instilling hope a rebellion could succeed, however, was the 1789 French Revolution and its Caribbean offspring, the 1791 slave revolution in the French colony of St. Domingue. Everyone in the room was inspired by it and had worked hard ever since to find a way to make it happen on Grenada, too. Fedon took a deep breath, savoring the sensation of their collective efforts and dreams coalescing into this culminating moment. He spread his arms wide for a moment before he spoke.

"My friends. My brothers and sisters. Citizens! The time to prepare is over and it is finally time to act. We have suffered British persecution in silence for far too many years."

He paused a moment to scan the faces around him for emphasis before he bellowed out a question.

"So are we ready?"

The crowd roared with inarticulate fervor. Several people raised fists in joyous defiance. Their eyes gleamed in the light of the lanterns and candles about the room. Fedon saw some were moved enough tears were streaming down their faces.

The crowd was a curious mix of people. Most were in their late twenties or early thirties like Fedon, but all ages were represented. A small group of mulatto women was present and a few white

The Sugar Rebellion

faces were sprinkled throughout the crowd. The majority were mulatto men and this was the key group Fedon focused his attention on, for they were the backbone of the leadership cadre supporting him. Each had personal grievances with the British.

Two of his senior commanders stepped forward at the same time to speak. One was Jules Besson, a huge man with a hard face. The other was Jean La Valette, smaller with a lean, wiry frame, but an equally determined air about him. La Valette deferred to Besson.

"Julien, our people are as ready as they will ever be. Give us the signal and unleash us."

"I shall. The time has come to follow our brothers in St. Domingue and bring revolution to our island too! We must seek to be citizens of our own republic and rule ourselves. Freedom from British oppression and freedom for all people of color, like St. Domingue! Yes, we shall be citizens. Think of the meaning of the word! But before we begin, you must know I bring good news that I believe is an omen of future success."

Fedon smiled at the hopeful looks appearing on their faces and he waved a hand in the direction of the two white men who had followed him into the room.

"You all know we have been planning for this night for a long, long time. How incredible is it then that on this particular night word has come from our friends here that the tyrant Ninian Home has left his fortress in St George's and could be within our reach?"

Fedon laughed to see the ferocious looks

appear on the faces of his men. Several clamored for more details and begged to be chosen to hunt him down. Even with Fedon gesturing with both hands palm down for calm to allow him to resume, it took almost a full minute for the excited buzz of talk to subside.

"Yes, my friends. Our Governor has conveniently left the safety of Fort George and gone to the other side of the island. I have no idea why and I don't care, I just think it is a sign heaven is with us this night. My friend Besson, I know you want the honor of capturing him, but you are needed to lead the men as planned in Gouyave. My friend La Valette, we will detach you and a small party of your men to see to the task, for the Governor has gone to Grenville. We will have to make adjustments, but I have some ideas and the time is now to strike. I am sure your junior commanders will be capable of dealing with the town of Grenville itself as we had planned you would do."

"Julien?" said La Valette. "What are your orders for him? Please, tell me we can just cut his head off and put it on display here at Belvedere for all to see?"

Fedon grimaced in response. "As much as I would love to see his head on a picket at my estate, I very much desire you to capture him. We have discussed the issue of prisoners before, my friends, and you know we may need something to bargain with. The British will not capitulate easily."

"Julien," said Besson. "We know this and yes, we have had this conversation before. The problem is this has become like a hurricane that may be

The Sugar Rebellion

impossible to avoid. The people's anger is a wild animal. We can talk all we want about taking prisoners, but there is going to be much blood shed before this night is out."

"I know. Much blood was shed in St. Domingue and I expect in the end the outcome will be no different here. At a minimum I ask wherever possible we capture the British aristocrat owners and especially their families. Anyone with any importance will be valuable, especially Governor Home. I promise you can beat him to the point where one more blow would end his life, but we need him alive. Beyond this, I would ask we all try to spare lives where we can, especially innocent ones. We have no need to kill women and children or men who willingly surrender to us."

Fedon paused to give them chance to speak, but none did. "Very well, let us make adjustments to our plans. I want everything in motion within the hour."

Julien's brother Jean stepped forward and the two men embraced each other with hard affection.

"Julien. My wonderful brother. We know you will lead us to success!"

Turning to face the crowd, Jean grasped his brother's hand and lifted it into the air to the raucous cheers of the others. Taking this as a sign the time for speeches was over the babble of several excited conversations burst out. Fedon looked over at the two white men standing impassively against the wall and smiled before turning away and moving to join his lieutenants. One of the white men nodded acknowledgement to Fedon before looking to the

man beside him. He signaled it was time to leave with a jerk of his thumb toward the door and they left unnoticed by the rest of the crowd.
***

The sleepy guard standing watch at the entrance to the military barracks in the coastal town of Gouyave looked bored. The men watching him standing slumped against the wall of the building knew he likely had an almost overpowering desire to let himself slide down the wall and sit with his back to it. The guard's problem was if he succumbed and his Sergeant caught him sitting down or worse, asleep on duty, he would find himself tied to a post and his back would feel the harsh sting of multiple lashes from a whip. As the guard yawned and shuffled to change his position and stay awake, a distant pounding of drums began.

The guard gave a start and took a few steps away from the wall to look for the source, but the brief burst of drumming ended within seconds. Despite this the man had identified the drumming came from the distant darkness of the island's interior and he remained peering that direction, but the drums didn't resume. The night sky was overcast with light clouds, making it difficult to see in what little moonlight was available.

Everyone was aware slaves used drums to communicate over long distances, but there had been minimal recent activity and the rebels were careful in the days leading to this night to give no indication of more than normal unrest in the slave population of the island. After a few more long moments to be certain the guard shrugged and

The Sugar Rebellion

turned to go back to his post, only to have the dark shape of a man loom in front of him. The guard tried to back away as the man was not alone and he opened his mouth to shout a warning, but a strong hand clamped his mouth shut and a knife was driven deep into his back. The killer cut the guard's throat after withdrawing the knife to be sure of his work.

Besson smiled in the darkness, knowing he had taken the guard in complete silence and his victims within remained unaware. The drums were the signal to begin and the thought blows for freedom were being struck all over the island made him grin even more. He turned to find his junior commander and some of his men had crept up in silence to stand beside him.

"What fools they are," said Besson. "The only other entrance to this building is in the rear and it is both locked and unguarded. Take your men and cut them down if they try using it to escape. The windows are too small for any of them to get out that way, but they will be useful for our purpose. I will give you a few moments to get your men in place and then we begin."

As they left Besson turned to another who had remained behind. "Bring the torches."

Within moments a burning torch was brought forward, producing a flickering, garish light that reflected off the dark pool of blood drained from the dead guard. Several other torches were soon lit and Besson signaled for the men to begin. The small, high windows lining the wall of the barracks were smashed in almost as one and a flaming torch was

The Sugar Rebellion

flung into each. From inside the barracks initial cries of surprise and alarm from the sleeping men turned into jumbled, inarticulate screams, rendering shouted orders from their officers unintelligible. Watching the windows, Besson was gratified to see the torches were doing their work. Bright flames could already be seen flickering inside and, as he watched, long tongues of fire came licking out of the windows as it took hold, fed by the steady flow of air through the smashed windows.

Within moments the first of the soldiers struggling to escape the flames burst through the door. As he did a wickedly sharp machete dropped him in his tracks, striking him so hard his head was almost severed from his shoulders. Four more men were dead before the remainder in the barracks realized what was happening. A brief pause ensued before three men with swords at the ready tried bursting through the door at the same time. Besson had anticipated this and his strategy to counter it was to meet their desperate charge with a forest of makeshift spears made for this purpose. The doorway was soon blocked with a pile of bodies. Screams of burning men and the stench of burnt flesh filled the night air.

Besson smiled. Unlike Julien Fedon, he had no qualms about killing the British and he didn't care if a few innocent victims were numbered among the dead. As he stood watching the growing flames his second in command appeared at his elbow to report.

"They tried using the rear entrance, but we got every one of them. The rest inside are finished. Can we proceed to deal with the rest of the town?"

The Sugar Rebellion

Besson turned to look behind him at the town and saw it was no longer in darkness. Several lights were visible to show the alarm was raised, but the attack had come fast and he knew confusion likely reigned.

"Of course. There is no rush now. They have no soldiers to protect them. They probably still don't even realize what is happening yet. Our only opposition now will be plantation overseers if any happen to be in town, and we have enough men they won't be a problem. You may begin. And Marcel? Remember to save a few for Julien."

The man laughed, knowing his commander was joking.

***

Julien had left the town of La Baye for another of his mulatto senior commanders to take. Like Fedon, Etienne Ventour owned various properties throughout the island, but only half the number of slaves of his commander. Despite his experience in giving orders and commanding men, the situation in La Baye was on the verge of chaos. People seeking orders were tearing Ventour in multiple directions.

Several English plantation overseers were mounting a spirited, desperate counterattack on his forces, disrupting all of the careful planning. The attack was being beaten back with big losses on both sides, but Ventour knew he could afford them far more than the English. With the defeat of their resistance almost assured Ventour's men were now on a rampage through the town. Plantation owners were being dragged into the streets and beaten to death in front of their families. In the distance he

The Sugar Rebellion

could hear the faint screams of women and children.

Ventour was grateful a few of his senior men were still with him. He ordered them to band together everyone they could find that hadn't completely lost all control and to bring the others to heel by force if necessary. As the men about him dispersed to their tasks he felt a tug on his arm. Turning, he found his mulatto sister Sophie Ventour standing beside him. Her light brown skinned, attractive face wore a desperate, anguished look.

"Etienne, my God, you must come at once!"

"Sophie, what are you doing here? You were supposed to stay behind our lines and come out only when we established control. This is not safe!"

"It doesn't matter, Etienne. You must come and stop them now. They are attacking French people!"

"What? Oh, my God! Where?"

"Follow me!" She pointed and began running down the street before he had a chance to hold her back.

Groaning, Ventour signaled for three of his men to follow him and he went after her. As they ran down the main street lit by the roaring flames of a fire started in one of the big mansions he saw it's owner and his men with their backs to the fire struggling to break free, but fighting a losing battle with his forces. The owner's wife and children huddled in a piteous group behind them. Everywhere he looked there were small knots of men struggling. Several unmoving bodies lay strewn on the ground where they had been cut down. But at least some of his men were obeying orders, pushing groups of frightened prisoners back

The Sugar Rebellion

down the street toward their temporary headquarters. His sister kept going past all of this. Ventour was angry, knowing she had strayed far from where she was supposed to remain.

She finally stopped and pointed at another mansion at the far end of the street, where the scene greeting him was appalling. A small group of his men were on the verandah of the mansion taking turns holding and punching two white men, one older and one much younger. Blood streamed down their faces and both were barely conscious, still standing only because their captors kept them this way.

As Ventour came closer he saw another larger group of his men clustered inside the front entrance. All of them appeared intent on watching whatever was going on inside. Sophie clutched at his arm as he finally caught up with her.

"Etienne, these men are French owners! These madmen have no idea what they are doing. We must make them stop!"

Ventour recognized the older man and knew she was right. A blazing anger filled him as he strode forward and shoved one of the two black men about to strike the prisoners to the side.

"Stop what you are doing, you fools! These men are friends."

The man he shoved recovered fast and shoved Ventour in return. "Who are you to stop us? Go away or we will beat you too!"

Ventour responded with a crushing punch to the face of the man, who fell to the ground and did not get up. Pulling out his sword, Ventour pointed it

The Sugar Rebellion

at the remaining men.

"You idiots. Who am I, he says? I am your commander and if you don't release these men now I will carve all of you into scraps of meat for the dogs!"

The remaining three men in the group let the prisoners drop to the ground without a word and stepped back, sullen looks on their faces. The older prisoner moaned in pain while the other lay comatose where he fell. Ventour stooped to touch the shoulder of the older man, but once again he felt his sister tug at his arm.

"Etienne! My God, they need your help inside too!"

Ventour whipped his head about to look at the doorway and for the first time realized there were screams of pain and terror coming from inside the mansion. Ventour groaned, knowing what he would find, for the people screaming were women. The dark anger that had begun to subside flared within him once again.

Two men staring at the scene inside blocked the doorway. Ventour shouldered his way past them and stepped inside, followed close by the three men who had come with him. One of the men Ventour had shoved was angered and made to retaliate, but was felled by crushing blows from clubs wielded by Ventour's followers.

Ventour was appalled at the scene before him, finding his worst fears realized. The owner's wife and two younger women, presumably his daughters, were all being brutally raped. Five other black men were watching the scene, waiting their turn.

The Sugar Rebellion

Ventour waved his sword and scowled at the watching men before reaching down to grab one of the rapists by his hair. The man screamed as he was dragged off the woman. Once the man was free of his victim Ventour let go. The man turned to look at Ventour, an equal mixture of anger and puzzlement written on his face. Ventour let every ounce of his frustration vent as he kicked him hard in the groin. His victim howled in pain as he crashed to the ground.

The men with Ventour had already taken their cue and pulled the other two rapists off their victims as well. The remaining attackers were furious and shouting abuse at Ventour, but they made no move to stop him.

Ventour roared out his own anger and waved his sword in all directions once again.

"Silence!"

With murderous looks they all finally complied, but the tension in the air was palpable. All of them were clutching the clubs and knives they carried hard. Ventour knew they would not hesitate to use them, but he didn't care.

"You stupid fools. These people are French! They are friends!"

One of the two rapists pulled off the other women stepped forward. He was big, with muscles hardened from years of brutal slave labor rippling as he moved. His rage was clear as he stuck his face bare inches from Ventour.

"I should kill you for that. Who do you think you are?"

"I am in charge here, asshole," said Ventour,

The Sugar Rebellion

not giving any ground and bringing his sword point to the man's face. "And as your commander, I'm the one that can order you killed. So back away. Now."

The man scowled and remained where he was for a long moment before finally taking one step back. But he still wasn't cowed.

"What is the problem? We were only doing what is right. We are the victors, we have the right to do as we please."

"You are an imbecile! These people are French. They are friends and were not to be harmed."

The man snorted. "They are whites. Who cares whether they are English or French? The whites are all the same. They all keep us in chains of slavery."

"The French are supporting us. Listen to me, all of you idiots! They may be slave owners now, but they want a better future for everyone. Freedom and liberty for all! I am not going to argue this with any of you. If I catch any of you hurting our friends again you will hang. Is that clear? Now report to your leaders for orders and get out of my sight, all of you."

Several of the men remained looking sullen, but after another long moment they slowly began to comply. Within seconds the only people remaining in the room were Ventour and the three victims. Two were curled into unmoving balls of pain where they lay while the third had managed to sit up, lying slumped against the wall. She clutched at the rags of her torn dress to cover herself.

Sophie slipped into the room and came to stand beside her brother, tears streaming down her face. Ventour slipped an arm around her shoulders as she

The Sugar Rebellion

shuddered and spoke to him.

"Thank you for coming, Etienne. I just wish we could have gotten here sooner."

"I wish that too. We must do a better job of teaching and controlling this ragtag army we have raised. Sophie, you took a bad risk not following orders. We will speak of this again, later. I am needed elsewhere. I will post a guard to ensure nothing else happens. Do what you can for them."

***

Fedon was weary from lack of rest, but even if he had found time to try he knew sleep would not have come. A steady flow of reports came in from his field commanders around the island. He had remained at Belvedere, his estate located in the rough and mountainous geographic center of the island. Being roughly equidistant to anywhere on the island, it was a natural and logical headquarters. The estate was also a convenient place to keep a small force in reserve, as reinforcements could be sent as fast as possible to bolster his men wherever necessary should they encounter stiff resistance.

They were not needed. Instead, they found themselves serving as jailers to a small, but growing stream of prisoners. By the time dawn broke Fedon had a squalling, disheveled crowd of forty men, women, and children locked in a large, unused storehouse on his estate. He had hoped for more. None had come from Gouyave and he wasn't surprised, as Besson's cruel streak was well known. Most of the prisoners had come from areas his friend Ventour and his brother Jean Fedon had led their forces to.

The Sugar Rebellion

The one remaining town he had received no reports from was Grenville, on the windward side of the island. By itself Grenville was no more important a target than anywhere else, but the fact Ninian Home travelled there the day before for whatever reason changed everything. Fedon was desperate for La Valette to capture him, knowing his value and that the success of the entire rebellion could depend on it. The lack of news ate at him, but enough reports on the situation elsewhere had finally arrived and Fedon knew he no longer needed to be concerned about other towns. Striding out of his mansion he signaled to a group of his men and their commander standing ready and waiting for orders.

"Louis, half of your men will remain here with you. You are in charge until I return. The rest of them are with me. We need to find out what is going on in Grenville. Let's go."

***

They rode into Grenville an hour later. Despite it being straight downhill from Belvedere to the coast they pushed the horses hard, leaving them lathered with sweat. Fedon slowed them as they rode into the outskirts of the town and he sighed as he took in the destruction greeting them.

Grenville was a massacre. Dead bodies were strewn all over the streets. The stench was already bad and would soon be worse as the sun climbed higher in the sky. Buildings were vandalized everywhere he looked. They saw no living beings anywhere until they got further into the center of the town, where they found several men milling about.

The Sugar Rebellion

In the main square several bodies were hanging from the limbs of a large tree. All were gently swinging back and forth in a strong breeze coming from the ocean. The breeze was welcome as it wafted away the reek from a large number of dead men still lying where they had fallen.

Fedon sighed and dismounted. He looked about in vain for the junior lieutenants they had designated to lead the men for the Grenville attack. He recognized none of the waiting men who were all staring at him. None of them spoke.

"Well?" said Fedon, an exasperated tone in his voice. "I am Julien Fedon. Who is in charge here?"

Once again the men all looked at each other until one finally shrugged and stepped forward.

"I am Joseph. I am not one of your leaders. All except one were killed in the fight for this town. There were soldiers here who put up a strong fight. They made a stand over there, but we overcame them all."

Fedon looked where the man pointed and saw a mansion further down the street. Fedon realized at once an even larger pile of dead bodies was strewn haphazardly about the front verandah of the mansion. He turned back to the man.

"You say there is one leader left. Who is he and where did he go?"

The man pointed further down another street at the ocean shimmering in the distant sunshine, where Fedon knew the town docks were located.

"His name is La Valette. The old white man the soldiers were defending tried escaping by boat and he went after them. He has not come back."

The Sugar Rebellion

Fedon sucked in his breath in dismay. He saw the men awaiting orders and knew he had to keep them occupied. He looked back at the man who had spoke up.

"I will go find out what is happening. For now, I want you in temporary charge of these men. Get them organized and lets start cleaning this up. We don't have time to dig separate graves because of the heat, so have them dig a big grave in the local cemetery and put all of these dead people in it as soon as possible."

Fedon turned to the men who had come with him to Grenville. "Follow me."

As he strode onto the main dock of the town minutes later Fedon scanned the horizon for signs of activity. One of the men with him cried out and pointed to the distant southern horizon not far out from the shoreline of the island. A smudge of white patches that could only be the sails of more than one ship was visible, but it was impossible to make out any details. Worse, Fedon couldn't tell whether they were sailing further away or returning to Grenville, leaving his only option to watch and wait. Knowing it would take time he ordered some of his men to find water and food while the rest settled down for the wait.

As the men were leaving the dock two white men rode up on horses and dismounted. The four heavily armed black men with them remained where they were. Fedon recognized the two whites as they walked toward him. The three men shook hands as Fedon greeted them.

"Montdenoix, I wondered what had happened

The Sugar Rebellion

to the two of you," said Fedon.

One of the white men, stocky and muscular and with an air of command about him, looked around to ensure they were out of earshot of Fedon's men. Seeing a few too close for his liking he motioned to Fedon and his companion to step further away. When he finally appeared satisfied he turned back to Fedon with an exasperated look.

"Julien, please be careful. We do not want the names Hubert Montdenoix or Flemming Linger to be known around here. In fact, we don't want anyone to know we were within a hundred leagues of this island."

Fedon bowed his head in contrition for a moment. "I'm sorry, you did tell me this. Lack of sleep is affecting me."

"We understand," said Montdenoix, a grimace appearing on his face. "And yes, being white we thought it prudent to disappear until things settled down. A few of our own men to guard us also helped matters. But enough, the town has obviously been taken. What news is there of the Governor?"

Fedon explained the situation and as one all three men turned to look at the sails in the distance. Flemming Linger, taller and thinner than his superior, peered hard into the distance and was the first to speak.

"I think they are coming closer."

"You are right," said Fedon, exhaling the breath he was holding with relief. "I wasn't sure, but they are definitely closer than they were a few minutes ago. God, let's hope they caught him."

Montdenoix pulled a flask out of his pocket and

after taking a long drink of the contents offered it to the others.

"We may as well enjoy ourselves while we wait."

***

An hour later a motley collection of ships were finally close enough details of the people on board could be seen. Fedon's spirits soared, as he was able to make out La Valette prancing about with a huge grin on his face on the deck of a small cutter. One other ship of similar size and design was with them along with a larger sloop, but the only one showing any damage was the cutter La Valette was on. An entire section of the starboard railing was gone and shot holes could be seen in the sails. What could only be dried blood had run down the side of the ship in two places. As soon as they were close enough to be heard La Valette shouted across the water.

"Julien! We have him!"

Fedon breathed a sigh of relief and Montdenoix slapped him on the back in congratulations. As they waited for the ships to be secured to the dock Montdenoix spoke close to Fedon's ear, ensuring he would not be overheard.

"Well done, Julien. You have succeeded with everything you planned so far. My colleague and I must now take leave, for we have other tasks here in the Caribbean. We want the British to lie awake at night in fear everywhere, including even places they think are invincible like Jamaica. But we will be back. In the meantime, you know what to do."

"I do. We will not let up."

The Sugar Rebellion

Montdenoix nodded and the two men left as a gangplank was put in place. Within minutes a dispirited and disheveled group of thirteen prisoners were being led onshore. Two of them were badly bruised and wounded white soldiers, but the rest were white men, women, and children. The oldest was a grey haired male with a massive bruise and dried blood on the side of his face. Julien knew the man was Governor Home, having seen him before at events in the capital of St. George's. La Valette preceded them and reached Julien first.

"It was hard fought, Julien, but we have him! The Governor had several soldiers with him, but our men fought well. I wanted more prisoners for you, but the soldiers made that impossible. As you can see he tried escaping with this ship, but soldiers know nothing of sailing and they didn't have enough men that knew what they were doing to be effective. I, on the other hand, had plenty of people that know how to handle a ship."

As he finished speaking the guards made the party of prisoners shuffle to a stop in front of Fedon. Governor Home saw they were being deliberately led to Fedon, an obvious signal he was someone of importance. As the Governor stepped to the front of the crowd a sense of recognition of appeared on his face. Standing as stiff and straight as he possible he mustered a show of outrage.

"Who are you? Damn me, I've seen you before. You are a plantation owner, aren't you? Are you in charge of this gang of murderers and cutthroats?"

Fedon laughed. "Governor Home, to me they are just people fighting for their freedom and

The Sugar Rebellion

liberty, and I hardly think that makes them cutthroats. Who is right? Well, since I am in charge here I'd say I am, while you are no longer Governor of anything. I am Julien Fedon and you are all my prisoners."

Governor Home scowled. "It's the Goddamn French behind this, isn't it? They're using the free mulatto population as puppets. We should have packed all of you bloody spawn of frogs back to Africa where you belong long ago. Well, you have me, but are you civilized enough to show mercy to the women and children and set them free?"

"I'm afraid no one is going free, Governor. You may all be valuable to me at some point in the future. But not to worry, I am certain my people will be civilized enough to treat them at least as well as you barbarians treat your own slaves."

Governor Home's face suffused with outrage. "You, a slave owner yourself, dare to call me a barbarian?"

He shoved away La Valette's man standing guard at his side and swung a punch at Fedon that never landed. Another of La Valette's men anticipated the move and drove the cudgel he was holding hard into the Governor's stomach. The Governor doubled over, clutching at his belly and gasping in pain. Another made to strike the defenseless man, but Fedon called for him to stop.

"There will be plenty of opportunity for that later. We have too much else to do for now. Take them to Belvedere and put them with the others. La Valette, I need to question the Governor later about a few things like the defenses they have in St.

The Sugar Rebellion

George's and I need him capable of responding, so please restrain the men for now. We have done well this day, but we still have to make our final effort and take St. George's. Once I am my answers and we know whether I can use him as something to bargain with, I will consider turning him over to you to do as you please."

"I pray that day comes soon, Julien."

"And Jean? I congratulate you and your men. Well done."

***

Situated on a prominent, hundred-foot high hilltop right at a point of land jutting into the ocean, Fort George dominated everything in the capital of Grenada. The point effectively created the St. George's inner harbor as well, providing excellent shelter and a deep-water port for ships of all sizes.

As Kenneth MacKenzie made his way almost two weeks after the rebellion began to the Governor's office in Fort George he had no interest in enjoying the excellent view of the Caribbean sunset the Fort offered. He and the three other men with him had far weightier matters on their minds. Their distress over what was happening was etched in the men's faces. An Army Lieutenant was standing with the guards at the entrance to the Fort awaiting their arrival and he escorted them direct to the Governor's meeting room. Another officer was already there, rising to greet them as they came in.

While the Lieutenant stepped into the background and began pouring a glass of wine for each man the other officer stretched out his hand. This man was tall and imposing, sporting a broad

The Sugar Rebellion

moustache stretching well beyond the corners of his mouth.

"You are Colonel John Walter, I assume?" said MacKenzie as he walked up and shook hands with the man.

"Sir, I am."

"Thank you for meeting us. I am Kenneth Mackenzie, senior member of the King's Council for Grenada and these men are my colleagues on the Council."

MacKenzie introduced the others and motioned for everyone to sit around the meeting table.

"Colonel, we understand you have been rather occupied with the military situation. We also understand you arrived just in time to be appointed senior Army officer for this island at the worst possible moment. But we have heard disturbing rumors about the status of Governor Home and we felt we could wait no longer. Is it true he has been captured?"

The colonel sighed. "Gentlemen, it appears to be true. We believe he is still alive and being held captive, but cannot be certain as we have not received any communication from these rebel slave scum."

"Have you made any attempts to actually communicate with them, sir?" said one of the Council members.

"Good God, no," said the Colonel, with an incredulous look on his face. "Don't know why we would do anything like that and we won't be, either."

"Colonel," said MacKenzie, with a sharp tone

The Sugar Rebellion

to his voice that made the Colonel's head snap back in surprise. "That is not your decision to make, sir. If the Governor is indeed a captive then that means my Council members and I are in charge here. As senior member of the Council I am assuming the role of Acting Governor as of now. Given the circumstances it was acceptable to let the military take the lead on dealing with the situation and military matters will continue to be your domain. But this has gone on long enough and you need to understand we are in charge here. Am I making myself clear?"

The Colonel paused for a long moment, before offering a curt nod. "Sir, you are."

"Fine. We would now like a full report on the situation, please."

The Colonel paused once more before stiffening in his chair as he began to speak, sitting as if he was standing on a parade ground being reviewed.

"Gentlemen, as I expect you know by now a full scale rebellion was launched in key centers in the north of the island on the night of March 2nd. I am sorry to tell you we have reports of total massacres of the British population in some places. We also believe they have taken a number of prisoners, but we are not certain who they are or how many."

The faces of the men on the Council grew grim as the Colonel related what little news they had of the Governor's capture. He had little to offer as to who was behind the rebellion, other than word Julien Fedon seemed to be a prominent leader.

The Sugar Rebellion

"In the two weeks since this blew up the rebels have continued to make gains," said the Colonel. "Unfortunately, we lost several members of the Grenada Garrison defending the Governor when he tried to escape from Grenville. The animals also trapped several others in their barracks in Gouyave and proceeded to burn them to death, if you can believe it. I have lost well over a hundred and fifty valuable soldiers. I have been forced to deploy several men to try and help refugees that escaped the rebels gain the safety of St. George's. There were numerous attacks in the south of the island soon after this began, too. Effectively, we have been in fights on several different fronts with fewer resources than necessary for such a fluid situation. I deemed it appropriate to fall back and establish a defensive perimeter around the capital. As I expect you know, they made several determined assaults on our positions, but we have beat them back with heavy losses on their part each time. Unfortunately, though, the only part of this island we now control is St. George's itself."

"Yes, yes, you were quite right to fall back," said one of the Council members. "Colonel, what are your sources of information? Do they have anything more than just a name to give us as to who is behind this and what they seek to achieve?"

The Colonel raised his eyebrows in disbelief he was unable to hide, before turning to the waiting Lieutenant standing silently to the side.

"I haven't spoken to anyone personally so I wouldn't know. Lieutenant Ramsay?"

"Sir, I believe what little we have comes from

The Sugar Rebellion

the house slaves of our plantation owners who escaped or were let go because of their status as slaves. As for what the rebels want, we have no idea. It is clear they are targeting British plantation owners only, so some obvious conclusions can be drawn from that."

"This man Fedon, his name rings a bell," said MacKenzie. "Isn't he a colored owner with an estate somewhere in the north?"

"Look, ah—Governor MacKenzie," said the Colonel. "What does it matter who they are or what they want? These animals are killing our people. As soon as we have consolidated the situation to a point I am satisfied we will strike back to repay them in kind. We are already working on a draft plan that I hope will be ready soon."

MacKenzie remained still for a few long moments while he thought about a response. He glanced around at the other members of the Council. One of them spoke up.

"I think we should proceed as discussed, Kenneth."

As the other two men nodded agreement, Mackenzie turned his gaze back to the Colonel.

"Colonel, has it occurred to you there may be more going on here than meets the eye? It is not lost on us that French owners are not being attacked like us."

"Oh, bloody—look, sir, with respect, I will be launching an attack very soon. We will capture enough of these bastards you can spend all the time you want talking to them for information."

"Colonel, please proceed with your plans, but

The Sugar Rebellion

you will not proceed to the attack until we give you the word. We will be making some effort on our own to find out what we want to know and we will also be attempting to communicate with this Fedon, if he doesn't contact us first. We need to know more about what is going on here. More importantly, do you have sufficient resources to get the job done, sir?"

The Colonel chewed on a corner of his moustache for a moment and shrugged. "I've never met an officer that thought he had enough men to work with in situations like this. Look, as I told you, we've lost some men, but overall I'm quite certain we will find a way to make do."

"Colonel, do you know how many men the rebels can field?"

"Well, no, but I am confident every one of my men is worth a hundred of theirs."

"I see. Well, I think that will be all for today, Colonel," said Governor MacKenzie. "We have a few matters to discuss among ourselves and perhaps we can meet again tomorrow, sir. Please carry on."

The Colonel remained sitting stiff where he was for a few long moments before nodding to the Council and standing. He waved for the Lieutenant to join him and the two officers locked eyes briefly before leaving. As the door closed behind them MacKenzie sighed and turned to the other men in the room.

"Well, gentlemen. What do you think? Is he the buffoon I think he is, or am I being too pessimistic?"

"You are not being pessimistic, Kenneth," said

The Sugar Rebellion

one, while the other two nodded.

"Well, we feared this would be the case," said MacKenzie. "We should have stepped in sooner. The man has no idea what forces his opponent can muster, how they are deployed, or anything of what their strategy may be, but he blithely assumes it'll all be just fine once he has at them. I fear there are far more enemies facing us than he thinks and at a minimum we should seek to have our losses replaced."

"Kenneth," said one of the Council, a worried look on his face. "Are there any soldiers to spare anywhere? This situation with the Maroons on Jamaica growing restive sounds dire. If our political masters face a choice between saving Jamaica or saving us, we all know what the decision will be."

"I know. We can but ask. We may be forced to keep this fool in check and fight a siege until help can be freed up. Well, I shall be up half the night writing letters, so let's end this now. We can figure out how to make some contact with our foes tomorrow."

As they rose to their feet MacKenzie sighed one last time and lifted his glass.

"We may be deep in the shit, gentlemen, but we are not without help. If we have to be in what is effectively a siege here, at least we have the comfort of knowing there is one thing we can rely on without fail. Thank God for the British Royal Navy."

Without a word the other men raised their glasses and drained the remaining wine in silent agreement.

The Sugar Rebellion

Chapter Two
January 1796
St. Domingue and Antigua

Royal Navy Commander Evan Ross looked up from the paperwork on his desk as the sailor entered and saluted.

"Sir? The bosun sends respects and desires you on deck. Our party has signaled a problem."

Evan swore under his breath and rose from his chair, reaching for his sword as he nodded to the man. Having lost his left arm in a fight with American smugglers over ten years before he had long since mastered the process of arming himself fast, despite having only one hand to do the job. Within moments he was on his way.

He reached his quarterdeck in time to see the remnants of a red signal flare dying out in the distance. His ship, *HMS Alice*, a brig sloop of 100 feet in length, was lying at anchor in the darkness on the western side of the entrance to Jacmel Bay, off the southern coast of the island of Hispaniola and the French colony of St. Domingue. The moon was only now beginning to rise and would shed some light on the scene soon enough, but for now the night was close to pitch dark. With a sense of foreboding he strode up to the hulking form of his bosun, Wallace Mitchell, who was staring intently at the flare.

"Report," said Evan.

"Sir. It's the trouble signal. Two flares, both red. The first was straight in the air, but as you may

The Sugar Rebellion

have saw before it died out the second was pointed east toward Jacmel. That second flare has to be telling us the frogs in Jacmel are awake and after them. Haven't seen any gun fire, at least not yet."

"Damn me, that might not take long," replied Evan, before bellowing a stream of orders that turned the *Alice* into a hive of manic activity. To a casual observer the scene would appear chaotic, but in reality it was a well-practiced dance the crew had performed many times before. More often than not in recent years it was done with the threat of desperate action looming in their future. Evan displayed no outward sign of worry, knowing he had no reason to cajole the men into greater speed. They all knew what was at stake and they would give their best.

On the inside, however, Evan couldn't help feeling worried for his men. He always did. After over two years together with this crew, facing dire action on numerous occasions, an unspoken bond of having been tested and survived had grown among them all. If trouble was at hand, he couldn't think of a better crew to deal with it.

With the anchor secured they were soon underway, standing into the bay with a breeze strong enough Evan knew would get them to the scene fast. He hoped it would be in time. But even as the thought came a swivel gun barked in the distance, followed instantly by the popping sounds of small weapons fire. Evan cursed under his breath again and pulled out his night glass, focusing on the location he had seen the pinprick flashes of the discharges. As he did the intensity of the fight grew.

The Sugar Rebellion

Another bigger flash of light stabbed out, followed instantly by the report what sounded like a small two-pound chase gun. More swivel guns barked in response. After several long moments studying the confused scene he called for his Gunner and within seconds the man was at his side.

"Ah, Smith," said Evan, finally lowering the glass. "As near as I can see our people are engaged with a small sloop, but it's hard to tell them apart at this distance. We have the weather gauge on them both, so we will stay this course for now. They are close together, but I think our cutter is still some ways ahead of the chase. We will know in another minute or so. Be ready with the port side carronades, as if I'm correct they are what will tell."

"Sir? What kind of shot?"

"Grape. I want their deck raked completely. We're not here to take a prize, we just want to get our people and get the hell out of here."

As Smith left the bosun grunted, still standing impassively watching the scene unfold.

"Sir, are they fools to maintain the chase? Anyone with a brain would realize those flares were a signal to someone like us for help. They are acting as if no one else is around."

"They are either fools or they are desperate to catch our people. I suspect the latter. Either way they are about to discover they have gambled and lost."

Moments later the moon finally made an appearance, sliding from behind a cloud. While it was nowhere near being full, enough light was now on the scene Evan's night glass was no longer

The Sugar Rebellion

necessary. He realized his guess was correct and he called orders to alter course slightly. His new course would bring the *Alice* parallel to that of the cutter and the small sloop chasing her. The staccato bursts of firing between the two vessels continued unabated and Evan clenched his fist in frustration, willing the *Alice* to clutch at every whisper of wind with her sails.

Not for the first time, Evan also found himself cursing the necessity of being armed only with carronades and light swivel guns. Having six pound cannon with their much greater range would have enabled him to engage the enemy far sooner, but his disguise as a lightly armed merchant vessel not normally carrying such weapons made this impractical. The carronades had their benefits, however. Although they were short-barreled weapons with a much more limited range, the punch they packed was enormous. The *Alice* was fitted with carronades delivering eighteen-pound shot and Evan knew all he had to do was get close enough to his foe to turn the tide.

Carronades had one other benefit, too. Unlike larger cannons, carronades were smaller and lighter, and they could be shifted about without too much effort. This made available on short notice a much wider arc of fire and Evan used this to his advantage, rapping out orders to shift them to bear on the sloop. As they finished and Smith signaled readiness, the bosun called out a warning.

"Sir, I think they've finally realized we are here! They—yes, they are making to come about and run back to safety."

The Sugar Rebellion

"Hmm, I think we should make sure of that," said Evan. "Fire!"

The night was lit with three flashes of light, so bright Evan was still blinded for several long moments despite shading his eyes from the flash with his hand. Simultaneous ear splitting reports from the three carronades mounted on the port side of the ship were followed by the sulfurous stench of spent gunpowder as it was wafted by the wind to the quarterdeck. After a few long moments the bosun laughed.

"Well, that did for them. They are falling off and I'd say they are ripe for picking. Too bad we can't take her as a prize, sir."

"Not part of our mission, Mitchell. We also don't want to hang around and see if the frogs we just took care of have friends bigger than us."

Evan scanned the horizon for their cutter after satisfying himself Mitchell was indeed right. Seeing the cutter tacking to join the *Alice* he issued orders to heave to and take it in tow. As the cutter closed on them Evan gave a sigh of relief to see his two officers, Lieutenants James Wilton and Timothy Cooke. Both were alive and appeared uninjured.

The cutter had not escaped damage, however. The aft section of the ship had taken several direct hits and was pockmarked badly. They also appeared to be missing a few men and Evan grimaced at the thought. But huddled in a small group near the forward mast was a small group of civilians and Evan hoped this was a sign the mission was a success. After ensuring a lookout was posted to watch for more enemy ships and the situation was

The Sugar Rebellion

in hand, he gave orders to get the ship underway for Antigua when everyone was safe on board. With one last look about he went below to his cabin, knowing the men and his officers knew what to do. Less than fifteen minutes later he felt the ship get underway at the same time as a knock came on his door.

"Enter," said Evan, knowing it would be James Wilton, his first officer.

The Lieutenant came in and stiffened to salute, but Evan forestalled him by waving a hand and pointing to the chair in front of his desk. Forgoing the formalities of paying respects to a commanding officer would in other circumstances be most unusual, but not for these men when they were alone with each other. The two men had been firm friends for years now. Evan studied the man before him, seeing how tired he was. This was not the first such time they had been sent on missions like this and Evan's thoughts were drawn back over the years.

They had met over a decade before while serving on a frigate in the Caribbean. Both were injured in the same fight with American smugglers and left to recover in the hospital at the British Royal Navy base of English Harbour on the island of Antigua. With time in the hospital on their hands, the spark of friendship had grown. The friendship was unusual as Evan was a Lieutenant at the time, while James was a Master's Mate. Even more unusual was the fact James was the son of a black female slave and a white Royal Navy officer.

But the two men found they were much alike in

The Sugar Rebellion

their thinking and, with the shared prospect their careers could be over, they had plenty to cement their friendship. Without a war on at the time, opportunities for employment of injured men were practically nonexistent. They had despaired for their future until Captain Horatio Nelson appeared on the scene.

Nelson was assigned to lead the northern station of the Leeward Islands Squadron, based in Antigua. His primary task was to stamp out the rampant smuggling in the area and he seized on the opportunity to employ the two men as spies. They succeeded at that and more, as in the process they uncovered and put a stop to a plot by French and American spies to incite revolt among British possessions in the Caribbean. Both were rewarded with promotions and assignments to carry on serving as spies, using their overt assignments as officers in charge of the Dockyard in the English Harbour base as cover. Over ten years later they were still on the job.

"You need a drink," said Evan, not waiting for a reply as he got up from his chair and poured two glasses of wine.

Evan saw the grateful look on James's face as he downed a big portion of the contents in one gulp and knew he was right. After countless missions all over the Caribbean in the service of their spymaster Sir James Standish, based in Barbados, Evan could read his friend with ease. Perhaps it was his imagination tonight, but the fatigue brought out the fine wrinkles that had begun to appear around the eyes and on the face of his friend, making them seem a little bit deeper. Both men were still only in their early thirties in age, but the toll of time, their duty, and a life spent outside in all manner of weather was beginning to show. Evan knew hints of grey had appeared along his hairline and he had his own share of lines on his face now, too.

While their careers in the Royal Navy had went in a direction neither of them would have foreseen, let alone requested, both men had long since accepted their role as spies and decided to simply be the best they could be at it. War with the French ongoing since 1793 meant the demand for their services was such no one would have contemplated using them for any other purpose anyway.

Of necessity they had to focus more and more of their time since the war began on St. Domingue. British forces insufficient for the job first invaded in 1793, with more following the next year. St. Domingue was seen as a lucrative source of potential income and, at the very least, it would be a highly valuable piece to bargain with in negotiations with the French should peace be sought. But the shifting sands of allegiances in the quagmire of St. Domingue, combined with the growing devastation of yellow fever, were playing havoc with the imperialist designs of the British government. The Army was increasingly desperate for any intelligence to help turn their limited success to date into something more lasting, which put Evan and James under constant, heavy pressure to help. The cost of their need continued to mount.

"Three dead, Evan. Johnson, Sanders, and Davies. Two others injured, but they'll live."

The Sugar Rebellion

James shrugged as Evan winced. "They died at their post. Those bastards gave it to us pretty heavy before you showed up. As for the mission, we managed to get one family out. It was too late for the others."

Evan swore under his breath and sighed. "Tell me more. What happened?"

"The guy working as a clerk for one of Sonthonax's commanders and his family are the ones we brought out. I confess I might be wrong about him, but I'm still not sure. I figured he was a plant when he first made contact and starting feeding us information, but I guess he's the real thing. Still, when we showed up to get him out he and his family couldn't wait to get on the ship. Evan, they all had small bags packed and ready to go. And those bastards that followed us out were conveniently awake enough to spot us rowing out to the cutter. I don't know. This could all have been a set up. On the other hand, they weren't pretending at anything when they were shooting at us and this guy has brought his family with him. So all that means is it could well be we've got someone very good at this business rolling up our sources."

Evan tapped his fingers on his desk while he thought about it. Over time Evan and James had established a variety of sources in St. Domingue, along with ways for them to pass information.

"I tend to think we should trust his information, but I'll talk to this clerk when there is time. Even if he is a plant foisted on us by some clever French bastard he won't have opportunity to start feeding information back anytime soon. We'll pay someone

The Sugar Rebellion

to have an eye on him and it'll be fine. But what happened to the others?"

James shrugged. "Word is the guy we blackmailed was sent to the guillotine two weeks ago. Interestingly, they called it fraud and theft, but didn't give a lot of details. So who knows, it may be they didn't know we were squeezing information out of him. He was such a total arsehole I wouldn't be surprised if he finally found himself in a corner he couldn't get out of. At least I'm sure what we did get out of him was good. And as for the house slave working for this nephew of Toussaint L'Ouverture, he is currently rotting in jail along with his entire family. Asking questions about him brought attention on us and not in a good way. That was when we went after the clerk and his family and ran for it. You know the rest."

"Shit," said Evan, after downing a good portion of his own glass of wine. "This is the same as what happened in Gonaives last month and Cap Haitien before that. I think we need to face it, there really is some clever French bastard rolling up our networks and he clearly knows what he is doing."

"Maybe more than one, Evan. I didn't have time to stand around asking a lot of questions, you understand, but this clerk we brought out made mention of a couple of white Frenchmen nosing around. Nothing firm, but it may be more than coincidence that these two appeared right at the same time as the heat turned up."

"Yes, not the first time we've heard about them. I discounted that before, but I fear we can discount it no more. We have to assume from here on we are

The Sugar Rebellion

facing some serious opposition and be that much better. But the timing of this couldn't possibly be worse. The Army is screaming for more and better information just as we are losing sources everywhere we turn. Right, this is enough for now. I'm sure Cooke has the crew in hand, but check on them and then get some rest. Send this clerk to me so I can see what else we can get from him about our opponents. When I'm done I'll take the deck and Cooke can get some rest, too. I need the time on watch to mull over what we're going to do about finding some new sources the next time we are back here, which will have to be soon."

James downed the rest of his wine and rose from his seat to leave. Evan forestalled him, as he was about to open the cabin door.

"James? I know you and Cooke did the best you could. Well done."

James nodded. "I just wish it hadn't come to a fight. We lost some good men."

Evan nodded too, lips tight in a grimace as James left the cabin.

***

All Evan wanted was sleep by the time they tied up at the main dock in the safety of English Harbour late in the day. Had it been summer the heat would have been an unbearable combination with his weariness, but the weather in January was much more tolerable. He was forced to push his fatigue away the moment he stepped off the ship, as the Dockyard Shipwright was waiting to brief him along with his personal clerk bearing messages from the Governor of Antigua.

The Sugar Rebellion

Two hours later Evan had managed to address the most pressing demands for his attention and the sun had gone down. Since the war had begun in 1793 the Dockyard was abuzz with activity seven days a week and sometimes at all hours of the day. Today was no exception. A big thirty-two gun frigate was competing for the attention of the Dockyard workers along with three other smaller vessels in various states of repair. One was careened on the beach on the far side of the Harbour having her bottom scraped clean of growth.

The constant demands for repairs meant maintaining sufficient stores of paint, tar, pitch, spars, powder, and other necessities essential for keeping warships afloat was a never ending, gargantuan task. Constant, unpredictable needs on one hand and a parsimonious Victualing Board in London on the other, all too ready to question why the Dockyard needed such large stores of supplies, meant the inevitable result was occasional shortfalls. Having to explain to a Royal Navy Captain his needs couldn't be met was never a pleasant experience.

But in the years since Evan began managing the Dockyard he had grown proficient at creatively juggling the various needs and at being diplomatic when he had to. Lieutenants Wilton and Cooke had grown too, and between the three of them the Dockyard ran with the precision of a fine watch. Their problem was the covert side of their work taking them away from Dockyard duties. On occasions such as this last trip to St. Domingue, where Evan deemed it necessary for all three of

The Sugar Rebellion

them to make the journey, the Dockyard suffered without firm hands to guide it. The need for all three of them to be away at the same time was happening with increasing frequency.

Evan looked up from his desk as his two Lieutenants knocked and entered. Evan knew the haggard looks on their faces were mirrored on his own. As they finished their terse reports Evan nodded.

"Well, I know what you two are thinking, because it is the same as what I'm thinking. This is the fourth time this has happened and we can't make do anymore. I will see about getting help from Captain Mason in the morning. I doubt I can get another Lieutenant, but someone must be able to spare a suitable midshipman or two we can train and leave in charge here when we are away."

"That would be welcome, sir," said Lieutenant Cooke. "A day or two is one thing, but there is no escaping that things go downhill when all three of us are gone for a week or more."

Evan waved at the pile of correspondence stacked on his desk. "That's for certain. I haven't even had time to sort through this mess to see if any of it is of real importance. Well, let's get some sleep. You are dismissed, gentlemen."

An hour later Evan trudged up the path to his home, located near the Dockyard midway between it and the nearby village of Falmouth Harbour. The moonlight helped to find his way, but it wasn't necessary, for he knew the path well. He had shared this home with his wife Alice for many years now and it was a welcome sight. As he neared the

The Sugar Rebellion

verandah an old three-legged mongrel dog that was sleeping on it perked up his head and wagged his tail.

"Hello Nelson. It's good to see you," said Evan, stooping to scratch behind the dog's ear. Someone had abandoned him years before, but the dog was a tough, scrappy fighter and he survived to grow grey around his muzzle. Evan and James had taken him in and named him after Horatio Nelson. Evan was still bent over paying attention to the dog when the door crashed open and Alice rushed out. Evan found himself enveloped in a crushing hug, enough to make him stagger and almost lose his balance.

"Ease up, woman. You just about knocked me on my ass," said Evan with a laugh, although he was enjoying the feel of her body and her scent enveloping him to the fullest.

Alice responded by going on tiptoes and sliding her full breasts up his chest to give him a long kiss on the mouth. As she finally pulled back a little she looked him in the eyes. Her eyes were moist and Evan knew she was on the verge of crying.

"God, I missed you so bad, lover man. I hate it when you leave, but it's heaven when you come back. You look tired."

"I am," confessed Evan, as he reached up with his hand to caress her face and wipe away the single tear now coursing down her cheek. "Hungry, too. Any leftovers I can wolf down?"

Evan sat at the table as Alice bustled about in the kitchen. The savory scent of a fish stew she was heating up made his mouth water, so he chewed on a piece of bread and butter to keep his growling stomach in check. As he watched her, his thoughts went back over the years they had been together and he found himself grateful once again this wonderful woman had chosen to share her life with him.

That they were together as husband and wife was unusual, for Alice was the daughter of a white plantation owner and a black slave who had worked for him. When Evan met Alice over a decade before she was a slave herself, working as a prostitute in a tavern her father owned in St. John's, the capital of Antigua. Still dealing with recovering from their injuries, Evan and James had needed to get away from the hospital to boost their morale. They had ended up at The Flying Fish tavern and, given the need, found themselves seeking solace in the arms of the local women.

Alice and Evan were attracted to each other from the moment they met. When Evan and James were assigned by Horatio Nelson to work as spies ferreting out American smugglers circumventing British tax laws, Evan turned to Alice for help. The key to their success was using the local slave networks she connected them to along with their own efforts trawling for information. Alice was keen to help, as the father she abhorred was an integral part of the plot designed by the French and American spies trying to destabilize the island enough for the locals to declare independence and side with the Americans.

Along the way Evan found he had fallen in love with this spirited, intelligent, and beautiful woman. More than a few men had declared she was by far the best looking woman on the entire island, with

The Sugar Rebellion

her soft, flowing dark hair and light coffee colored features. Using an intermediary, Evan purchased her freedom and they had lived together ever since. She continued to work with him when he needed information, making connections with locals both on Antigua and other islands. Almost three years ago they had married.

Evan had known there would be consequences, but he didn't care. Racism underpinned the entire slave economies of all of the Caribbean islands, regardless of whether the masters were English, French, Spanish, or other European nations. Antiguan society had overtly ignored the fact the Navy officer in charge of the main naval base on their island married a former slave woman, but the consequence was invitations to society events were not forthcoming. One of the Antigua Militia officers who had married a local mulatto woman also was ostracized to the point he resigned his commission.

The Royal Navy was different, though. While there were exceptions, the only thing most officers in the Navy were focused on was whether someone did their job well. A small but noticeable proportion of men serving on Royal Navy warships were from countries all over the world and more than a few of those were black. Having grown up in the Navy, Evan was among this group of officers and he had no time for plantation owner's prejudices that made no sense.

The real consequence was to his career. A lot of senior officers were of the opinion officers shouldn't marry while serving, and being married to a black woman didn't help. But Evan had long since

The Sugar Rebellion

made up his mind his life was here with Alice and he knew change was in the air. The constant pressure of William Wilberforce and his followers in England seeking the abolition of slavery was beginning to bear fruit. The Government of Upper Canada took the bold step to ban slavery in July of 1793 and in 1794 the French followed suit.

Evan gave thanks in silence that she was still with him as Alice put a steaming bowl on the table. Although healthy now, she had almost died soon after they married. She was pregnant with their first child when she developed problems. The child had not survived and Alice had come close to losing her own life. Ever since they had taken precautions when they were together, but the question of whether to try for a child once again lingered.

The smell of the hearty, spicy soup drove all coherent thought from his mind as he downed it with pleasure. By the time he was done he could only drag himself off to bed, lacking the energy to even shave the rough stubble of two days growth of beard from his face. He never saw the worried look on her face that lingered as she crawled in beside him, for he was already fast asleep.

***

Evan's first stop the next morning was to see Captain Mason, the senior commanding officer in charge of all Navy forces in the northern division of the Leeward Islands station. Evan knew he was fortunate to find him in port. On hearing the situation Captain Mason sighed and agreed he would do what he could to get Evan help. Evan hated adding more to the man's workload, but he

The Sugar Rebellion

left satisfied knowing the Captain was a good man and, if anyone could find help, it would be him.

After checking in with his two Lieutenants at the Dockyard and establishing who was doing what for the day, Evan steeled himself to the thought he would likely be trapped in his office the entire day trying to clean up all the paperwork. Settling into his chair with a strong cup of tea to fortify him, he sorted through the pile of correspondence and put several aside as he knew they were simple updates on supplies and other matters that could wait. The remaining smaller pile would not be so easy to deal with.

Correspondence from diplomats around the Caribbean briefing him on developments and seeking his advice on intelligence matters comprised the bulk of it. Some were from sources Evan had cultivated on French or Spanish possessions who had found ways to smuggle their letters out to be sent onward. Others were letters from sources sent to innocuous addresses in neutral islands and then forwarded on to him. All of it needed careful attention.

But one envelope in particular caught his eye and on seeing it he shoved the rest aside. The letter bore the seal of the First Lord of the Admiralty in London and Evan gave it a speculative look. A letter from the First Lord himself was rare and always meant something was happening. Using a small knife blade he had set into a wooden block on his desk to make it easier for him to open envelopes with one hand, he slit the letter open.

The letter was brief, but it was enough to make

The Sugar Rebellion

Evan first gape open mouthed and then curse aloud. The First Lord was ordering Evan and James to drop whatever they were doing and come to the aid of the Governor of Grenada, who would provide details in his own letter. The letter added that their work in St. Domingue was not to be ignored, as Lieutenant Cooke was tasked with continuing efforts there. After a quick search through the diplomatic correspondence Evan found a letter from the Governor of Grenada, but he gave no details other than to specify he had need of their services.

Another letter from Evan's superior, Captain Sir James Standish in Barbados, acknowledged he was aware of the request and supported it. His letter, at least, alluded to the reason. Evan was aware of the rebellion on the island of Grenada the year before, but as the issue was ostensibly in the hands of the Army and Evan had no lack of other problems to address, he had not paid much attention to developments there. Sir James gave no details, but made it clear the Governor in Grenada was desperate for help and Evan knew this meant matters were not going well.

Calling for his clerk, Evan ordered him to have his two Lieutenants join him. As the two men came in and sat down Evan knew they could see the concern on his face. Evan shrugged and pointed to the letter from the First Lord on the desk in front of him. The two officers eyes narrowed, realizing whom it was from, and both men looked up at Evan at the same time.

"Well, gentlemen, as if we didn't have enough to do we now have more. James, you and I are off to

The Sugar Rebellion

Grenada and, no, I have no idea for how long. As to why, well, we all know they've got a fight on their hands there and while I don't have any specifics, you can guess what they might want us to be doing."

"Good God, sir," said James. "How could we be of help at this stage? Any contacts we had on Grenada have long since been lost because of the rebellion. Sir James told us to not to bother reestablishing them because the Army was going to deal with it."

Evan shrugged. "Who knows? But when the First Lord says go to Grenada, we go. I saw Captain Mason this morning about getting help and he said he will do what he can, but now he's going to have to whether he likes it or not. As for you, Mr. Cooke, you are ordered to take the lead role and carry on as we have been with St. Domingue. And yes, I know what you're thinking. I will talk to the Captain about getting you a ship to work with."

The young Lieutenant's face lit with interest. "Damn me, that would be wonderful, sir."

"Don't get your hopes up. It will likely be temporary. But unless you're going to swim there you have to have something to get you back to St. Domingue, because I'm not giving you the *Alice*."

The two officers laughed and James looked at his companion. "You lucky bastard. I'm going to be insanely jealous if you parlay this into a permanent posting."

"Not to worry, sir," said Lieutenant Cooke, a cheerful grin on his face. "I like working with you both and the work we do."

The Sugar Rebellion

"That's good, because I don't think the First Lord would free us up for regular duties for any reason anyway," said Evan. "Right. Let's target departure in one week. It will take time to finish setting everything right around here and training our new recruit. Mr. Cooke, you and I will have a talk tomorrow about St. Domingue. I used my time on watch sailing back here to think about what options we might have to find some new sources. So let's be about it, gentlemen. This pile of paperwork is still screaming for my attention."

As the door closed behind the two officers Evan couldn't help thinking about what might be behind the request from Grenada. St. Domingue was clearly on top of the list of situations driving events in the Caribbean and demanding Evan's attention, but he had no lack of others fighting to be noticed, too.

St. Domingue was not alone in feeling the consequences spawned from the French revolution. Power struggles in France continued after the King was beheaded in 1793, culminating in a reign of terror beginning in September of the same year. Thousands of people were sent to the guillotine and many more were jailed, left only to die in prison in France and her possessions around the world. In the midst of the terror early the following year the British took the nearby islands of Martinique and Guadeloupe, but it wasn't to last.

A French squadron with a thousand troops led by a fiery revolutionary named Victor Hugues arrived in June of 1794. His forces would have been insufficient for the task of retaking the island, but his orders from the French National Convention were to declare an end to slavery in addition to driving the British out. With several thousand now freed slaves supporting the effort, it took only days to do the job. Evan wondered whether the slaves Hugues had freed now saw the irony of the man's cynical decision to force them to continue unpaid labor on behalf of the new administration.

Hugues didn't stop there, however. Making the best of what he had to work with, Hugues used his authority as the new Governor to authorize a host of French privateer warships to operate out of Guadeloupe. In the year and a half since his arrival British shipping around the Caribbean had suffered enormous losses. He also actively incited resistance on several nearby islands. On St. Lucia he succeeded, taking the island from the British in 1795.

Evan had responded to it all by building an extensive network of sources everywhere he could. The amount of gold flowing through his office to pay bribes or support his sources reached staggering levels as a result. Evan knew Grenada was likely one of the targets and wouldn't be surprised if Hugues were the mastermind behind what had happened there.

The timing fit. Hugues arrived in the Caribbean in June of 1794 and less than a year later open rebellion had broken out in Grenada. But Evan knew Hugues was simply the background guiding hand. What he didn't know was who was taking care of the details. The more he considered the possibility, the firmer his conviction grew that the

The Sugar Rebellion

timing of the various setbacks the British encountered was spread out enough to point the finger at a master spy working behind Hugues and opposing Evan. He simply had to find and deal with whoever this was and Evan sensed Grenada could be where he would find his opponent. But that would be later and with a sigh he shook his head to clear his mind as he drew the stack of paperwork closer.

***

During dinner later the same night Evan sat across the table from Alice and told her what was happening. He could see her thinking through the implications and he knew she had been around him long enough to absorb plenty of nautical knowledge. Although Grenada wasn't as far from Antigua as St. Domingue, it was still a long trip and Evan could give her no idea of how long he would be there. He also knew what she was thinking.

"You want to come with me," said Evan, voicing it as a statement and not a question.

Alice's face was a mask for a long moment before she couldn't hide it any longer and she began to laugh. She reached out and took his hand, giving him her most winning smile.

"I guess we've been together long enough I'm that easy to read, am I?"

"I guess. Look, you do realize we're under siege there, right? Conditions are probably not good and I don't really know how safe it is."

Alice shrugged. "I've been in tough situations with you before, haven't I? Besides, I'm not talking about just being a simple passenger. I could help."

The Sugar Rebellion

Evan raised an eyebrow in question as he responded. "You want to nose around in St. Georges and listen to people? Hmm."

"Evan, I really have been around you long enough to know how this works. You have sources feeding you information about your opponents. They are doing the same to you and maybe I can find some of them for you."

Evan grunted, lost in thought. "Well, I can't disagree with your thinking. I confess I'm not happy about the danger you might be in, but you're going to insist on this. I guess you win, because I love you and can deny you nothing. You must promise me to be extra careful."

Alice reached across the table to grasp his hand. "I know you worry for me, you wonderful man. Evan, I want to live life. I *like* helping you and if it means a little danger in the process I don't mind. But I was thinking about more than just coming with you on this trip. I want to live life to the fullest and because of that I want our future to be full. Yes, I am talking about trying one more time to have a child."

Evan sat a moment in silence as he gripped her hand. "Alice, are you certain? You almost died the first time. I don't know what I would do without you. I know, I deferred to you for a decision about this, but I want to be sure. You do not have to do this."

Alice bit her lip before replying. "Evan, we live in dangerous times. I don't know what I would do without you either. With this endless war on every time you go away I live in fear it will be the last time I see you. But we just need to live our lives and I want to try. I want to live it all."

Evan remained sitting in silence for several long moments before he nodded his agreement and finally replied. "Well, as I said, I can deny you nothing. So when do we get started on trying for a child?"

Alice flashed him a wide smile and laughed. "Cleaning up the dinner dishes can wait. How about right now?"

***

Nine days later Evan was standing on the dock beside the *HMS Alice* with James at his side, having finished issuing final orders to the two young midshipmen Captain Mason assigned to them. Evan turned to James as the two new recruits walked away to attend to their duties in the Dockyard.

"Well, what do you think?"

"I think we'll be lucky if the place is still intact by the time we get back. Someone took this as an opportunity to get rid of their deadwood."

Evan sighed. "We work with what we must, James. I think the one named Jeremy has at least a modicum of sense in his more lucid moments, but that other blockhead is a disaster. Well, we did our best to cram as much information into their heads as we could, but we are already two days later in getting away than I wanted. At least Mr. Cooke was able to get underway."

"Too bad the Captain had no command to offer him, but that pretty sloop he is a passenger on will get the job done. When he has to go ashore they will have to make sure there is no one else about."

The Sugar Rebellion

"Yes, we are better served by pretending to be merchants and using the same approach as we have with the Alice. I have already written to Sir James about this. With any luck he will find the money to purchase another merchant ship and we can convert it on the sly to meet our needs. How does the thought of sharing the use and command with him as needed sound to you?"

James grinned. "I'm a sailor, Evan. Give me a ship, any ship."

"It was a question I knew the answer to before I asked it. Well, Alice is already on board and everything is ready. The tide is with us, so let's go."

The Sugar Rebellion

Chapter Three
January 1796
Grenada

The young officer leading his patrol gave the thick patch of brush off to the side of the path a wary look, knowing other patrols along this route of the defensive lines around St. George's faced ambushes many times before. Those earlier attacks had come further down the path and he was mentally steeling himself to be ready for anything in the next few minutes, but he should have done it sooner. As he turned his gaze back to the path his mind finally registered and processed the subtle signs of movement deep in the brush. Whipping his head about he screamed a warning as he pointed in the direction of the movement.

"Ambush!"

This proved to be the last word he would ever speak. Three men bearing muskets rose from their hiding place and brought their weapons to bear. His officer's uniform made him the natural primary target and the musket balls cut him down in an instant. But the men with him knew what to do and instantly charged his killers before they could reload. Two of the three attackers were cut down without even the chance to bring a sword to bear while the third man ran for his life. The Sergeant now in charge of the patrol wasn't paying the scene any attention, however, certain the three men weren't the lone attackers. Barking orders he organized the bulk of his men into two groups to be

The Sugar Rebellion

ready to fire their muskets in coordinated volleys.

He was proved right as with a howling rush a swarm of foes came at them from behind. The constant training and discipline of the men paid off once again as the first volley cut down the entire leading edge of the line of attackers, forcing those behind to stumble and slow. As the first group of soldiers knelt to reload the second stepped to the fore and as one delivered another volley, creating further havoc in the ranks of their enemy. But despite their losses the attackers surged forward.

The Sergeant wasn't paying any attention to this scene either. Being a veteran with almost twenty years of service he had seen it all and he knew the third prong of the attack would come from the direction the patrol was heading in before the attack started. With this in mind he had held a small, third group of his men in reserve. He quietly ordered them to pretend to be focused on the fight blazing away while he kept a wary eye using his peripheral vision for movement. When he was certain the third group of attackers had broken cover and were making their move, he barked his orders out.

"Third cohort! About face and fire!"

As one the three remaining men who had not engaged their foes as yet turned, found targets among the seven attackers running at them, and fired. The Sergeant did the same with his own musket, but a misfire with one of his men's weapons meant four of the now howling attackers were still coming fast. The Sergeant risked a quick glance behind him and realized the larger group of foes

The Sugar Rebellion

was also almost upon them.

"Bayonets!" he shouted, and as one those of his men still trying to reload stopped and joined the line of defenders.

As the remaining attackers smashed into their lines the Sergeant's men stood their ground, surrounded now by a ring of men screaming and waving long machetes and clubs. A light rain the night before had wet and softened the path, and within seconds the struggling men churned the ground into enough mud to make finding solid footing almost impossible. Men screamed in agony as blades cut them down and their blood splashed on the mud, making it even more difficult to find purchase.

The Sergeant found himself engaged with a huge black slave, who whipped his machete back and forth as if it weighed nothing in his hand. But the Sergeant stood his ground, knowing he had to read the man's intent. His opponent was trying to mesmerize him with the dance of his blade, but the Sergeant was watching his eyes and how he bore his body for clues to the attack. When it came he was ready for it, for he had seen the move many times before.

Dancing to the side he avoided the downward slash of the machete and stepped closer, stabbing at the man with his bayonet. His opponent's youth and blazing speed saved him, although the Sergeant's weapon cut a slash in the man's side. The man bellowed in pain as the blood began flowing, maddening him enough he began a series of hammer blows attempting to smash the weapon

The Sugar Rebellion

from the Sergeant's hands. But the Sergeant knew it couldn't last and he simply bided his time, parrying each blow and waiting for the man to tire.

When he saw the time had come the Sergeant unleashed his own attack, pushing the man hard with long practiced ease. As the man stepped back to escape a thrust he slipped in the mud, leaving an opening even a raw recruit couldn't miss. The Sergeant drove his bayonet hard into the man's torso and his opponent screamed as he fell.

The Sergeant knew he had no time to enjoy the victory and turned to find another foe, but as he did the scene changed once again. He heard a bellowed order in the distance followed instantly by musket fire from the direction they had come and he knew reinforcements were coming. An instant later a brief burst of drumming came in the distance, an obvious signal to the attackers. Within seconds they melted away into the forest around the path.

The Sergeant sighed after taking a deep breath to settle his nerves. Even after almost twenty years and more skirmishes like this than he could count, he still needed time to wind down from a fight. The bottle of decent French brandy he was hoarding would be opened tonight. As he looked around to see the toll taken on his men the Lieutenant in charge of the relief party marched up.

"Report," said the officer.

"Ambush, sir. Lieutenant Walsh was the first one killed. It's a bad spot, sir."

The Lieutenant's lips pressed hard together and he raised an eyebrow as he stared in silence for a moment at the Sergeant. A long few moments later

The Sugar Rebellion

he finally spoke.

"Right, well, let's get this cleaned up and get back. Looks like you've lost three men and have a few wounded. We'll take them all back with us."

"What about their dead, sir?"

"That's their problem, not ours."

As the Lieutenant stalked off to return to his own party of soldiers the Sergeant grimaced to himself. He had told his now dead officer the spot was a bad risk to their patrol in this particular area, to no avail. His simple attempt to plant the same thought in this other officer's head garnered the same reaction as that of the dead man. The officers simply had no interest in listening to a non-commissioned officer, despite the years of experience behind him.

If it were left up to him, the Sergeant would have established another redoubt in the area and manned it properly, rather than exposing the men to exactly this sort of attack. He shook his head and wondered why he bothered, but even as the thought came he knew the answer. The lives of the men in his care were at stake, so he would keep trying. He would also keep doing what he was told. A vision of the flask of brandy flashed into his mind once again as he began barking commands to his remaining men.

***

Fedon was unhappy and he let his displeasure show to the men around the table. Besson, Ventour, La Valette, and his brother Jean Fedon were all there. The only woman at the table was Ventour's sister Sophie.

The Sugar Rebellion

"Eighteen men lost? Good God, Besson. You are calling this a success?"

"Of course. The British lost another officer and three of their men. To my thinking this was a good day's work and a fair trade. We are far better able to sustain losses than they are, especially when we can kill yet another of their officers."

"But the cost in lives, Besson. If the toll continues like that even on minor raids no one will want to go. I can give all the pretty speeches you want, but if we aren't making progress and all the men see is their doom facing them, we will lose."

"Julien," said Ventour. "You know the British are too well dug in on the perimeter of St. George's. You also know they have superior weapons and training. Our strategy of wearing them down and starving them out isn't working. There has been a steady stream of supply ships keeping them fed. In fact, I think their strategy is to wear *us* down. We've had to use far more of our men doing basic tasks like growing crops to feed everyone than we would like. So unless you are prepared to authorize an all or nothing assault to take St. George's, these limited attacks are the best we can do. And we will lose more men than they will."

"Julien, I don't see the problem," said Besson. "These are just slaves we are losing. They hate the white people and are willing to die if they must, because they have nothing to lose. And once again, I say we should just throw everything we have at them. We have thousands of men that will do it."

"I'm not sure about that," said La Valette, as Ventour nodded agreement beside him. "They have

The Sugar Rebellion

seen what the British field artillery can do. They have also seen how well trained they are. I think too many of them will balk at being fodder for their cannons unless we can show them something to guarantee success. We are making some progress with our men to try and match British discipline, but it takes time. So while I too would like to see the British pushed into the ocean, it's not clear to me that simply sending men to their certain doom is a winning strategy. Julien, what we really need is more and better weapons."

"Bah," said Besson. "Why don't we kill all these hostages? They are just eating food we could instead be feeding to our men. I think we should take the prisoners to where the British can see them and hang them all on the spot. It will provoke the British cowards into coming out to fight us in the open."

"Well, all I know is this looks like a stalemate to me," said Fedon. "They come out a little and raid us periodically and we try to ambush them periodically and nothing changes, except we keep losing far more men than they do. We've tried threatening them with an all out attack as you are suggesting and they told us we were the ones that should be surrendering. Even the offer to let them withdraw without bloodshed and a promise to free the hostages got us nowhere."

Fedon turned to face Besson direct. "And it's not clear to me that actually doing what you suggest with the hostages will get us anywhere, either. They have rejected all attempts to gain concessions from them in return for their release. But even so, I still

The Sugar Rebellion

think if we can find the right circumstances these people might be useful."

Besson frowned. "I still think their only use at this point would be to kill at least some of them to show the British we are serious."

Fedon shrugged. "Well, I don't know. You may be right, but the time for that is not now. Look, I know some of you probably think I am soft, but I am just trying to find the winning strategy our friend La Valette talked about. And I am not opposed to losing men. I know we will lose many more before this is over. I just don't want to commit to something unless I am certain we can make it work once and for all. But see here, I think La Valette made a good point about weapons. We have done the best we can with what we have and it is not enough."

"I agree," said Ventour, sitting forward for emphasis. "And the question I have is what has become of the support we were promised? Our friends from Guadeloupe have made lots of fine promises, but beyond a small supply of old muskets and ammunition they have done little for us. Too little. The only real weapons we have are ones we bought and paid for with our own resources."

"Yes," said Fedon. "I am not happy with the lack of tangible support. They have just returned and I am meeting with them shortly. I intend to bring this up and make it clear they must do better. I—ah, this may be word of them now."

Everyone turned to look at the servant who had poked his head in the door to announce the arrival of the two Frenchmen. Fedon told the servant to have them wait for a bit.

"Julien, can we join you in this meeting?" said Besson. "I do not trust these white men and I would like to make it clear they will have to do more than talk."

Fedon sucked in his breath in frustration. "These men agreed they would help us on the condition they deal only with me. Look, we all know they are spies sent from the National Convention in Paris and because of that they want their profile kept low. So do you all still trust me on this? I guarantee I will not mince words with them."

The four commanders looked at each other and slowly, one by one, they nodded agreement. Ventour spoke as he rose from his chair in unison with the others.

"Yes, Julien, we trust you. We have come a long ways and I don't think anyone wants to change course now, especially when we are so close. But something does have to change if we are to succeed. I agree with La Valette about our need for better weapons and you must make them see this. If they are not willing to help I am afraid the kind of bloodbath of our men that you fear will be a reality and, our only choice, if they don't help us. The longer the British hold out in St. George's, the more time they have bring in reinforcements or even more weapons. If we can drive them out perhaps they will give up on our island and focus their energy elsewhere. Julien, I want to see your dream of having our own republic here, just like in St. Domingue, become a reality."

Fedon rose from his seat to face the others and

The Sugar Rebellion

nodded to his commanders. One by one they gripped each other's forearms to reaffirm their commitment to each other. Jean Fedon embraced his brother hard for a long moment.

"I will not let you down," said Fedon.

Before the four men finally left the room Besson turned to Fedon to speak.

"If nothing else, Julien, we do still have your support as discussed for the attack on their southeastern fortification, correct?"

Fedon paused to take a deep breath before speaking.

"Yes. Yes, you do. I confess I fear we will lose far more men than you think, but I agree we must test them in this spot. Who knows, I may be wrong and you may be right they are in fact vulnerable there."

Besson nodded and closed the door behind him.

As Sophie Ventour made to leave Fedon reached out and touched her arm to forestall her.

"Stay a moment, Sophie, and tell me your thoughts. You know I value your opinion."

She remained silent for several long moments before finally speaking.

"Your commanders are divided and frustrated, Julien. But I am merely telling you the obvious. What you want to know is whether they really mean the words they have said about believing in you. The answer is yes, at least for now. As you know, Besson is the one you should most be concerned about, but the others keep him in check. As long as we have success he will happily stay in check. Your commanders have made good points, though. It is

The Sugar Rebellion

coming close to a year since we began and it is well over six months now we have been in the stalemate you correctly identified. Something has to change here. And I think my brother is right about what will have to be done if these men from Guadeloupe cannot help us."

Fedon rubbed his chin, obviously deep in thought. "Thank you, Sophie. As always your thoughts are clear and helpful. I will push them hard."

As Sophie made to leave once again Fedon stopped her and pointed to a door on the other side of the room from which the three commanders had left.

"Sophie, don't go just yet. The Frenchmen don't know you are here. Please, hide inside my chamber by the door and listen to the conversation. You know I value your perceptions. I will call you out when they have left."

With a silent nod she disappeared through the door and Fedon went to the main entrance to usher the two Frenchmen in. As Montdenoix and Linger came in both men looked around to ensure the room was empty before sitting down.

"We are sorry we have been delayed," said Montdenoix. "The British have been making our lives difficult in St. Domingue and on other islands. How are matters here?"

"No different than when you were here two months ago. As you saw I just finished a meeting with my commanders and they are even more frustrated than they were then, as am I. But lets get to business, shall we? What do you have for me?"

The Sugar Rebellion

"I am pleased to advise we have more muskets and small arms for you. Not as many as I know you wanted, but I'm sure it will be enough to make a difference with your efforts."

"And that is all?"

"It is."

Fedon slammed a fist on the table hard enough to make the two Frenchmen flinch.

"It is not enough! Do you not see the problem? We have been in a stalemate here for months now. The British are better armed than we are and they are dug in deep. You know we need field cannons from you and lots of them. You promised these would be found and given to us. Where are they?"

Montdenoix shifted in his seat, looking uncomfortable. "Julien, you must understand we have many demands on our resources and what you ask for is a precious commodity. I assure you we have tried, but our masters have had to make hard decisions about where the need is greatest. We will continue to try, you understand."

"Not good enough," barked Fedon. "The only choice left to us is to try to overwhelm the British with fodder for their cannons. Our men are already growing reluctant to be sent to certain death. We may win a skirmish here or there, but we always lose far more men than they do. Meanwhile, the strategy you suggested of starving them out is not working because the British are still being well fed by a steady stream of supply ships. Where is your navy? You assured us effort would be made to blockade the port."

"We have made effort to do that, Julien. But

fewer ships than we wanted were assigned to the task because of needs elsewhere. You also need to understand the cursed British Royal Navy is a force to be reckoned with. You may think what you will about the British overall, but the reputation of their navy is well deserved. But see here, the cache of muskets and weapons we have brought you? One of our privateers captured these arms from a British supply ship on its way here. So you see, we are doing what we can for you."

Fedon shook his head. "Fine words, Montdenoix. They are not enough. Look, I can't say it any clearer than this. If you and your masters want us to succeed you *must* do better."

Montdenoix spread his hands wide, allowing his own frustration to show on his face.

"I don't know what else we can do beyond what we already are. I assure you, we will make your needs known to our master in Guadeloupe. I shouldn't tell you this, but there is a possibility another ship can be freed up to deal with British shipping. You must understand I cannot guarantee this will actually happen, though."

"And what about information, Montdenoix? You are spies, are you not? What is the state of the British forces in St. George's? What is the possibility of reinforcements being sent to them?"

"I'm afraid I can offer you little about what is going on inside St. George's, but elsewhere is another matter. Our privateers based in Guadeloupe have been making life difficult for British shipping everywhere. In Jamaica the Maroons are still fighting with the British and we think they are tying

The Sugar Rebellion

down plenty of resources there. And St. Domingue, well. Matters there are complicated and will continue to stay that way. In some ways that is a stalemate, too, at least for now, but I think the British are paying a far higher price than they want and will rue the day they invaded. So for now, at least, I don't see an imminent threat of reinforcements appearing here. I counsel you to continue small raids to wear them down while we try to step up our efforts to cut off their supplies. They need food to survive and it must be having an impact."

"My God, I know more about what is happening in St. George's than you do, and you two are the spies," said Fedon, wearing an incredulous look on his face. "Yes, I have found a way to get a source in and out of St. George's. Food is not as scarce as you think. The British have been creative about planting crops everywhere they can within the area they control. They are doing just fine with this and the supplies coming by sea, despite the fact they have significant numbers of slaves and free coloreds that remain sided with them. They have also been getting soldiers. Not many, we think, but enough to replace their losses. Well, enough of this for today. I have other matters to attend to and I think I have made myself clear about what we need. If you want us to succeed, you know what to do. The day is not upon us yet where we will be forced into gambling on a full-scale attack, but I fear it is coming soon. And I won't be able to guarantee success unless you do better. Good day, gentlemen."

The two Frenchmen looked at each other and

rose from their seats, leaving the room without speaking.

Fedon remained sitting where he was in silence for several long moments, shaking his head in dismay over the encounter. With effort he finally pushed his chair back and went to open the other door. He waved Sophie in and went back to sit at the table. She joined him and sat opposite. Fedon rubbed his chin and sighed before speaking.

"Well?"

Sophie shrugged. "You did what you had to do, Julien. I think they actually are trying to do the best they can for us, but they have too many demands and it is too easy for this man Hugues in Guadeloupe to simply shortchange us. He may be trying to do too much with too little. This leaves us in a hard place and I hope your words will get us results, but I am not optimistic."

Fedon grunted his agreement. "So what does being in this hard place mean?"

"It leaves us needing more than ever to wear them down as fast as possible. You may have to step up the size of the attacks and, yes, that means sacrifice more men. We also need more information about what is going on in St. George's. If there is any hint whatsoever of large numbers of reinforcements coming it will force your hand."

Fedon was silent for a long moment. "So you think you have to go back to St. George's again?"

"At some point. Julien, there is no choice."

Fedon sighed. "Are you certain the fishing boat route will work again?"

Sophie shrugged. "I see no other option. The

The Sugar Rebellion

British lines are too well defended for me to try slipping through them. But they send fishing boats out just like we do and a little gold for the fishermen to bring me in while asking no questions works. The man we dealt with last time told me he regularly fishes that same area, so we will find him again. And no one pays attention to the fishermen and the fact a woman happens to be with them. Yes, there is a danger someone will be suspicious of me, but in truth the only attention I got last time was from men thinking about what they could do with me in private."

Fedon reached across the table and grasped her hand. "I am a man too, Sophie, and you know I have confessed to those thoughts before myself. But I fear for you also. You really will be in danger. If you are caught and accused of spying, the British will show no mercy."

"I will have to stay with my half sister again. She tolerates me and I think she knows what I am doing, but gold works with her, too. She also provides me with a cover story. Look, I am willing to risk it, Julien. What choice do we have?"

Fedon sighed. "In that, I fear I must agree with you, although I do not like it. It seems strange to me I must rely on you for this, but perhaps it makes sense for a woman to be a spy. Men do not give women much credit for anything beyond what they do in the bedroom, but you are not an ordinary woman, are you? No, of course not. But look, we do have choice today, Sophie. I want you to stay with me tonight."

Sophie eyed him for a long moment, still

clutching his hand, before she rose from her seat and came to stand beside him. Fedon's hopes soared as her scent enveloped him and she put an arm around his shoulders, her enticing breasts bare inches from his face.

"Yes, Julien, I choose to stay with you tonight."
***

Governor Mackenzie looked up as Colonel Walter was ushered into his office in Fort George and he steeled himself for the meeting to come. Waving the Colonel into a chair, he ordered his aide to bring wine for both of them. The two men remained silent until the wine appeared and the aide closed the door behind him.

"Colonel, thank you for coming today. What do you have for me?"

"Governor, the situation is unchanged except for the attack yesterday on one of our southeastern redoubts. I confess they threw rather a lot of their men at us there, more than the pattern of past attacks would suggest was the norm. I am not certain why, but they may have thought they had an opportunity there. In point of fact they did manage to flank us to a certain extent by sending a force through a rather thick patch of bush filled with thorns I had not anticipated they could get through. Fortunately their numbers that used this route were small and we were able to beat them back. We lost a dozen men along with a little more than that same number wounded, but they lost well over four times our losses, both dead and wounded. We also captured a couple of them. We are fortunate to have light artillery we can bring to bear while they still

The Sugar Rebellion

have none. In any case, we will not be caught with that ruse of theirs a second time."

"I see. And what are your plans from this point on?"

The Colonel shrugged. "I have kept our operations beyond our perimeter extremely limited as you requested. I still think I could damage their morale were we to expand our operations. I also think we should use the free colored population and the slaves we have on hand to help out, as much as I would rather not. Having lost this many men yesterday doesn't help matters. But Governor, with respect, you already know this, for we have had this conversation before. If your thinking has not changed, then the tactics will not either."

"Colonel, it has not changed. I know you don't believe it, but the limited sources I have suggest the rebels have far more resources than we do. We are in a stalemate here and I am concerned they are trying to wait us out, hoping we will lose patience and do exactly what you suggest. They want you to come out and fight them, Colonel, and that is exactly why you shouldn't do it. The losses you have sustained to date have been barely manageable and we have been fortunate the Army has been able to at least send replacements for the fallen. I also think the longer this goes on the more they may fear we will eventually be able to bring far more of our own resources to bear. If I am right, they may be massing forces for an all or nothing attack even as we speak."

Colonel Walter raised his hands wide to show his frustration. "I agree with you this is a stalemate, given the restrictions I have. Do you have something different in mind?"

"Sir, I do. I thank God every day we have been able to avoid starvation, given prudent management of our food supply and help from the Navy, but we need more and better information about the size of the forces arrayed against us. We need to know what their morale is, and most importantly what their strategy will be from this point on. Even better would be some way to deceive them as to our situation and intent. I have tried to no avail to build some sources to get this information, so I am now seeking help elsewhere."

The Colonel frowned. "Help? What kind of help?"

"Our friends in the Royal Navy have some fellows that specialize in this kind of thing. I know it's a bit out of the ordinary, but they have had some success and I have an idea they can help us. Yes, yes, I have once again requested you be provided enough additional resources to assure us you will have the upper hand, but it simply isn't possible right now. On the other hand, I have succeeded in convincing London we need help gaining the intelligence to prove we are in grave danger. If these men find that to be true, their word will help the case for more men. So at least help with this is on the way."

The Colonel's face wore a look of total disbelief and as the Governor finished speaking he shook his head as if to clear it of cobwebs.

"Governor, what can the *bloody* Navy do for us? Is this some kind of joke?"

The Sugar Rebellion

"Colonel, I do not joke about matters like this, and you would do well to remember that," said the Governor, unable to keep his annoyance from his voice.

The two men stared at each other for several long moments, neither willing to give in. The Colonel finally sighed.

"Sir. What do you expect of me?"

"At the moment, carry on as you have been. I am expecting our Navy friends to arrive at any time. You will not speak of this to anyone. When they do arrive, I will have you attend to brief them on the tactical situation here. And then we shall see what they have to offer."

"I see," said the Colonel, the stiff tone in his voice unmistakable. "Is there anything else for today, Governor?"

"You are dismissed."

The Sugar Rebellion

Chapter Four
February 1796
Grenada

Alice was standing on the leeward side of the quarterdeck of the *Alice* watching everything with obvious fascination as the ship tacked to stand into the inner harbor of St. George's. The late morning sun sparkled on the water as a light breeze filled the sails. Evan knew from the broad smile on her face how much she was enjoying herself. While she had sailed with him before, this was her first visit to the island of Grenada. Surrounded by the hills in the distance the colorful shops and homes around the harbor came into full view. Alice's smile widened and she came over to where he was standing on the windward side of the deck. On a normal Navy warship he would be watching his men work the guns to salute to the fort, but the *Alice* never gave away her true nature to anyone in such an obvious way.

"My God, Evan, this island is beautiful too. I can't believe how alike and yet different the various islands are. Thank you for bringing me."

"Let's not forget this is business, my love. And speaking of business, here you are, intruding on the Captain's personal domain again," said Evan, trying for a gruff tone to his voice, but unable to keep from laughing as he spoke.

"Oh, right, you did tell me this is your side of the deck, didn't you?" said Alice, allowing a sheepish look to appear on her face.

The Sugar Rebellion

Evan laughed again and put his arm around her shoulders. Out of the corner of his eye he saw James and a few of the other hands on the deck smothering grins of amusement.

"Not to worry, permission granted. Seriously, my love, I want you to be careful here. We don't know the situation and there may be opposition here. What do you plan to use as a cover story?"

"Why, I'm just going to bend the truth a little. If pressed I'll confess I'm the wife of a businessman, sent here by my husband and brought here by you as a favor to him. I'll say I've been asked to look at whether or not it might be worthwhile to open an inn with a tavern in St. George's. I do have some experience with taverns, you know. But that means I have to ask questions of people and find out what the situation is here."

Evan rubbed his chin in thought. "All right, I guess that works. But be careful with the questions, please. If you get any hint of suspicion I want you to pull back right away."

"Don't worry, lover man. Remember, I have done this before. And I know what you want. An assessment of the morale here and anything anyone can tell me about the state of affairs on the rebel side. Most of all, you want to know if there is anyone from their side in St. George's spying on us."

Evan nodded and gave orders to nose into an open spot alongside the Wharf Road dock. As Evan turned back to Alice he pointed to the fort on the hill looming over the harbor.

"Well, the Governor has his offices in Fort

The Sugar Rebellion

George and I expect he will be wanting to see me without delay, so that is where I'm going to be. I have no idea how long we will be there, but I expect I will be back on board before sundown. I would like you back by then, too. Most of the shops you will want to sniff around in are over there. Say, I almost forgot. Do you have your knife with you?"

Alice smiled and patted her left arm. One of the small sheath knives he had given her was strapped to the inside of her underarm, hidden from sight by the long sleeved dress she wore.

"I am armed and dangerous, my love. The other one is strapped to the inside of my thigh. Since I know you like dangerous women, why don't you make the Governor wait for a while and you come inspect me in our cabin?"

Evan laughed.

***

After securing the ship he left it in the hands of the third midshipman Captain Mason had found for him. Francis Hardman was the most promising of the three they were given, despite having turned seventeen only a few weeks before. Like Evan and James, he grew up in the Navy and had already proved a degree of competence with the ship, which was the reason he was chosen to join the ship and not the Dockyard.

As always, neither Evan nor James was wearing their uniforms, so the soldiers on guard at the base of Fort George hill eyed them with suspicion. But Evan's orders were clear, so an escort took them up the hill to the entrance to the fort. The fort was bustling with activity, but several of the

The Sugar Rebellion

soldiers and local militia eyed the newcomers with curiosity. The curious looks grew more pronounced as the two men were ushered straight into the Governor's office with minimal delay. Governor Mackenzie was alone, but greeted them with obvious warmth as introductions were made.

"Sirs, I had no idea you were in port or I would have been better prepared for your arrival. I have sent word to the one other person who needs to attend this meeting. Hopefully he will be here soon."

"We make a point of trying not to advertise our presence with things like rendering salutes when we come into harbors, Governor. It is far better not to be noticed, given our line of work."

"Yes, quite. That would explain your lack of uniforms as well. I—oh good, here is our other attendee."

The Governor made introductions as Colonel Walter came in and joined them. The Colonel looked both of the newcomers up and down with an expression on his face that somehow contrived to be both appraising and dubious at the same time. Without ado the Governor turned the meeting over to the Colonel, requesting he provide a full debrief on the current military situation.

"Sirs, Grenada Garrison currently numbers close to six hundred personnel, but not all of these are field soldiers for deployment. That number is closer to five hundred at best, officers included. The local Militia we can call on, as needed, effectively doubles our resources, but they are nowhere near as well trained as the Garrison. We also have local free

The Sugar Rebellion

colored men and slaves at the ready for use if we really must, but I wouldn't use any of them unless my life depended on it. We have sufficient resources in terms of weapons and ordnance with powder to spare, but we could always use more. Our forces are confined to a series of redoubts and fortifications we have constructed surrounding St. George's. Some also man the cannons in Fort Frederick on our easternmost lines. The rebels regularly test our defenses and we have beaten them back every time, with losses on their side far worse than ours."

Evan let the man drone on, absorbing and processing everything he offered. After almost ten minutes the Colonel was down to detailing the minutiae of his work, but Evan knew some things were missing, so he signaled he had questions.

"Thank you, Colonel. This is most helpful. I do have question or two for you. What forces do the rebels command and how are they deployed?"

The Colonel took a moment before responding, giving the Governor a quick side glance before he did.

"We do not know for certain. My officers and I estimate perhaps double the numbers we can field, based on the size of the attacking parties they send against us."

The Governor cleared his throat and spoke. "My colleagues and I on the Council fear that is an underestimate, gentlemen. We do not have any sources in the rebel camp, but anecdotal reports from people that fled to us when the fighting first broke out suggest it is far more than this, perhaps

The Sugar Rebellion

even ten times our numbers."

James spoke up for the first time. "Sir, what kind of weapons have they been fielding against you?"

"Mostly small arms, muskets, machetes, swords, whatever they can get their hands on," replied the Colonel.

"No field artillery?"

The Colonel shook his head and Evan nodded his understanding.

"So the reason they haven't overwhelmed you, if they indeed have that many people, is your field artillery, the defenses of the Forts, and what trained soldiers you have at your command."

"Yess," said the Colonel. "That would likely be a fair statement. *If* they have that many people. They were given a full taste of our defenses when we finally pulled back to our current lines. After they lost large numbers of men they realized it was getting them nowhere. Ever since it has been small raids to test our fortifications and our patrols. Opportunities to utilize our artillery with effect have been minimal."

Evan turned to the Governor with his next question. "Sir, what do we know of their leadership? Do we know where they are based? Have you communicated with them?"

The Governor grimaced and relayed what little he knew about Fedon, speculating the rebels might be using his estate in the mountainous center of the island as a base. He also told Evan of the hostages.

"The only communication we've had with them was to hear their demands we surrender. They sent a messenger with a white flag to tell us that nonsense. The messenger threatened they would murder the hostages and Governor Home, but we did not cave in. On hearing that he offered to free the hostages if we simply withdrew from the island. We sent him away and told him to tell his masters they should free the hostages and surrender or face the consequences. They tried more or less the same message a second time and got the same response. We haven't heard from them since."

Evan paused in thought, wary of the alarm bells ringing in his mind. He looked over at James and knew without question the same concerns were going through his mind, too. That they knew so little about their opponents at this stage in the conflict was worrisome and it was a safe bet finding out more would be part of what Evan and James would be expected to do. But orders were orders.

"Governor, I think we have a basic understanding of what is happening now. The orders I received lacked detail of any sort about what you desire my colleague and I to do. Is this a good time to discuss this?"

"It is, Commander. But first, I want to be sure you understand the context. I expect you are familiar with the wider situation throughout the Caribbean and, if so, you will know this is the real problem. We have significant military resources tied up on St. Domingue and that doesn't appear likely to change for some time. Meanwhile, in Jamaica the Maroons have been creating havoc and tying down help that could be sent our way. While I am hopeful that may finally change in the next few months, there is no lack of things for these soldiers to do. I have few expectations of help from back home any time soon. In fact, if it weren't for what is happening here I believe some of the resources protecting us would already have been sent elsewhere. Realistically, this is a minor sideshow compared to what is going on elsewhere."

Evan nodded agreement. "Sir, that tallies with my understanding of the situation."

"Good. So, as you heard, it is not clear what forces are arrayed against us and we have no idea of what their plans are. My fear is they have far more men than we think and that the longer this goes on the more they will be tempted to simply overrun us with men. Yes, their losses will be enormous, but I think they know sooner or later a relief force will be sent. I think the bloody French in Guadeloupe are behind this, damn them, and I also fear they may make an attempt to overwhelm us at the same time with an attack from their warships to help turn the tide. I don't know. I fear the French may be thinking of sending them better weapons, too. You would likely be better placed than I to assess whether or not any of this is possible. Thus, what I need from you at a minimum is a far better understanding of what forces they have and anything you can give me about their intentions. I would like to know how firm their resolve is. And I need this as soon as you can get it. If we are indeed in imminent danger then I will use whatever information you get to agitate for immediate help. If I'm wrong, well, we'll all sleep better at night."

Evan remained sitting in silence for several

The Sugar Rebellion

long moments before he responded. "Hmm, I'm not certain the French could get enough ships together to get past the Royal Navy and make the combination with the rebels here that you fear, but then this bastard in Guadeloupe is proving resourceful and anything is possible. Governor, you perhaps need to understand how we work. Our normal mode of operation is to slowly cultivate sources, all the while making certain we can actually rely on what they are telling us. This always takes time, which may be something you don't have. It usually also involves a lot of gold, but I think we can manage that issue."

"Actually, Commander, I was hoping for answers fast. I know, you aren't in the business of making miracles happen, but you gentlemen do have a reputation for getting things done when you have to. To be honest, Sir James Standish is a good friend of mine and he has told me about you two. Your colleague Lieutenant Wilton here came to mind."

Evan and James looked at each other for a long moment and then James spoke directly to Evan.

"Sir, we both know this means someone has to infiltrate the rebels. I volunteer."

Evan slowly nodded his head. "Governor, I think my colleague and I need some time to digest everything we have heard here today. In particular, we need to give thought to exactly how we might accomplish this. I fear this could be extremely dangerous. Could we meet again tomorrow to discuss this further?"

Before the Governor could respond Colonel

The Sugar Rebellion

Walter spoke up. His voice carried a hint of disdain.

"What, is our vaunted Navy going to try to wiggle out of this?"

Both Evan and James turned and scowled as one at the affront, but the Governor slammed a fist on the table to get everyone's attention.

"Colonel, that remark is uncalled for and displays a serious lack of professional respect. You will apologize immediately to these officers."

The Colonel glared back at them for several long moments before finally relenting.

"Sirs, the Governor is right. I apologize."

The tone of his voice left Evan in little doubt the Colonel's apology was insincere, but to cool the situation he nodded his acceptance.

"Right," said the Governor, still wearing a frown on his face. "Let me look at my calendar. Yes, I can see you gentlemen tomorrow at the same time here."

"Thank you, Governor," said Evan. "We will be here. The key to success with a mission like this will be having a well thought out plan and to accomplish that I do have one request for now. I wonder if the Colonel here can spare us maps of the interior of the island and he can show us where exactly his defensive lines have been established?"

"Yes, I can do both. If you gentlemen will join me in my office?"

"Excellent," said the Governor, "But Commander Ross, there is one other thing. If Lieutenant Wilton here does indeed infiltrate the rebels, it would be most helpful if any opportunity to sow discord or deceive them were seized. I think

The Sugar Rebellion

Colonel Walter here would be most appreciative if, say, bad information about our intentions or a deployment could be fed to them. Any opportunity to strike them hard with an ambush and put them on their heels in a significant way would be welcome. It shouldn't be anything that would put the Lieutenant at risk, of course, but if there is a way to buy us more time I will be forever grateful."

"Governor, something like that will definitely take time and thought. We first have to find a way to gain their trust."

"I understand, Commander. I know this can't be an easy task. I will leave you to it. Good day, gentlemen."

***

As Evan and James made their way the next day through the busy crowds on the cobblestone streets of St. George's to attend their second meeting with the Governor, Evan's mind was still abuzz with everything they had learned since their arrival. He knew James was preoccupied too. While trawling the taverns for information the night before they discussed the situation and the conversation carried on throughout the next morning. Both men proposed and discarded several possible ways to run the mission. They all carried high degrees of risk without any way to avoid it.

Evan sighed. "Well, I don't like this, but we have our orders. You are going to have to be ready for anything."

James grunted. "We're at war, Evan. If I wasn't being exposed to risk like this I'd be serving on a regular warship with just as much chance of being

The Sugar Rebellion

blown apart or shot. I knew what I signed up for."

Reaching Fort George once again they were shown into the Governor's office without delay. The Governor was alone and motioned for them to sit.

"It's just the three of us today, gentlemen. Wine?"

The two men looked at each other before Evan responded.

"Thank you, but I think we'll pass, Governor. We were in the local taverns last night looking for information and I think we both had one too many in the process."

The Governor gave a start before laughing aloud. "I suppose I shouldn't be surprised at that. Well, did you find anything of interest?"

"Sir, we did. Morale here seems good overall, but many are definitely worried about exactly what you are. And more than a few people confirmed they would put faith in your estimates of how many men the rebels can command. We were surprised at how many slaves seem to have stayed true to our side and perhaps even more surprised there are a number of free colored men who have done the same. It seems clear they are very divided on this island, but the real source of this rebellion seems to be the mulatto population. We did not find evidence or any hint of spies, either from the rebel side or even the French themselves. However, I must tell you one of our, hmm—associates found hints pointing to a possible exception. We didn't have time to get details before coming here, but we will be investigating further and will let you know."

"Yes, please do. Do you think the French

The Sugar Rebellion

would be so bold as to plant spies or informers here?"

"Absolutely. Even if they haven't been successful, I am quite certain the thought has crossed their minds. We have rumors of some Frenchmen out of Guadeloupe making mischief for us on other islands. It is possible these same bastards are operating here, or may be using cut outs to further their ends. Well, if they are here we will do our best to put a stop to their business."

"I may be able to help a little. I neglected to mention yesterday that the rebels had launched a fairly large raid on our lines just before you arrived. We beat them back, of course, but what is significant is we captured a couple of their men. They were injured and one died, but the other is alive. He was in no position to talk until yesterday. It turns out the one that survived is interested in saving himself from in depth interrogation and has been giving up what he knows."

Evan and James both sat forward with interest. "That would be helpful, Governor. We would like to talk to him ourselves if we could."

"By all means. He is just a slave and knows little unfortunately, but for starters he does corroborate our rough estimate of over ten thousand men under the rebel command. He can't be certain of exact numbers, of course. He confirms the rebel headquarters are indeed on the Belvedere Estate owned by this man Fedon. However, the one piece you will find interesting is he talked of seeing a couple of white Frenchmen coming and going to see Fedon on different occasions. No one knows much

The Sugar Rebellion

about them, but our man overheard them talking as they passed him by during one visit and he swears they are French and not locals. In any case, I suspected you would want to talk to him. Simply go to Colonel Walter's office after we are done here and you will be taken to the cells. So gentlemen, what are your thoughts on how to get what we need?"

"Sir, we are still building a plan, but we are doing so as fast as possible. I confess the possibility of success may be slim. As you may know from Sir James, Lieutenant Wilton here does have some command of French and can converse without much difficulty, but there will be no mistaking it is not his mother tongue. That he is black will help, but the challenge to ensure his survival is to concoct a believable story. In any case, we need a few more days to explore possible ways to even get him to the rebel side of the lines. I also think it likely we will have to involve another of our crew and, unfortunately, this man has little experience with this sort of business, but we shall see. But Governor, even moving expediently, I fear it will be a matter of weeks before the Lieutenant here will be in a position to offer us anything material."

The Governor sighed. "I know. Sir James Standish already told me this in his last letter. It's this sense we are sitting on a bomb that could explode at any time that drives me. I am sorry to be demanding about this and to be putting the Lieutenant here in such risk, gentlemen, but I am doing what I have to."

"Governor, we understand," said James,

speaking for the first time. "We know you are simply doing your job and we will do the same. I appreciate the concern both of you have shown for my safety, but this is my job and I will do it to the best of my ability. The Commander and I have been through more than a few tough situations together. I can't think of anyone better to come to my aid if that becomes necessary."

The Governor paused a moment, appraising the two men before him.

"I think Sir James has sent me the best men anyone could possibly want for the job at hand. Look, there is one other thing. I know it is highly unlikely anything can be done, but I fear for the hostages the rebels have in captivity. The rebels confirmed they have over fifty of them, including a number of women and children in addition to Governor Home. They included a note from him in his handwriting confirming this in one of their messages to us. If you can see any way at all we could mount a rescue mission for them then we should do it. We owe it to these people to at least consider the possibility and try, if there is a way. Well, God speed to both of you."

***

The sun was going down by the time they left the dank holding cell the lone surviving prisoner was in. Glad for a reprieve from the gloom of the prison dug into the hill beneath Fort George, Evan took a deep breath when they reached the fresh air. But the visit was worth every second spent with the man.

"Well, what do you think, James? Can we trust

him?"

"Yes. He is like a caged bird that knows he will be fed to a cat unless he sings. Did you notice him flinch when that Sergeant escorting us went in first? I suspect some of those bruises our man was wearing came from previous visits by our escort."

"Yes. Well, we know more than we did yesterday about our opponents. If nothing else this rough map he gave us of the layout of the estate they are using may prove useful to you. But I see little hope for those hostages."

"I agree, Evan. I didn't understand why anyone would have an estate on a bloody mountain until he explained they are growing coffee beans there. Any rescue mission would be in their gun sights for far too long just climbing there."

By the time they reached the ship Alice was waiting for them.

"Evan? I wasn't certain earlier, but I do have something for you."

"Do you now? Excellent. Unless it's urgent, you can save it for dinner. I think after all our efforts we deserve a little treat tonight. I know of a little place that served very good food the last time I was there a few years ago and I am hoping it will be just as good tonight. I sent word earlier we would be coming and they have a spot for us. Let's wash up a bit and go."

* * *

The unobtrusive little inn tucked away on a small bluff overlooking the inner harbor of St. George's was unchanged from what Evan remembered. His last visit to the inn was over seven years before. His dinner companion that night was a French spymaster named Captain Marcel Deschamps. They had enjoyed a wonderful meal as they probed each other's defenses, each trying to learn whether the other man was their foe. Both concluded they would have to look elsewhere for the unknown enemies smuggling arms to slaves in their respective islands. Rogue French aristocrats seeking to provoke a slave revolution around the Caribbean were to blame.

Years after the dinner Evan found himself mounting a rescue mission to St. Lucia to save the Captain, imprisoned as a royalist supporter by French revolutionaries. Evan and his men freed the Captain, but he died soon after from the brutal interrogations he had endured.

Evan introduced himself to the couple that owned and managed the inn, reminding them of his prior visit. Both gave a start of recognition and remembered the occasion, as they were relatives of Captain Deschamps. The couple treated Evan and his party like royalty from that point on. They asked no questions when Evan requested a table off in a corner, far enough away from most of the other patrons to ensure their conversation would be unheard.

In addition to affording them a measure of security, the table was close enough to the long verandah they could still enjoy an excellent view of the harbor. The night was pleasant, with a light, warm breeze. The lights of the numerous ships twinkled around the harbor and the docks. The room was filled with numerous plants in pots sprinkled near the tables. Vines were allowed to grow and attach themselves to a trellis attached to the wall framing the verandah itself. Unobtrusive paintings adorned the walls. The owner was apologetic as he went over the menu choices and the prices he was asking.

"I am sorry, but the current situation forces this upon me. Because I refuse to sell food that does not meet my standards I have to pay my sources more for the quality. We do not have rationing yet, but supplies are simply not as plentiful as they would normally be."

"We understand," said Evan, as the three of them took turns ordering. As the man left Evan smiled at James and Alice.

"This is my treat to you both. If the food is anywhere near as good as the last time I was here, you will love this. We don't often get to enjoy ourselves and I fear we have some difficult days ahead of us, so lets enjoy it while we can. Let's save business for later and just enjoy dinner."

The first to arrive was a bottle of French wine carrying an outrageous price, but Evan knew it would work well with most of what they had ordered. Fresh bread with butter was soon followed by a variety of small appetizers he had ordered for the table. A small dish of cold crab he remembered from the last time he dined at the inn was accompanied by a delicious plate of goat cheese covered with savory herbs, oil, and zest from a lemon. A small bowl of spicy fish soup filled with herbs and peppers for each of them rounded out the beginning of the meal.

The Sugar Rebellion

At the suggestion of the owner all three of them had the local grilled fish with an aromatic mix of rice and pigeon peas for their main course. Grilled and sprinkled lightly with garlic, oil, parsley, salt and pepper, and a touch of lemon juice, the fish made their noses twitch in anticipation and was done to perfection. They rounded the meal out with a dish of crème brulee for each of them.

"My God, Evan, that was incredible. These people know what they are doing," said James. "Beats what you get served by the Navy."

Evan laughed. "That wouldn't be hard to do. But our cook Baptiste does well with what he has to work with."

"Yes, thank you, my love," said Alice. "You can take me out for a dinner like this anytime."

Evan sighed. "The price for a dinner like this is we have to get down to business sooner or later to pay for it. I'm glad you two have enjoyed it, you in particular, James. While I appreciate the confidence you showed the Governor about my ability to rescue you if you run into trouble, I fear this time is different. The only way I can see to complete this mission is to get you into their camp and I won't even know if they toss you in prison the second you arrive."

"Evan, I trust you. You know that. Look, as we discussed the big problem is communication. If I can win their trust, how do I get you word of what is happening? We talked about pigeons, but there are too many things could go wrong with them and it's too obvious. Even if we could find a way to stash a cage full somewhere, if I'm caught with

The Sugar Rebellion

them the game would be over. Dead drops? Well, maybe, but even if I can gain a measure of trust they might be watching every move I make. That's what I would do if I was them."

Evan rubbed his chin and sighed. "Yes, I think there is nothing for it. I will have to see if Baptiste will serve as your conduit for messages."

"Baptiste?" said Alice. "Isn't he that slave you brought back with you from St. Lucia a few years ago?"

"Yes, I know you don't know him well. He is the house slave that stayed true to his French royalist owners. When French revolutionaries murdered his owner, he killed the man that was trying to rape the owner's wife. That landed him in jail waiting to be sent to the guillotine and we brought him with us when we rescued Captain Deschamps. He was so grateful he basically attached himself to us and joined the Navy. We've had him doing everything from serving as our cook to our ship's doctor. The men were even training him in how the ship is handled. But doing what I have in mind for him—well, I don't know."

James shrugged. "I think he's more capable than we know, Evan. He adapted fast to life on the ship and I confess his cooking is a major improvement over what we had before. I'm willing to trust him, if he is willing, and you think he can do it. He'll be able to fit in way better than I will among the rebels."

"Yes, there is that. Well, we shall see. We need to do a lot more planning before we reach a point you can be sent in. I think that idea I floated to you

The Sugar Rebellion

will work, but it is only the beginnings of a plan and I need time. That, and a few pieces like Baptiste being the man we think he can be for this job. I expect we will need to spend more time with our reluctant friend Colonel Walter on plans as well, but then no one ever said this job was going to be pleasant. Well, one piece of the puzzle at a time. Speaking of which, you mentioned you may have something for us, Alice?"

"Yes. I've made a few new friends around town in the last two days. Amazing how fast that can happen when you have much in common. Most of them are whores in the local taverns, but some are slaves that work in the local shops owned by white men. Things work the same way here as they do in Antigua. You will be happy to know my story is working, at least so far, and once they realize I am a former slave they are happy to talk."

"How do they figure that out?" said Evan.

Alice gave him a rueful look. "I'm not the first good looking black woman to be bought out of slavery by a white man. I just approach them and show some respect while I give them my story. It doesn't take them long to understand my background and they just ask me straight out. Amazing what showing people respect and valuing what they tell you can do. You should know. You use that approach very well yourself all the time."

Alice grinned as she grasped his hand and Evan smiled. "Anyway, you wanted to know what morale was like here, right? The answer is it's good so far, but there does seem to be some unease. They fear an all out attack and they know sooner or later

The Sugar Rebellion

something has to change. There are actually a lot of slaves that were forced to take refuge here in St. George's. I find it interesting many did not trust the rebels. It seems to boil down to a distrust of the French. They seem to think the French are the real drivers behind all this, but no one has any proof of that."

She paused a moment to sip her wine before continuing. "But the real news is I think there was someone here looking for information. A mulatto woman no one seemed to know much about was here some time ago asking questions around town. My new friends tell me she wanted to know about the state of affairs here, much like myself, but she also hinted at being willing to pay for any information about the Army and it's plans. They also tell me she is quite good looking and is even a rival to me."

"Damn," said James. "Lead me to her."

"Not possible, you beast," said Alice with a laugh. "Apparently she has not been seen for a while. But I will stay on the lookout. The one other point of note is my friends don't think she is a slave or even ever was one."

"And how do they know that?' said Evan.

"Simple. She is far too used to ordering people around and it shows. She may actually be a freeborn mulatto, Evan. And if she is as good looking as they say she could be someone's mistress or wife."

Evan grunted, deep in thought. He turned and motioned the inn's owner over to the table and ordered snifters of cognac for all of them before reaching for Alice's hand once again. Evan waited

The Sugar Rebellion

till they appeared on the table and the owner left before responding.

"Well, this is interesting. I wonder how she got in and, presumably, got out of St. George's again. If anyone figures it out do let me know. In any case, Alice, you have done well once again. Please keep it up and if you get any hint of this woman's return you will have to be on your guard. You must assume she will be as armed and dangerous as you are."

"I can take care of myself, lover man."

"You both must take care of yourselves," said Evan. "This could well be the riskiest task we've ever been given and I don't feel right about it, because you two are the ones doing the dirty and dangerous work. You both mean a lot to me and I don't want to see you come to harm."

Evan and Alice were stilling holding each other's hand across the table and James reached his own out to place it on top of theirs for a brief moment.

"Evan," said James. "We all mean a lot to each other. We know if there is anyone that can dream up a plan to see us safely through this, it's you."

The Sugar Rebellion

Chapter Five
February 1796
Grenada

Evan called out a command to enter and the door to his cabin opened. A slim, but well built black man a few years younger than Evan came in and saluted. Evan motioned for him to sit, studying the man before him as he complied. Evan knew he was about to ask much of the man sitting patiently before him and he cursed himself for not taking the time to learn more of his qualities before now.

The moment Evan had freed him from the reeking jail in St. Lucia Baptiste had sworn a vow he would be Evan's man. Evan had paid little attention at the time, but Baptiste was true to his word. Evan thought he was a simple house slave in St. Lucia before being thrown in jail, but he was wrong. Baptiste was in fact the senior slave in the entire organization of his former owner, trained and educated to a high level to oversee administration of his owner's estate. When Evan returned to Antigua from the mission to St. Lucia his days were a blur of demands on his time because they needed to go back one last time. Somewhere in this blur of activity Baptiste approached him and begged to stay at his side to be of service.

Baptiste himself suggested joining the Royal Navy. He freely admitted to knowing nothing of ships and sailing, but swore he would learn. Evan knew the man already had a degree of skill with medical problems, as this was one of his additional

The Sugar Rebellion

tasks on the plantation in St. Lucia and Evan had no one on the *Alice* with such skills. When Baptiste offered his services as a cook Evan had him prove he could do it by serving him dinner the same night. The meal was so good Evan made arrangements to give Baptiste the signing bounty as a volunteer and added him to the ships roster before he got to the dessert course.

Baptiste also made it clear he could both read and write, and had done much of the paperwork for his now dead former master. Evan tested him by delegating some minor paperwork from the never-ending flow of correspondence, reports, and invoices coming across his desk for Baptiste to handle. He managed it all without effort and soon had work as a part time clerk for Evan added to his duties. In the three years since Baptiste joined the Alice he had become an indispensible part of the crew.

As a condition of joining the *Alice* Baptiste was sworn to secrecy about the true role of the ship like everyone else. That he had fit in well, made himself so useful, and in particular obeyed the rule to keep his mouth shut about the activities of the ship boded well. But Evan realized he didn't know Baptiste on a personal level and, for what he was about to ask of him, this had to change.

"Thank you for coming, Baptiste. It has been three years since you joined the *Alice*. I suppose I should have asked you this sooner, but how have you fared? Have you enjoyed your life with us?"

The only outward sign Baptiste gave he thought this line of questioning from his commanding

The Sugar Rebellion

officer was unusual could be seen in the slight crinkling of the lines around his eyes for a brief moment.

"Sir, I have enjoyed every moment of my time on the *Alice*. I like cooking, even in the somewhat primitive conditions aboard the ship. I like helping the men when they have medical problems and I'm trying to expand my knowledge in that area. I like helping you and I have made many friends on the ship. I hope I have performed my duties to your satisfaction."

"You need have no concerns about that, Baptiste. You have made yourself indispensable. I seem to remember quite some time back you expressed interest in learning how to sail. You also wanted to be trained in using weapons and the bosun was going to help you with all that. I am remiss in not following up to see it was accomplished. How did you fare?"

"Sir, the entire crew has been most helpful on all accounts. I confess I didn't much enjoy climbing up the mast onto the yards to handle the sails, but I did it. I like working the guns. I am very comfortable handling small arms and the bosun has deemed me good enough with a cutlass I no longer need his advice."

"Very good. So I expect you know we are dealing with a serious rebellion here on Grenada and you probably know the word is the rebels want to establish a black republic, just like in St. Domingue. Does it bother you we are here to help put a stop to that?"

This time Baptiste couldn't hide a momentary

The Sugar Rebellion

flash of surprise at the question.

"Sir, I am your man. If our orders are to do that then it is not for me to question them."

"But you are a man of color, like they are. Isn't the freedom to run their own lives a worthy goal?"

Baptiste took a long moment before answering, clearly giving thought to his response. He sat straighter in his chair as he did.

"Sir, it is. Every slave desires to be free and they should be. I am but one man and I do not have the power to change the world. If there were one thing I could change, ending slavery would be it. But nothing I've said changes what I said earlier. I am your man and will follow orders. Willingly."

Evan reached across the desk and extended his hand. Baptiste eyed it and did the same so they could shake hands with each other.

"That was well said and, yes, I agree with you," said Evan, withdrawing his hand. "I too would like to see an end to slavery. Unfortunately, I suspect there are French revolutionaries behind this and I very much question their motives. It's not clear to me they really want freedom for their slaves."

"You don't need to convince me of that, sir. I have no trust for them either."

"Look Baptiste, I am sorry to be asking difficult questions of you, but I had to. I have you in mind for something that is much more difficult than anything you have ever done. I needed to know a bit more about you, but I am still thinking you are the man for this job."

"Sir. Those revolutionary animals would have cut my head off were it not for you. I told you the

The Sugar Rebellion

day you saved me I was your man and that hasn't changed. Not only did you save me, you have given me a new life here on the *Alice*. My former masters are dead and on the *Alice* I am a free man. I love it here and I'm not alone. Sir, I don't know if you realize it, but the men have the highest respect for you. You are a firm and fair commander. So if you have a task for me then simply command me and it shall be done."

"I appreciate that, Baptiste, but I think in this case it would be best if you understand the task first. If you do not believe you can do it simply say so. I would have you do this willingly or not at all. Please understand, though, the mission is confidential. If you choose not to do this you must still keep what I tell you now to yourself."

As Baptiste nodded Evan took several minutes to give him a detailed outline of what was at stake and what the Governor was asking of them. As he finished he sat forward in his chair to emphasize his final point.

"Lieutenant Wilton will obviously have the most dangerous task with the basic plan I have outlined, but you will be in danger, too. The Lieutenant has to have a way to get information out. He will be under suspicion, but by using dead drops that you monitor, or even better, by finding ways to communicate verbally with each other, it could work. You will be able to fit in with ease as you speak French and have served as a house slave. We will have to concoct some story that will work for you. The object is to somehow get you as close as possible to him without being under suspicion. But

The Sugar Rebellion

you will be in danger every second while you communicate with him and in turn while you pass messages to us. I am still working on figuring out the best ways to do that, but there is no escaping the danger. If you are caught they will likely show no mercy."

"I've seen the kind of mercy they offered my former masters, sir. Lieutenant Wilton is a good man and I am willing to support him. Count me in, sir."

"Very good. He will appreciate your help. Right, that will be all for now. We will speak more of this once we have our plans in place. You are dismissed."

As the door closed on the young man Evan felt better. His major concern to this point was James would have no help on the other side, but with Baptiste appearing both capable and willing the situation was improved. But there were still many gaps to fill in the plan and with a sigh Evan turned his thoughts to those. After musing in silence for a while he made his decision. Tomorrow would see the *Alice* leave harbor.

***

The morning sun glistened off the water, forcing Evan to shade his eyes as the *Alice* left port and tacked north toward Gouyave. The maps available to him hinted he might be able to find what he was looking for along the way, but he had to see the coastline to be certain.

Alice and James were on the quarterdeck with him and, as usual, the scene fascinated Alice. Evan marveled yet again she had never shown any hint of

The Sugar Rebellion

seasickness and appeared born to sail. The light swells and wind kept them moving at a steady pace, stirring up schools of flying fish bursting from the waves as they went. Seeing them always brought a smile to Alice's face, but she danced with joy at seeing a cluster of green turtles on the surface as they passed a small cove.

Evan told James what he was looking for and together the two of them watched the coastline for signs of what they sought. Every so often the two of them would raise their telescopes as one to study a particular section of the coast. As they got closer to Gouyave the intensity of the search grew. With sharp eyes James found a spot with promise and pointed the feature out to Evan. Scanning the coastline around it intently Evan saw no signs of life.

"Excellent, I think it will do. James, bring her about and let's take one more cruise past it a little closer inshore. I think we can risk it."

As they came about Baptiste appeared and signaled for permission to join them on the quarterdeck. Evan waved him over.

"I was just about to send for you. Here, take my glass and have a look at this spot. The plan is to hide a small cutter here. You see the little inlet there with the heavy brush around the sides and a fairly steep slope to the water?"

"Sir, I do. What about the mast?"

"I think the surrounding trees will screen it from casual view. The water won't be deep enough for the *Alice*, but I think it will be fine for a cutter. That odd shaped peak of rock just to the south can

The Sugar Rebellion

likely be seen for a long ways and will serve as a good reference point. All we need do is secure it to the trees and you and Lieutenant Wilton have a means of escape should it be needed."

The return sail past confirmed their thoughts and Evan decided to return the next day to drop off the small boat. He also decided Baptiste would join him to establish a message dead drop location for Evan to check periodically, one far enough from the hidden boat to ensure its location would remain secret. Evan kept the *Alice* under a light press of sail to buy them plenty of time to scout the coastline, continuing onward to Gouyave in search of the second location he wanted. Not far outside of the town was a golden sand beach, partially obscured from anyone in town by a point of land that made for a gentle, curving bay. The beach sloped gently up to the thick, green jungle of the tree line.

"Perfect," said James, as he lowered his glass and looked at Evan.

"Yes," replied Evan with a firm nod. "Far enough from town we won't risk anyone being shot by onshore guards, but close enough they will come and see what we want them to see. Close enough too that the row to the beach isn't long, while the water looks shallow enough a warship wouldn't risk their bottom coming closer in."

Evan turned to Baptiste. "So the plan is you will be dropped here first, two hours before the Lieutenant goes in. Once the show is over you will follow them into Gouyave. We are hoping the Lieutenant will sooner or later be taken to this man Fedon. You follow and use your cover story that

The Sugar Rebellion

you are a house slave from the south of the island who wants to help Fedon. It is unlikely you will get close to him, but your real goal is to find a way to shadow the Lieutenant and serve as a conduit for information. You and the Lieutenant will have to improvise based on the situation you encounter. I recommend the two of you establish a series of dead drop locations to hide messages as soon as you can if verbal reports are too risky."

"I understand, sir. I won't fail you or the Lieutenant."

***

A week later the pieces were all in place. Several long sessions with Colonel Walter produced plans for a pending raid James could reveal to Fedon as proof of his sincerity. A second opportunity was identified should he need to provide further proof. The meetings included the Lieutenant commanding *HMS Keene*, a Royal Navy sloop that was part of a larger nearby force. He and his ship were in port for temporary repairs and the Governor requested he stay a little longer than planned to help. Evan sent word to the man's commanding officer of the need, and orders to remain and help soon arrived.

Evan knew the best story James could use to explain his presence would have to contain as much truth to it as possible, leaving minimal opportunity to be caught lying. The *Keene* was a necessary piece, as James would be cast as a deserting master's mate throwing his lot in with mulattos like himself to help with the rebellion. The *Alice* couldn't perform the role as she was made to appear

The Sugar Rebellion

more like a merchant vessel than a Navy warship.

A key piece of the puzzle was the easy decision to have James hide the fact he could understand and speak French. He had learned the language from Manon Shannon, the woman he was going to marry until she was murdered by the French three years before.

The Governor was pleased Evan had made progress as fast as he had on building a plan and readying to begin. He confessed in private his expectation was it would take far longer, although his hope was the opposite. Evan left the Governor's office with mixed feelings. While pleased it was all falling into place, he was unable to escape the sense the man who was his best friend for years now was going into extreme danger, despite Evan's best efforts to mitigate it.

Evan knew it was the burden of command, having sometimes to give orders that might bring harm to others. Even sending Alice into the streets of St. George's every day to keep watch for the mystery woman gave him pause, but he knew it was necessary. She had found no further sign of the woman, but Evan knew this could change at any time.

When the day came for James and Baptiste to board *HMS Keene*, Evan stood on the dock and gripped his friend's arm for a long moment.

"Stay safe, my friend," said Evan.

James nodded. "I can take care of myself, Evan. I'll come back."

After Alice had given both James and Baptiste a quick hug each the Keene slipped from her berth

The Sugar Rebellion

and headed out to sea. Evan and Alice remained standing on the dock with an arm around each other, watching it leave until it disappeared around the headland of Fort George.

After returning to the *Alice*, Evan turned to the only thing he could to take his mind off his worry. The mountain of ever present paperwork on his desk together with occasional trips into town to trawl the taverns for information and be on the lookout for spies would be his only solace until Baptiste could get word out of the situation behind the rebel lines.

When it became clear they would be stationed on Grenada for an extended period Evan sent word to Antigua to have correspondence for him and the crew forwarded regularly by packet ship. As he shuffled through the latest batch of letters and reports, one letter in particular caught his eye. He recognized the handwriting on the envelope and he shoved the rest of the letters to the side to concentrate on this one.

On opening it he was proved correct the letter was from Captain Horatio Nelson. Having given Evan and James the opportunity over a decade before to prove themselves in a career as spies Nelson had kept his interest in the two men alive. Ever since they had maintained a sporadic correspondence with each other. Every time a new letter arrived Evan marveled at his dedication to keeping in touch with two men.

While true the success Evan and James realized a decade ago reflected well on Nelson, favor was often fleeting in the world of the Navy. But Evan

The Sugar Rebellion

knew Horatio Nelson was not a fair weather sailor. He was the kind of leader who stood fast with the people he led and would do so to the end of his days.

But as Evan read the letter he grew more and more concerned. Evan knew from Nelson's last letter that since resuming command of a warship in 1793 he was active in the Mediterranean. The Captain was involved in the fall of Toulon in December of the same year, while in July 1794 he was injured when struck by a splinter of rock while at a forward gun emplacement during the siege of Calvi on Corsica. The price was losing sight in his right eye. The year 1795 had not been any kinder.

Evan was shocked at the degree to which Nelson was criticizing the admirals above him in the letter. Nelson had spent much of the year conducting operations out of both Corsica and Genoa, a small state on the Italian coast. As of the time of writing the letter, Nelson felt everything he had done to sustain British support in Italy and to hamper the French at sea was for naught. Evan had never seen such a dispirited tone in any of the letters Nelson had sent over the years.

Admiral Hotham was Nelson's senior officer for most of 1795 and he seemed the antithesis of the man of action Nelson embodied. Admiral Hyde Parker replaced Hotham late in the year, but proved little better as he behaved like a caretaker and showed little interest in stirring himself to action. The one ray of hope Nelson could hang onto was the rumor a more active officer might be appointed soon to reverse the decline of British power. Nelson

The Sugar Rebellion

feared it possible a full retreat from the Mediterranean was coming.

Evan was appalled. To even contemplate turning the entire Mediterranean over to the French was unthinkable. After a few long moments mulling over everything the Captain had said, Evan put the letter down and began to pen his response. Evan and James would stand firm and do their part to ensure the same thing did not happen in the Caribbean. Evan knew the Captain needed to hear that.

***

Even with the minimal moon light available Baptiste was able to scout the area they dropped him off at two hours before. By the time a hint of dawn appeared to the east over the island he was established in what he felt was the best possible spot. They hadn't seen the well-worn path down to the beach from the ship during their reconnaissance, but he found it right away and he knew if the rebels came this was what they would use. He discovered a small, rocky rise in the ground covered with scrub brush between Gouyave and where he knew Lieutenant Wilton would soon appear suited for his purpose. He settled in to wait with only the mosquitos for company, certain he would not be seen.

The wait was not long. *HMS Keene* lay at anchor well over a hundred and fifty yards from the beach. As the birds in the trees began to stir with the dawn the silence was broken by the sound of a shot from the direction of the warship. Within seconds a man rowing the ship's jolly boat toward shore as if his life were at stake appeared. The boat was over

The Sugar Rebellion

halfway to shore when more small arms fire sounded from the deck of the warship, but the man in the boat never faltered.

By the time he was almost on the beach a second boat was pulling away from the Keene while the small arms fire continued. Baptiste shifted his focus to watch the path for signs the rebels were coming and he was rewarded by the first hint of movement through the trees in the distance. Turning back to the beach Baptiste was in time to see Lieutenant Wilton jump out the second he touched shore. He reached back into the boat and pulled out a musket, which he quickly loaded. Taking shelter as best he could behind the boat he aimed for his pursuers in the second boat and fired. His shot had no effect.

The Lieutenant was undeterred and quickly reloaded. His second shot was better, as one of the passengers kneeling to return fire threw his arms in the air as if hit and fell among the men rowing. Lieutenant Wilton reloaded once more and sent another shot their direction as the *Keene* responded with a swivel gun. The shot ripped into the sand near the boat Lieutenant Wilton was hiding behind. The Lieutenant turned and fled up the beach into the trees with his weapon. As he reached the tree line a half dozen rebel soldiers appeared and made their presence known by firing at the boat chasing the Lieutenant.

Baptiste smiled, as their arrival signaled time for the second boat to retreat as planned. He knew it was all a charade for the benefit of the rebels and that the Lieutenant had not actually shot his pursuer.

The Sugar Rebellion

But as the boat turned and retreated the *Keene* wasn't pretending at anything when they turned their sights on the rebel soldiers. Two swivel guns barked at virtually the same time, cutting a swath through the enemy. Baptiste saw two of them fall and not get up. The others melted away into the brush. With no obvious targets to shoot at, the *Keene* did not fire again. The *Keene* made a show for anyone watching of using a sling to hoist a limp, unmoving sailor from the second boat to the deck.

With the show over Baptiste focused on watching for contact between the Lieutenant and the remaining rebel soldiers. When he spotted movement through the trees as they all came out of hiding, Baptiste made his move. Creeping slowly down the rise he wormed his way closer to where he had seen them. By the time he got there Lieutenant Wilton was disarmed and being searched by two of the remaining soldiers. When he got close enough to listen to the conversation he was elated to realize the plan seemed to be working.

Fortunately, the big black man that was their leader seemed to understand English to a degree. Between him and Lieutenant Wilton using a few atrocious, stilted French words the Lieutenant made them understand his story. The leader still wore a suspicious look, but Baptiste could see the worm of doubt on his face. Baptiste smiled as the man made his decision and they all turned to head into Gouyave. That they had accepted Lieutenant Wilton at face value to this point was a good sign. Baptiste followed at a discreet distance until they reached Gouyave.

The Sugar Rebellion

Once in town Baptiste simply blended in with the people who came out of their houses to see what was happening, as the distant weapons fire had woken everyone. All eyes were on James and no one paid attention to Baptiste at all, exactly as they had expected. The soldiers took James to a squat stone building Baptiste surmised was their headquarters and they all disappeared inside.

The task now was to wait and remain undetected. The hope was James would be taken to meet the leaders of the revolt and that it would be soon. If not, Baptiste's task would be much harder. After walking about the town Baptiste settled on a small tavern with an inn above it near the headquarters building. Pretending to be a house slave from a plantation in the south of the island in Gouyave on business for his master, he secured a room and then went to the tavern for breakfast.

As he sat at a table with a view of the entrance to the headquarters James was still in, a pretty young serving girl approached to take his order. Baptiste sat straighter and offered his most winning smile, hoping the Lieutenant would be held overnight and he could get to know the girl better.

***

They kept referring to James as their guest, but he knew it was otherwise. He also knew sooner or later it would change. On the third day they led him out of the tiny room he was kept in and gave him a mount with an escort of four men without explanation. Fortunately, the same man that understood English was leading the party and as they left the outskirts of town James asked what

The Sugar Rebellion

was happening. The man eyed him as if he were a simpleton before shrugging in response.

"Fedon wants to see you."

James could see the man had no interest in answering any further questions, so he turned his attention back to the road ahead. Several curious people were standing along the roadside watching them leave and James made a point of ignoring their stares as if they weren't there. He was buoyed by the sight of Baptiste standing further back from the crowds, waiting in the shadows of a building they passed. Baptiste made no move to draw attention to himself and James made a point of not looking in his direction, although he tried signaling he had seen him with a wave of his hand that he passed off as an attempt to brush away a fly.

As they left town the road soon became little more than a worn, narrow path snaking its way ever inland. The path began winding its way gradually upward toward the green, lush hills and low mountains in the distance. At times they intersected other, wider paths that were obviously used to haul the products of the plantations they passed out of the interior of the island down to the shore. Fields of sugarcane in various stages of growth swayed in the breeze, but those weren't the only crops he saw. As they wound their way higher into the hills the plantations of sugar cane gave way to fields on the slopes holding row after row of exotic looking coffee plants with bright red berries. Tropical birds flitted back and forth everywhere he looked, giving voice to their musical cries as they went.

What was unusual was the lack of activity on

several of the plantations. Over the years James had learned about the cycle of planting and harvesting on sugar plantations, and he knew they were in harvest time right now. While some of the plantations had people cutting cane and working in the fields, many more did not. They also passed by several buildings James knew were dedicated to crushing and processing the cut cane, but many showed no signs of activity. The picture was the same with many of the coffee plantations.

As he thought about it James realized that at best only a third of the plantations were actually being worked. Of those he also noticed the level of activity was nowhere near what would be expected on a normal plantation. Whether this meant a level of disorganization in the rebel cause or something else was unclear. But they also passed several small plots of land serving as gardens to produce various fruits and vegetables and these were all being tended carefully. James surmised the simple need to put food on the table explained why effort was focused on them.

After over two hours of steady climbing on the winding paths James found himself entering the boundaries of yet another coffee plantation. This one was set on the slopes of a small mountain with commanding views of the surrounding terrain. Having studied the maps with Evan, James felt certain he was close to the center of the island. Lush green vegetation covered everything in sight. Rolling hills and taller peaks were everywhere, while occasional glimpses of the ocean shimmering in the far distance could be seen between them.

The Sugar Rebellion

James was sure a nearby peak was Mount Qua Qua, with its sheer height and particularly steep slopes making it easy to identify.

James soon had more than scenery to concern himself with. He quickly realized this plantation was a hive of activity, unlike all of the others he had passed. The difference here was no one was working in the fields. Several small buildings that were clearly temporary shelters had several men lounging around them. In a small open field James saw others being drilled to fight by their commanders. Some were practicing on dummies fighting with machetes, while others were using makeshift pikes. Another group was being drilled on using muskets and even as James watched a volley crashed out. No one seemed curious about the new arrivals.

Once past the makeshift shelters James found the small mansion of the plantation's owner. Across from it and separated by a pleasant, open patch of ground were yet more buildings. These had an air of permanence to them and were much sturdier. What caught James's eye were the armed guards posted at the entrance to a large, but dilapidated, older building off to the side. They passed close enough to it on their way to the mansion James thought he could hear the sound of many voices coming from it. A woman's cries mingled with the voices. James had no time to study it further as soon enough they reached the mansion and stopped in front. The leader of the group dismounted.

"You will all wait here," he said, before mounting the steps to the wide verandah of the

The Sugar Rebellion

mansion and disappearing inside.

The wait wasn't long. He returned and beckoned to James to join him. The inside of the mansion was as much a hive of activity as it was outside. They passed several rooms with people in discussions, some sounding heated. After knocking on a door at the rear of the building a voice within bade them to enter. As James walked in a door on the far side of the room was closing, but not before he had a brief glimpse of what he thought was a woman leaving. But a handsome, coffee colored black male sitting behind a desk immediately drew his full attention.

"He is unarmed, Julien," said his escort.

"Fine. You may leave us. I will call you if needed."

As the guard left the room and closed the door the two men studied each other with interest for several long moments before Fedon finally spoke.

"Well, I've had many men flock to our cause to do what they can, but you are the first to flee a British warship to do so. I'm told your name is James Williams? I need to hear your story, James."

James cleared his throat. "Sir, I was a Master's Mate in the Royal Navy, but I am now a deserter. If they catch me I will hang. I am aware of what happened in St. Domingue and when I heard what you have done here I longed for the freedom. I seized my chance and here I am."

"Come, James, I need to hear more. How did you, a black man, come to be in the Navy? How did you manage to reach the level of Master's Mate? This is a senior position, is it not?"

The Sugar Rebellion

"Sir, it is. My father was a white man in the Navy and at a young age I chose to follow him. I am not alone, as there are more than a few black men serving on Royal Navy ships. For the most part the officers care only if you do your job. If you do it well, as I did, it is possible to rise in the ranks, but I was at the limit. The white officers have no interest in seeing a black officer on their ship and many are all too willing to disregard evidence before their eyes of my competence and simply dismiss me. I have grown weary of their ignorance and prejudices. It may not seem like it to you, but my life in the Navy felt like a form of bondage. Not outright slavery, perhaps, but the sailors are slaves in all but name, given the way many Navy officers treat their men. So here I am, sir. I assume they told you I can offer news of a raid they are planning on you to prove my sincerity?"

Fedon leaned back in his chair and studied James for a long moment before responding.

"Yes, they did tell me of this. I welcome the opportunity to blunt their attack, but I need my senior commanders to hear what you have to offer. I have sent word for them to join us and they should be here in the next day or two at most."

"Sir, unless they change something, the raid is planned for a week from now at the beginning of March. You do not have much time."

Fedon raised an eyebrow and let a look of incredulity appear on his face. "We will not rush into anything, you understand. Make no mistake, James, we must be certain you are who you say you are. If we deem it necessary to act, we can do so in

The Sugar Rebellion

a hurry. So, I still have some critical questions I need answers to. Do they know that you know of the raid? And why is it the Navy knows of a raid in the first place? They have not been directly involved to this point."

"There has been talk of the Navy taking a more direct role in this conflict for quite some time now," replied James, giving Fedon a small shrug of indifference. "And no, they do not know I am aware of the details. I was standing watch late in the evening recently and overheard the Captain and the First Officer discussing the details. The Captain's cabin has a skylight he keeps open on warm nights and, although their voices were low, I heard them clearly enough. The reason our ship was off the coast near Gouyave was to scout out a landing beach near the town. They want to retake Gouyave and open a second front to weaken your resources facing St. Georges. They also hope it will weaken your resolve, sir."

"All right, that at least makes some sense. Well, then we will have much to do when my commanders arrive. Please consider yourself my personal guest. We are pretty full, but I can assign you a room here in my home."

Fedon raised his voice and called for the guard to return, issuing orders to assign James a room and to cease guarding him. As James rose to leave Fedon spoke once more.

"I will send someone to show you around the estate and help you with settling in. We will speak again, Mr. Williams. Or should I say, James. And by the way, you can stop calling me 'sir'. We are not formal about this. I am plain old Julien to everyone."

"Thank you for your hospitality, sir—ah, Julien," said James, giving him a rueful smile. "Sorry, force of habit. It may take me a while to get used to the change."

***

Once the door closed behind James, Fedon remained sitting behind his desk for several long moments, staring at nothing while he digested what he had heard. He finally sighed and rose, crossing the room to open the other door. As expected he found Sophie waiting patiently for him. Without a word she came in and took the seat James had vacated as Fedon returned to his desk.

"You heard?"

"I did, Julien."

"Well?"

She shrugged. "We will obviously have to be careful with him. He has a story that is perhaps believable, but he could equally be a professional spy like our friend Montdenoix. I think it logical he would have a good story for us if that were so, wouldn't he? This raid he is talking about could be a trap, but if it is then the first thing we will do afterwards is kill him. That means he is either a real deserter or the raid will be a show to get him into our confidence and learn our plans."

"Indeed. Well, we will see what the others think of him. Sophie, we need to know more about him, much more. I told him someone would be assigned to help him settle in. Can I ask you to be that someone and work on learning more about him

The Sugar Rebellion

in the process?"

Sophie stiffened and gave Fedon an appraising look before responding.

"Julien, what does that mean?"

Fedon sighed and rubbed his forehead. "Sophie, we must know whether this man is a spy planted on us or whether he truly is who he says he is. I could simply have him taken out and beaten to get him to talk, but I have always felt such information is suspect. If you beat someone long enough and bad enough they will say anything to get it to stop. I prefer using something subtler, like you. Work your way into his confidence. You can speak English and you have your considerable feminine charms. This makes you the best possible choice for this task. Do what you must."

"Do what I must?" said Sophie, her face a frozen mask. "Julien, are you telling me to sleep with this man to get information?"

Fedon grimaced at her stiffness. "Sophie, please believe me I would prefer that was not necessary. But we are at war and we all must do what we have to. If he is a spy we may be able to learn something of British intentions and turn him to our advantage. Sophie, I have been doing things like keeping women and children hostages because I must, despite how distasteful I find it. You know I care deeply for you. But I need your help and for you to do whatever is necessary, however distasteful it may be for you."

As he finished speaking he reached across the desk with his hand open, hoping she would take it. She stared for several long moments at his hand,

The Sugar Rebellion

long enough he began to fear she would slap it away. With a deep breath, though, she reached over and grasped his hand for a few moments before letting it go and rising from her chair.

"Yes, Julien, I will do what I must. I will go see to his needs now. This may take time, but if I learn anything I will let you know."

As she door closed behind her Fedon clenched and unclenched his fists in silent frustration. He had felt alone, more alone than he was at any point in his life, when he assumed the role of leader of the rebellion. The burden seemed almost too much to bear many times, but that she had chosen to come to his bed and into his life made a world of difference.

Now, deep inside, he felt a worm of fear gnaw at him that he may have driven her away, but he knew it had to be done. His instincts told him this deserter from the Royal Navy was somehow more than he appeared to be and he simply had to find the truth. The man who had sat before him moments before bore an unmistakable air of command and self-assurance. But Fedon knew it was more than this. Beneath it all he sensed this man was dangerous and he knew he simply had to find out for certain. That he knew he was right to sacrifice even Sophie to his rebellion against the greed born of the enormous wealth from sugar was of little comfort.

Fedon shook his head in dismay when the familiar sense of being so completely alone washed over him once again. And he was growing weary of doing what had to be done.

The Sugar Rebellion

Chapter Six
February 1796
Grenada

On the second night of his stay in Gouyave the serving girl tiptoed into Baptiste's room and woke him as she slipped into his bed. With her slim body molded to his all thought of rest disappeared and it was only hours later sleep finally came to both of them. If the sun hadn't been shining on their faces through the window they would have slept much later.

The girl proved a wealth of information and seemed to accept his cover story without question. His gentle probes for information soon gave him a good picture of what was happening behind the rebel lines. The only real work being done was on plantations owned by the mulatto rebel leaders. Money was scarce as the local economy was a shambles. The few merchant ships willing to risk the wrath of the Royal Navy were forced to dash in and dash out of port fast, while the price they were willing to pay was far lower than normal in order to compensate them for the risk they took. The fact Baptiste was able to pay for his bed and board with silver coin made him a valuable customer and the slaves running the inn on behalf of their mulatto owner had no interest in losing the stream of money by asking him too many questions. A few generous tips ensured it stayed this way.

Baptiste was surprised to find the people running the inn were still considered slaves even

The Sugar Rebellion

now almost a year after the rebellion began. Fine promises of freedom were made, but nothing firm had happened to make the promises a reality. The owners had explained to the people it had to wait until the British were finally defeated. Baptiste sensed a weary frustration on the part of the girl, but she had little she could do about it.

Baptiste considered and discarded the idea of following James the same day he left Gouyave, as he didn't want the timing of his arrival to give cause for anyone to connect the two men. Baptiste was in no hurry to leave, as by now he and everyone else in Gouyave knew exactly where James was going anyway. Besides, spending one final night with the girl was too tempting to resist.

The next morning Baptiste wished the girl well and promised he might try to come back for her, but they both knew how unlikely this would be. He left her a generous tip as he finished breakfast and departed the inn with the satchel containing his few belongings over his shoulder, striking out on foot along the same path James had taken.

Most people travelling alone and on foot would have been wary, but Baptiste had no concerns. Hidden within his satchel and covered by the few clothes he carried was a small pouch with enough gold and silver coins to buy his way out of trouble if needed. Beside it was his personal favorite knife in its usual sheath. His only other weapon was a second, smaller sheath knife strapped out of sight to one of his lower calves. He had trained long and hard in the use of both weapons since Evan decided to use him on the mission and he was confident any

The Sugar Rebellion

would be attacker would pay a harsh price.

Baptiste was also confident he would succeed in his mission. After confessing to the girl his real goal was to join Fedon and the rebels, the girl had given him invaluable information about more than just Gouyave. Her younger sister Jeanne was a house slave on Fedon's estate and they maintained contact with each other. Jeanne told her of an estate in disarray because the owner's attention was focused on everything but his own estate. Baptiste smiled to himself as he trudged along the path. This man Fedon would soon find a solution to his problems in the person of Baptiste, for he brought plenty of experience running a large plantation as the senior house slave for his former masters on St. Lucia.

The possibility Jeanne could be as good looking and willing as her sister also lent a spring to Baptiste's step.

***

James stood on the small balcony jutting out from the second floor room he was led to and leaned over the railing, studying the surrounding terrain. Were he not in potentially dire peril he would have enjoyed the stunning vista before him far more. From the balcony he was offered a sweeping view to the north of a string of lush rolling hills, valleys, and small mountains. A light breeze tempered the late February sunshine. To the west the first hint of rose pink tinges to the few clouds in the sky came from the sunset that was only now beginning. The knock on the door to his room broke his reverie and he went to open the

The Sugar Rebellion

door.

He found himself wholly unprepared for the sight of the woman calling on him, for this was no ordinary woman and he felt it instantly right to the depth of his soul. An indefinable quiver of energy rippled between the two of them as they appraised each other. When he saw her eyes widen he was certain she felt it too. Although this woman's beauty was stunning, he found her attractive to him in a way that was far more than physical. The strength of the energy encompassing him would have been overpowering were it not for the knowledge he was sending exactly the same raw energy and desire to her. As she stepped into the room her feminine scent enveloped him and he knew if there were some way to have this woman he would find it.

This was not the first time this had happened to James. He had always had an eye for beautiful women and wasn't shy about ensuring they knew of his appreciation, but this was different. James had slept with many women, but few bore this secret, intangible energy inside that lit the same fire of desire in him. Although he had succumbed to simple lust to have someone on many occasions, it was almost always limited to this. This, however, was a rare, overwhelming desire to totally merge with the woman on every level and in every way. James struggled to master himself, as he knew he couldn't jeopardize the mission for the sake of having her. The woman was the first to recover, although she betrayed the impact on her again by licking her lips nervously before she spoke.

"Hello—you are James Williams, I assume? I

The Sugar Rebellion

am—pleased to meet you. I am Sophie Ventour. Our leader Julien has asked me to see to your needs and to help you settle in. Are you satisfied with your quarters, I hope? Under the circumstances this simple room is the best we can offer just now."

James waved a hand in dismissal and smiled. "This is much more than I need. Believe me, I am used to living in far smaller quarters than this on a Royal Navy warship. Space is always at a premium."

"Of course," said Sophie, running her eyes over him. "I gather you came here with little more than the clothes on your back. We will find you some. I think you are roughly the same size as Julien and since I'm sure he has a plentiful wardrobe here, I doubt he will mind lending you some of it. I will look to that before we do anything else. But beyond that I think the only real need you likely have is to be fed, correct?"

"Yes," said James, realizing for the first time his last meal had been in Gouyave late that morning. "It has been a long day and I am rather hungry."

"Then we will dine together and you can tell me more about yourself. Julien has been called away and none of the other leaders are here just now, so it will be just the two of us."

James smiled. "It has been a long time since I was last able to enjoy the company of a beautiful woman for dinner and have her all to myself. I look forward to it."

Sophie returned his smile. "I think I do, too. I will have towels and warm water sent to your room

The Sugar Rebellion

so you can wash up. I will be back with some clean clothes soon."

***

An hour later they were seated across from each other, the only two diners enjoying a small feast set before them on a table big enough to hold sixteen people.

James dug into the food before him with gusto, as he was famished by the time it began to arrive. Fresh baked bread and a spicy fish soup helped take the immediate edge off his hunger, but he was far from done. He soon devoured the better part of a delicious roasted chicken done with savory herbs and served with local vegetables cooked in the same pot as the bird. Fresh fruit and cheese served as dessert. He washed all of it down with a pleasant French red wine, giving him opportunity for a short while to forget the real reason he was in the company of the beautiful woman across from him.

"I don't think the word 'hungry' does enough justice to you tonight, James," said Sophie.

James laughed. "Sorry, I know I haven't been much of a dinner companion. When I'm hungry I tend to focus on the job at hand. It stems from growing up in the Royal Navy, I expect. Most of the time the food on a warship is plain and basic. Something as simple as this fresh bread is impossible to get when you are at sea. When I was younger it never seemed like there was enough of any kind of food, either. So when a fine meal like this appears and I'm hungry, I don't talk much."

"That's all right, we have the rest of the evening to talk. Tell me about yourself. What's it like in the

The Sugar Rebellion

Navy? It must have been a hard decision to leave them and come to us."

They spent the next hour talking and finishing the bottle of wine. James gave her the same story he had given Fedon, adding more real examples of prejudice he had endured over the years from Navy officers. The irony was he knew he could easily have become discouraged by it all, but he also knew the picture he was painting for her was a distortion of the truth. The great majority of Navy officers were men of honor and cared only whether you did your job well. For them, prejudice about skin color was not a consideration. She seemed particularly interested when he spoke of his white father, who had served as a Royal Navy officer, freeing his black slave mother. Eventually she seemed satisfied she knew enough of his background and turned the conversation to the present.

"So you have come to help us and start a new life here, James. Do you have something specific in mind you can help us with?"

"Actually, yes. I told Julien I have details of a raid they are planning and, if we act soon, we can put a stop to it. I have something else you may find useful, too. But more long term I think I can help you deal with the Navy. I would be surprised if there was anyone here that understands them and knows how they operate better than I. We could even plan some attacks on St. Georges from the sea if you have enough of the right men and ships to do it. But I am willing to help in any way I can. I'm tired of the Navy and need a change in my life."

"Well, attacking the harbor is an interesting

The Sugar Rebellion

thought. That idea hasn't crossed anyone's mind here. Julien may find it useful to put yet more pressure on them."

"Forgive me, Sophie, but if you don't mind, I have to say I am curious about you. You are obviously not just a simple servant and you speak as if you are privy to the thinking of Julien and his commanders. Are you one of the leaders of this rebellion?"

Sophie smiled and shrugged. "Yes, I suppose you could say that. This is a man's world, of course, but I am playing a role here. My brother is one of Julien's commanders. Perhaps they are just indulging me, but I do sit in on their planning sessions whenever possible. I've never been shy about speaking my mind. I believe in freedom and I want to see everyone set free. Julien is a good man who has taken on a hard task and he needs all the support we can give him. We must end the madness of greed for the wealth sugar brings with our rebellion once and for all. If we can succeed like St. Domingue and become the second island to bring an end to slavery, I believe we will be an inspiration for the rest of the Caribbean islands. Who knows? Maybe even the people of color in America will take heart and throw off their shackles too."

James was watching her close as she spoke and he realized she meant every word she said with a burning fervor. He nodded slowly before responding.

"I can see you truly believe in this. I have made a good decision to join you, because I agree. But I would know more, Sophie. Tell me of your

The Sugar Rebellion

background. You seem very taken with Fedon. Is he the man in your life, if you don't mind my asking?"

Sophie paused for a long moment. "My brother and I were born here. Our father was a white Frenchman who settled here. My mother was a slave and both my brother and I were born into slavery. My father finally freed all of us when I was in my early teens. He never said for certain, but I suspect to this day he couldn't bear what he knew would happen to me, sooner or later, as a slave. My parents are both gone now, but my brother and I have not forgotten the stories my mother told us of life as a slave and the scars she bore from it. She inspired both of us and made us promise that if we ever had the chance to change the way things are that we should seize it. And that is exactly what we are doing."

Sophie sat back in her chair. "As for my personal life the answer is no, I do not formally have a man in my life. Julien is indeed an inspiring and attractive man and I look up to him. He is a good—well, to be clear, a very close friend. And with that I think we should end our night together. I have enjoyed our dinner and look forward to more conversations with you."

James rose from his seat at the same time as her. She told him to meet the next morning in the same location for breakfast and wished him good night before turning to leave the room. She briefly offered him her hand and he held it for a long moment that seemed to last far longer than it actually was. Her touch was electric and once again he knew they both felt the tremor of energy flow

The Sugar Rebellion

and pass between them, but then she was gone. James knew sleep would be hard to find that night.

***

A buzz of conversation came through the open door to the large anteroom Fedon used as his regular meeting place with his commanders. Besson, La Valette, Ventour, and the others were all there, having arrived back at the estate two days later in response to Fedon's summons. Sophie and Fedon huddled together outside the room in a hurried conference as Fedon himself had only now returned and had not had time to debrief Sophie. Fedon looked around to ensure they were unheard and signaled her to begin.

"Julien, I do not have much to offer at this point. If this man is indeed a spy he is very polished at it. There are no holes in his story. He is very self-assured and confident, which I suppose would be normal for someone who achieved a higher rank in the British Navy. I recommend remaining wary of this man and taking all possible precautions. He made mention of having another piece of information that could help us, which he didn't mention in his meeting with you. He gave no details. I suspect he is holding it back as something to bargain with, perhaps as additional material to prove he is sincere to us. His motivation for that is not clear."

"Well done, Sophie. I will hear this in mind. Is there anything else? The men are waiting."

"I spent a great deal of time with him yesterday and the day before. We've had dinner together both nights and went for a long walk around the estate so

The Sugar Rebellion

he could familiarize himself with it. As I said, if he is a spy he is very good at it and it will take me time to learn if that is so. But there is one thing. I can tell you he wants me badly. It would seem your strategy to use me might have potential. If I am in his bed his tongue may loosen. We shall see. But I will not let myself be an easy conquest."

Something in the cool tone of her voice rang a warning in Fedon's mind, but he had no time to delve further into it.

"A conquest only if necessary, Sophie. As I told you, I would have that only as a last resort. Look, the men are waiting. Let us join them."

They spent the next thirty minutes debriefing each other before the subject of James came up. As Fedon and Sophie told them what had happened along with the details James had given them, Fedon could see the doubt and concerned looks on the faces of the men around the table. Besson's face in particular was dark with suspicion.

"Julien, how do we know this is not a trap? This could be a diversion to get us to reduce our forces around St. Georges and that could be where the real push will come."

"Perhaps," said Fedon. "But from what we know of what is going on behind their lines nothing has changed. They do not have the resources to challenge us and break out. This could equally be a sign they are growing desperate. Our strategy has been to contain and weaken them to the point they leave willingly. Admittedly, this has gone on longer than I thought."

"Julien," said Ventour. "I agree with you that

The Sugar Rebellion

something is going on, but I'm not sure of what it means. We all knew something was going to change, sooner or later. The British did nothing about their situation before hurricane season last year and, so far, nothing this year. But I've said it before at this table that I cannot see them letting the opportunity to bring in more troops before hurricane season starts slip past them again. I guess my point is this could just be a test to see whether they need to do that or not."

"Julien," said La Valette. "We can speculate on this all day. Can we meet this deserter? I would like to judge him for myself."

James was waiting in his room, having been told he could be called to the meeting. Fedon introduced him to the men around the table when he walked in and explained no translation was needed as they all spoke English. James thanked them, pretending he had no French himself, and spent the next several minutes giving them his background and details of the pending raid on Gouyave. When he finished a brief silence ensued before Besson leaned forward and scowled.

Speaking in rapid French Besson looked around the table at his compatriots while keeping one eye on James to watch for a reaction. Besson told them he thought it was all a pack of lies and he was going to push James hard. James showed no outward sign he had understood as Besson turned and switched to English with unexpected speed. James was ready for the verbal attack.

"So, James Williams," said Besson, the tone of his voice harsh. "I think you are a goddamn English spy and we should take you to our lines outside St. Georges, cut your balls off in front of the soldiers, and hang you from the tallest tree to ensure they see everything. You need to tell us exactly how we can be certain you are not a spy leading us to our doom."

James shrugged. "I am not stupid. I knew you would be suspicious. Were I in your shoes the question would occur to me too. I have nothing that proves I am sincere other than what I have given you, though, and you must make up your own mind. Well, I do have one other piece of information that may be of use to you and I do have some ideas about how I could help the cause. I am, after all, quite familiar with how the Navy operates and we could take advantage of that."

The questions continued for several more minutes as the conversation turned to the operational details surrounding the looming attack on Gouyave and ways they could counter it. When it became clear nothing further was left to discuss and all that remained was the decision, Fedon stepped into the conversation.

"Well, I think we have all we need for now. James, we need to discuss this and make a decision. If you could return to your room we would appreciate it. You have the freedom of the estate, of course, if you would rather get some fresh air. I will see you at dinner tonight if not before."

James nodded and rose to leave. As the door closed behind him Fedon turned back to his commanders.

"Well? What do you think?"

The Sugar Rebellion

Besson was quick to respond. "I think we should cut his balls off and hang him in front of the British like I suggested. We have enough men we can push back this raid if it in fact happens. If we kill him we end the risk I think he poses."

La Valette rubbed his chin in thought. "You may well be right, Besson. However, we have nothing to lose by keeping him alive and, keep in mind, he did hint at having more information that could be of use to us. That means we maybe have something to gain. We didn't discuss any of that. I see no harm in keeping him around and simply keeping our eyes on him. If he proves false to us we can kill him any time we want. But Julien, do we have any more intelligence on the state of affairs inside St. Georges?"

Fedon nodded. "Not as yet, but I agree knowing this would help. As for James, I have already asked Sophie here to have an eye on him."

"Julien," said Ventour. "I need time to think about this. Why don't we start by making plans to counter this attack? If an issue comes up between now and then, we make the adjustment. We don't have the luxury of time and we have to make a decision about this. I really don't think ignoring it and leaving Gouyave on its own in case there really is a raid is an option."

"I agree," said Fedon, rising to signal the meeting was at an end. "Let's make the preparations."

As the men began filing out and a buzz of conversation began yet again Fedon motioned to Sophie to follow him back to his office. He waited

The Sugar Rebellion

until they were both seated once again, sensing she wanted to keep her distance.

"Sophie, I am troubled and of two minds."

"What do you mean?"

"Your brother is right, we need to know what is happening in St. Georges. Having that information would help to give us certainty over what to do about this raid. You know I wanted you to go back, but now I need you to deal with this man James, too."

"Julien, I cannot be in two places at the same time."

"I know and this is the problem. What is more important?"

Sophie shrugged. "Both are important, but to my mind I think I should keep an eye on this man as the priority, at least for now. There isn't enough time for me to get into and out of St. Georges before this raid anyway."

Julien took several long seconds, staring off into space as he contemplated the problem. He took a deep breath as he came to a decision and refocused on her.

"So be it. I agree. We will wait before we send you in again. I have an idea that may be far fetched and I need to think about it. But look, once again, Sophie, your counsel is proving valuable to me. Sophie, you are valuable to me."

Fedon stretched out his hand, hoping she would take it. Sophie looked at it for a few moments, but didn't hesitate and she grasped his hand.

Fedon bit his lip briefly before he spoke. "Sophie, come to me tonight. Please?"

She nodded. "I will, Julien."
***

Baptiste gave the girl Jeanne his most winning smile when he found her.

"Your sister sends her greetings, Jeanne. I am Baptiste."

He had found her within an hour of finally making his way to the estate. To his surprise they had no pickets set up around the perimeter and he simply walked right past several soldiers training with their weapons who ignored him without even a glance. He stopped a plump, older black woman sweeping the verandah of the mansion and asked for the girl. Jeanne proved to be a younger, even prettier version of her sister and she blushed at his attention. But she smiled back.

They went to the kitchen where she gave him food and drink as he told her his story. She accepted what he said, although her eyes widened when he told her he wanted to meet Fedon and to work for him. The girl was quick enough to understand she could be talking to her future superior and she became even more willing to accommodate his needs as a result. She left to deliver Baptiste's request and returned almost thirty minutes later.

"I apologize, Baptiste," said Jeanne. "Our owner Julien Fedon is very busy right now. We expect him to be busy for the next day or two. I can find you accommodation and show you around the estate while you wait for him if you like."

Baptiste smiled once again. "Oh, I'd like that very much."
***

The Sugar Rebellion

Two days later Baptiste was shown into Fedon's office and, after introducing himself, he began his attempt to be of use to Fedon.

"Mr. Fedon, I have come to offer my services to you. I was senior house slave to my former English master on his plantation in the south of Grenada. I was brought here from St. Lucia, which is where I was born, just before the rebellion began. He wanted me to serve his needs here. My former master was seeking to establish a coffee plantation and, as I am very familiar with every task there is to running such an operation, he obviously had need of my expertise. I would like to help you with your plantation."

Fedon sat in silence for a moment before responding.

"Well, you could be of use if you have the skills you say you do, that is for certain. Look, please just call me Julien. See here, I need a little more background, Baptiste. Why have you come to me now? What have you been doing for the last year?"

"Sir—Julien, I am not a fighter. It is not in my nature. My former master was away when the rebellion began and he simply never returned. I felt it my duty to the rest of the slaves on the plantation to try and hold it all together. People need to be fed and cared for. They need organization in their lives and someone to give them direction. I stepped into that role or, at least, I tried to. No one came to tell us what to do and people began thieving from us. Despite my best efforts it all gradually began falling apart. Several men and some women left to serve

The Sugar Rebellion

you as fighters or in whatever capacity. In a way that was a blessing as there were fewer to care for. Those of us that remained established a routine where we would grow what food we could and fish the ocean to feed ourselves."

Baptiste paused to give Fedon a pleading look.

"I grew weary of simply existing. I realized that while I may not be a fighter, I do believe in what you are trying to do. When I recently heard by chance that you had a coffee plantation here I resolved to come to you and help. I have been here two days and have walked about your plantation. You have a fine location for the coffee plants. The soil is not too soft and not too harsh and it drains well on the slopes. You are in just the right location, not too high up the slope, but not too low. You have plenty of sunshine the plants need. You appear to have planted crops at different times, as some plants are only now close to maturity while others are bearing you fruit. But you have a large section where the fruit is ripe and ready to be harvested. Julien, if that isn't done soon you will lose your crop."

Fedon laughed and threw up his hands. "All right, I am convinced. You do seem to know your business. And as it happens, I do have need of someone to care for my estate. Obviously, I have other things commanding my attention. Many of the people caring for my crops and my household are now serving as fighters. But look, I am afraid I cannot pay you much, at least not immediately. Because of the fighting we haven't been able to sell much of our produce."

The Sugar Rebellion

"I am not concerned about that. I know once we win everything will settle down and I have confidence you are a fair man. Everyone tells me you are."

"I appreciate that," said Fedon, reaching out to shake Baptiste's hand across the table. "Welcome to your new job as senior in charge of my estate. Let's see what you can do."

Baptiste smiled.

***

James knew Baptiste was proving himself to his new master in a hurry, made clear when James overheard Fedon remark to Sophie that in two days more work was done than in the previous two weeks. Baptiste seemed to be everywhere.

James saw him walking about with the girl on the first full day after he arrived, but made no move to contact or even acknowledge his presence. He knew it was only a matter of time and James was occupied in several meetings with Besson, poring over maps and discussing plans anyway. Besson was given overall command of the defense of Gouyave, meaning James had little choice but to deal with the man. Besson made it difficult, making sarcastic comments to test James at every opportunity. He also took a deliberately contrary approach to the defensive strategy. If James suggested something, Besson would suggest doing the opposite. James knew it was all a test.

Three days before the attack Baptiste and James finally contrived to talk to each other. Baptiste chose to pretend he was seizing opportunity to introduce himself to a resident of the mansion he had not met yet, talking loud enough for others nearby to hear him. Baptiste explained his interest in coffee plantations as the reason he was there and James took the cue, asking questions about coffee plants. The simple ruse enabled them to walk about, pretending to be looking at the plants while they talked.

As they walked toward the nearest rows of plants their path took them close by the makeshift jail the prisoners captured a year ago were still being held in. As they came by a party of slaves marched up to the guards at the entrance. Some of them carried empty pails while others were carrying trays of food. The guards unlocked the door and stepped back as the slaves entered. Curious, James and Baptiste stopped nearby to watch, but soon regretted the decision as a foul stench wafted toward them from the open door.

"Good God, those poor people," said Baptiste. "How can they bear it in there?"

James said nothing, knowing he had little he could do to change the situation. He had considered trying to find a way to get word to the prisoners they were not forgotten, but he discarded the thought, knowing how crushing a false hope would be if he could not find a way to save them. The party of slaves reappeared soon as none wanted to spend any more time in the jail than necessary. One slave carried out the now empty trays. The rest of the slaves strained to bear out several heavy, reeking pails of excrement filled to the brim of each. One of the slaves stumbled, spilling most of the contents of the pail he carried on the feet of one

The Sugar Rebellion

of the guards. This earned him a beating from the two-foot long club the guard carried. The beating continued as the slave struggled to shovel the mess back into the pail with his hands.

"What are you looking at?" said the other guard, scowling as he spotted James and Baptiste watching it all.

"Nothing," said James, as he motioned to Baptiste to move on. The second James was certain they were alone he spoke.

"Glad to see you, Baptiste. Have you reported back to Evan yet?"

"No, sir. I was waiting for a chance to connect with you. I have heard rumor of the attack on Gouyave coming. I assume that means you have gained their trust?"

James grimaced. "Not really. This man Besson is a pain in my arse. If I'm any further away than he can reach with the knife he carries in his belt then I am suspect as far as he is concerned. He'd rather see me dead with his knife in my back."

"Are you at risk, sir? I am willing to help if need be. A knife in his back could solve your problem."

"It could, but not just yet. We can't risk anything that would raise suspicions. And that means we should keep our conversations with each other to a minimum. I have a brief report for you to pass on, but for future we need a dead drop in case we cannot meet. Have you established one we can use?"

"Sir, I have," said Baptiste, as James unobtrusively slipped a small piece of folded paper into his hand. Baptiste secreted it in his pocket and surreptitiously pointed to a location at the base of a nearby tree with a rock beside it. Future reports would be left in a pouch Baptiste had hidden under the rock.

"Excellent," said James. "You will try and pass this report to Evan soon?"

"Sir, I am established here now and no one is questioning my coming and going. I am going to slip out tonight and do a drop at the location Commander Ross showed us. If anyone asks I will say I am off to see the girl I slept with in Gouyave and make sure she is all right. Her sister Jeanne here is the only one who might complain about that, but I don't think so. They both like me. I plan to be back by morning."

James snorted and held back a laugh as they walked back to the mansion.

"You have learned fast. You know, I'm beginning to think you could be as much of a rogue as I am. I'm betting you will end up doing both the drop *and* seeing the girl."

Baptiste grinned. "Perhaps."

As the two men walked back into the building they didn't see Sophie watching them go by as she stood in the shadows of a nearby shed.

The Sugar Rebellion

Chapter Seven
March 1796
Grenada

The night was cloudless. When the dawn came the change from dark to light was swift, as it always is in the Caribbean.

Besson and James were lying flat on the ground, peering over the rock they were hiding behind to watch the action unfold. Their hiding place was on top of a small rock cliff close to where Baptiste had hidden the day James made his dash for shore, for the location of the attack was in the same place. They would have a clear line of sight. James hoped all went to plan with as little loss of life as possible. Besson had brought far more men with him than Evan had anticipated and many of those were hidden in other spots along the rock cliff with muskets. More were stationed below them in the brush along the shoreline. If their marksmanship was good the potential for a bloodbath existed.

As expected, the same warship James had escaped from was anchored offshore. The ship was close enough everything in sight was still well within range of her guns, yet not so far off the pull to shore would be onerous. Beside her was a nondescript, shabby old unarmed troop transport that was finishing anchoring. The transport was towing behind it several smaller boats to ferry the men ashore. As the sun began rising behind them James could make out the distant forms of sailors on the transport bringing the boats to the side as

The Sugar Rebellion

expected, with more men queuing on deck waiting the order to disembark. James frowned as he turned his attention to the warship. After studying it for a long moment he scanned the entire horizon and turned to Besson.

"Something has changed," said James. "The plan was for the *Keene* to be using her ship's boats to ferry men to shore, too."

Besson gave James a cold stare. "If you are playing us false you are going to be the first to die."

James scowled back. "I'm just telling you what I know and can see, you fool. The plan I heard them talking about had the Keene's men involved. In war things can change. I have no idea why they are doing this differently, but they are."

The two men glared at each other in silence for a long moment before Besson finally hawked up some phlegm and spat off to the side, looking as if he was ridding himself of an unpleasant taste in his mouth.

"So what does this mean, Mr. big Navy man? Do we pull back or stay with the plan?"

James shrugged. "I think it means you wait and see. It looks to me like the transport is—yes, there is the first boat being loaded now. It looks like you will have some targets as expected."

As soon as the first boat finished loading men it pulled to the side and waited for the next to be filled and James frowned again. This time he said nothing, for he knew this also was not a part of Evan's plan. A single boat was supposed to look as if it were coming in to conduct reconnaissance on the shore and establish a defensive perimeter to guard the vulnerable troops as they offloaded to the beach. This was standard practice in situations like this and James knew Evan would deviate from it only if there were sound reasons to do so.

When four boats were loaded they set off as one for the beach. James counted at least a dozen men in each as they came ever closer to shore and he frowned to himself once again. This number of men being sent into certain danger was definitely not part of the plan. By the time they passed the midpoint between the ships and the shore, James knew for certain something was wrong.

Evan's original plan was for one or two boats at most to make for shore. At the midpoint someone on one of the ships was to pretend to sight the enemy on shore and they were to fire their muskets in disarray. Whether any of the rebel soldiers were visible and whether any of their shots came close would be irrelevant. Evan's thinking was this would tempt the waiting rebels into returning fire and this would be the cue for the *Keene* to rake the shoreline. After engaging the enemy for long enough to make it all look good, the British would make a scene of abandoning the attempt and sailing away. The hope was losses would be minimal, while the chance of killing a number of rebels on shore with the guns of the *Keene* was good.

As the first of the four boats touched the shore James was horrified to see one other significant difference. All of the men now scrambling to get out of the boats and on to the beach were black. Even the men rowing the boats were black.

If Besson saw and understood the significance

The Sugar Rebellion

of what he was seeing he gave no sign. Instead, he reached for his already primed and loaded musket and on seeing this James did the same. Besson took a few moments to aim the weapon, although he had little need to be careful. He had plenty of targets all bunched together, now standing in front of the boats on the shore. Numerous birds that only moments before were chirping in the morning sun rose in a squawking rush at the harsh sound of his musket being fired. One of the men on the beach was hit in the back and flung his weapon away as he fell, trying to claw at his wound.

Besson's shot was the signal for the rest. As one a file of men Besson had stationed below the cliff rose from their cover and let loose a devastating volley. James joined the crowd of snipers around him in firing, too, although James shot deliberately wide.

The carnage was horrific. In mere moments close to half the shore party had their lives snuffed out. More men were clutching at their wounds and screaming in pain. A pitiful few who weren't injured and had their weapons ready took aim and tried to return fire. Some of Besson's men were armed with two muskets and they brought their already primed and loaded second weapon to bear. More men fell and James could see pools of blood soaking into the sand. Besson was reloading his weapon and made to break cover and fire again, but James spoke up.

"I wouldn't do that were I you," said James. "Keep your head down."

Besson looked over at James with scorn on his face. "What, are you afraid?"

The Sugar Rebellion

As he finished speaking the warship guns spoke for the first time. The rock face they were hiding behind was lashed with a devastating hail of grapeshot. The numerous small metal balls fired from the warship cannons hammered into the rocks all around them, sending rock splinters flying everywhere. Several of the snipers around them screamed as they were struck either by one of the balls or the dangerous splinters flying past. With a quick mental calculation James guessed only half of the warships guns that could be brought to bear was used in the first broadside. He was proved right as a moment later the second slammed into the tree line below them, targeting the large file of men Besson had stationed there. Yet more screams of pain rose from those struck. James gave Besson a cold look.

"Sometimes it pays to have a good idea of what your enemy might do in response," said James. "You now have perhaps a minute or so at best to fire again before they reload. *If* you aren't afraid, that is."

James didn't wait to see the scowl of anger he knew was on Besson's face as he poked his head up to sight and fire once again. In the chaos of the battle no one saw his shot went wide yet again. James took an extra few seconds to read the situation and was pleased to see the survivors on the beach were scrambling to get their wounded men into a boat. In the last seconds before he ducked for cover again he saw them shove off and begin rowing back to the ships. Only two of the four boats that had come in were returning and neither of those bore anywhere near the number of men they had

The Sugar Rebellion

carried to shore.

The warship continued lashing the shoreline with grapeshot with several more volleys before they finally stood down. Realizing the engagement was over Besson shouted to pass word for his men to do the same. As they left their positions to regroup out of sight of the warship, James was troubled. Something was very wrong.

***

Evan was furious. "Good God in heaven, I can't believe you did this. This was not the plan we agreed to."

Colonel Walter shrugged, clearly showing his indifference. Governor Mackenzie, the other man in the meeting, raised an eyebrow and glared at the Colonel. The message was clear he wanted something better.

The Colonel relented and cleared his throat. "Sirs, I agree it was not the plan, but disposition of Army resources are my domain. Yes, this was not what you planned, but I thought about it and made the decision to change a few things. The Captain of the *Keene* had no questions about the changes and it seems to me the objective of the raid was accomplished, was it not? I fail to see any problem."

"Sir, I respect that these resources, as you put it, are in your domain," said Evan. "However, my plan was designed to achieve our goal with as little life lost as possible. You agreed to it. The Captain of the *Keene* had no idea this was an unapproved change. Your changes resulted in the loss of twenty-seven men dead and another round dozen injured. How is that not a problem?"

The Sugar Rebellion

The Colonel looked puzzled. "I still don't see what you are talking about. The men we lost were all local black militia we had recruited to help with the defense. They are soldiers. They did what they were told and some of them lost their lives. It happens."

"Colonel," said the Governor. "I think what Commander Ross is getting at is it didn't have to be this way."

"Governor," said the Colonel. "The Commander here wanted a good show to help his spy prove his value. We put on a good show. The Commander's plan would have put at risk some of our white soldiers and some of our Navy personnel. Even one of these men is worth twenty of this black rabble we have filling in the holes in our defenses. When I thought about it there seemed little reason to risk any of our truly valuable people on something like this, so I made the change. There really wasn't time to debate the changes. Like I said, it was a good show. I like to think the *Keene* made the rebels pay more than they wanted to, at least from what I saw from her deck. I'd love to have a few of her cannons and crew to fill in a few gaps in our defense. But in any case, I think you should be congratulating me."

Evan was appalled at the man's blatant prejudice and disregard for the militiamen's lives, but he knew the argument was lost. Were he to push the matter his complaint would go nowhere, getting lost in the ever present need of both the Army and the Navy to protect their own. He gave a small sigh and turned to the Governor.

The Sugar Rebellion

"Well, at any rate, we have achieved another objective. The reason I was not at Gouyave was I went to our drop location and picked up the first report from Lieutenant Wilton. He has succeeded in worming his way into the heart of the rebel base. He reports they appear to be following a strategy of trying to wait us out, as we surmised, but he has hints of unrest over that approach. He has little else to offer at this point as it is still early and he is still under suspicion. Hopefully the success Colonel Walter has given us here will go some way to helping the Lieutenant and make the loss of life worth something."

"Indeed," said the Governor, unable to hide the dry tone of his response. "What of the other man you sent in? I assume since a report was left at your drop location he is also operational?"

"Sir, he is. He too left a report and has succeeded beyond my expectations. He is now the senior man in charge of Fedon's estate. Although he has no military role, I am hopeful he may be able to provide us useful intelligence too. Time will tell."

"Well then," said the Colonel. "Since I have done my job, let's hope your men do their job, eh? Gentlemen, are we done here? I have other pressing matters."

The Governor and Evan looked at each other as one and both shook their heads. The Colonel smiled and left the room.

***

Once again all of Fedon's commanders were with him in the meeting along with James and Sophie. A questioning look appeared on Fedon's

The Sugar Rebellion

face.

"Besson, you don't seem overly pleased at the result. Yes, you lost some men, but we knew that could happen. But the British were turned back with heavy losses, so what is your concern?"

Besson chewed his lip a moment before responding in French. "Yes, Julien, I lost almost a dozen men, but that is not the concern. It has taken me a while to put my finger on it, but I think I finally have."

Besson turned to look directly at James and switching to English. "You said the plan had changed, correct? The warship was supposed to help with ferrying their men to the beach."

"That is correct," said James, on the alert because of Besson's use of French. "That is what I heard and what I told you. I have no idea why that changed."

"Did anything else change?"

"No," said James, not liking the direction Besson was going in. "Not that I am aware of."

"So tell me, Mr. Navy man, why was it all of the men they sent in were black?"

"I have no idea," replied James, thankful he knew the look on his face was truthful. "Yes, I noticed that too, but I assure you in the conversation I overheard no mention was made of the composition of the force being sent in."

A silence descended on the room as the people around the table digested what they had heard. James could see many of them, including Sophie, had furrowed brows as they thought about it. At length Fedon finally spoke, looking directly at

The Sugar Rebellion

James.

"This is the truth? Why would they do that?"

"Julien, this is the truth. I am surprised, too, and I have no idea whether this is something to question or not. Yes, something changed in their plan, but it seems to me it was a small element. This happens. As for why they were all men of color I have no idea. I do know I heard they have many black people fighting on their side. Perhaps someone formed an all black unit and trained them for this? Maybe they have fewer white soldiers than we all think and that has driven them to do it? I don't know."

Julien sat in silence once again for a long moment before he replied.

"Well, I believe you. There is a mystery there, but a small one and in the end I think it matters little. So, perhaps it is time to move on to our next opportunity. You mentioned you have other information that could prove useful to us?"

"Yes, if you have interest. It is nowhere near as specific as what I gave you about Gouyave and may prove not to be as useful as I think. But I can brief you on this if you wish."

"We are all here and we are interested, James."

"A day before we sailed from St. Georges to Gouyave I had a night of liberty in town. I went into one of the local taverns, but the place was packed. Some white Army soldiers knew I was Navy so they made room for me. They were already well into their ale, but I was quite sober, at least to start. All I did was ask them how it was going and that set them off. Aside from being universally bored of

The Sugar Rebellion

being on the defensive lines, they all complained about the position they were stationed in. To their minds the imbecile they report to has no clue about how to properly site static defenses. In short, their position is a redoubt on the northern side of the defensive lines and to a man they all think they are in a vulnerable location. If you have a map I think I can show you the location."

Within moments a map was produced and spread out on the table. As they all leaned forward James studied it for a minute before finally stabbing a finger at a spot.

"Hmm. I can't be certain, but I think this is it. You see this redoubt here? There is a larger gap between it and the next one than there really should be. And if this feature here is a small gully, then this is likely the spot."

"You aren't certain?" said Besson, wearing a frown.

James resisted the urge to scowl. "Of course I'm not certain. It's not like I could ask them to pull out a map and show me, is it? I am going by what they told me of the features of the terrain. They said they were happier with the other side of their redoubt as it butts onto a small cliff and, if I am reading your map right, this looks like a cliff, right?"

"It is," said La Valette. "I think I know where this redoubt is. The features you are talking about match this one. But why is it they are concerned?"

"A few reasons. One is the gully apparently has a fair bit of low ground cover. As far as they are concerned that should all have been ripped out long

The Sugar Rebellion

ago. Apparently it was when this all started, but no maintenance work has been done to keep it that way and the brush has regrown in the year since this all began. A man couldn't walk up unnoticed, but he could now crawl far too close for their liking. Also, they are of the opinion they have far too few men to hold the redoubt if it were assaulted directly. And no, I have no idea what far too few means to them. I could hardly start asking them for numbers, right? But most importantly they are guarding this redoubt with only one field cannon and they think they should have three. The rest of their weapons are small arms only."

Once again the room fell silent as they all contemplated what they had heard. Fedon rubbed his chin in thought, while several stared hard at the map yet again. Besson, however, kept staring at James and was the first to speak.

"So are we going to encounter a change in plans somewhere in this attack, too?"

This time James couldn't keep the scowl off his face as he leaned forward with his arms on the table.

"That's a stupid fucking thing to say. If you have a problem let's take it outside, you arsehole."

"Gentlemen!" barked Fedon. "That will be enough. Besson, please keep your comments constructive. Well, everyone, what do you think? Have we tried an attack on this particular spot before?"

La Valette spoke up. "Actually, no. I think we passed on that because of the terrain. I'm going by memory here, because I think I am the one that

The Sugar Rebellion

assessed it's potential and dismissed it. But now I think on it, if James is correct the ground cover has regrown then, yes, this could be an opportunity. We might send a flanking force in as close as possible under the cover first and then make a demonstration as if we were going to try a frontal assault. An unexpected attack on the flank may just get results."

"But is this going to be the hole in their defenses that would give us St. George's?" said Fedon.

La Valette and several other commanders around the table grimaced.

"Julien, I don't think we could say that, not unless we brought up a huge number of men and made preparations for attacks on other positions. The location is such they could get reinforcements there in fairly short order. I think the guns in Fort Frederick could also be brought to bear on this area if they felt they were too hard pressed, although I believe it is the limit of their range. So, no, I don't think this is the spot to make an all out push. However, we can certainly give them a very bloody nose. I am thinking a quick, hard strike to maximize the impact and then we pull back before they can react. If you want to continue this policy of trying to wear them down, then a significant attack where they suffer more losses than they want could serve the purpose."

Fedon looked around the room. "Anyone disagree with that?"

The commanders around the table were once again silent, so Fedon nodded.

"All right, let's do it. La Valette, you seem

The Sugar Rebellion

familiar with this spot and I think you have something in mind. I suggest you take the lead on planning the details of the attack. I will join you to observe. It has been a while since I have been to the front lines and the men need to see me. La Valette, we will await your word when you are ready to proceed, but I suggest we try to make this happen soon. The British have had a defeat at Gouyave and it might help to have a second defeat follow soon on its heels. Gentlemen, good day."

Several men rose from their chairs in concert with Fedon. A crowd formed around La Valette and an intense buzz of conversation ensued. James turned to leave, but Fedon signaled for him to join him. As James walked over Fedon did the same to Sophie, and as she joined them Fedon looked around to ensure they would be unheard.

"James, please forgive Besson his indiscretion. He may be a blunt instrument, but in a war sometimes men like him are useful. I will speak to him to ensure he is more respectful."

"I am not concerned, Julien. I've dealt with plenty of men like him. I understand."

"Good. So for tonight I would like the pleasure of having the two of you to dinner with me. Join me around seven thirty, please."

Fedon smiled as they both nodded acceptance.

"As much as I like my commanders I think you two will provide much more pleasant company tonight."
***

Sophie was wearing a creamy white colored, low cut gown for the occasion and as she walked

The Sugar Rebellion

into the dining room both James and Fedon stared in open-mouthed appreciation of her bounty. Fedon was in mid sentence talking to James and was the first to recover.

"Sophie, my dear, you look marvelous tonight. Please join us. James, I—damn me, what the hell were we talking about?"

"I have no idea," said James, a wide grin on his face. "But I'm sure it couldn't have been as important as Sophie."

Sophie laughed and grasped the sides of her gown, spreading it wider.

"I thought I would put on a nice dress for the occasion. Apparently you two like it."

"We do," said Fedon, laughing. "Well, I am looking forward to dinner tonight. You are an interesting person, James, and I'd like to hear more of your experiences. As for Sophie, well, she is always interesting. I confess, James, that I rely on her opinion far more than people know."

Fedon signaled to a waiting servant to begin the meal as he poured wine for his two guests. The meal began with cool, fresh caught crab meat sprinkled with a local cheese and fresh bread with butter. A thick and hearty pepper pot soup followed as the second course. James shared a love of spicy food and the three of them scraped every drop of the soup from their bowls.

As the servants began bringing in the main courses their conversation drifted to the life James had lived in the Royal Navy. Both Fedon and Sophie seemed fascinated by stories of a world so foreign to that of their own experience. Although

The Sugar Rebellion

Fedon confessed to having learned to sail when he was young, the only other island he had visited was St. Lucia for one short visit, while Sophie had never been off Grenada. James, however, had served all over the Caribbean and sailed as far away as England with the Navy. The broad scope of his experience was a source of complete fascination to both. That it would take many weeks on a ship to sail to England and back was a concept they knew on an intellectual level, but talking to someone who had actually done it was different. James was able to give a personal sense of what it was like, adding a whole new level of understanding.

The main course of huge, fresh caught grouper steaks was delicious, spiced to perfection with herbs and lightly sprinkled with lemon juice. Grilled plantains and carrots accompanied the fish. For dessert the servants put a dish of crème brulee in front of each of them. As he finished James sat back and thanked his host.

"Julien, that was the kind of dinner I could only dream of when I was in the Navy. You are too kind."

Fedon waved it off and ordered coffee for all three of them.

"We continue to have problems at times with ensuring there is enough to go around, but tonight is not one of those nights and I wanted us to enjoy ourselves. So tell me James, what finally set you on this course of action? I know you told me you've felt the prejudice before. But why now?"

James wiped his lips with his napkin. "It was my new Captain. He joined the ship a month before

The Sugar Rebellion

I deserted. From the moment he set foot on board I was a target. I've been on ships where other men of color were serving, but this particular ship, for whatever reason, had only me. The ordinary seamen had no problem with me, but the officers were another matter. I kept to myself and they tolerated me, but the Captain enjoyed blaming me for everything. The rest of the officers saw how the wind was blowing and actively joined in. I've learned patience over the years and probably could have outlasted them, but I had risen as far as I could. It was time for a change and for something better. I hope this is it."

"I hope so, too," said Fedon. "When this is all over, what do you hope to do here?"

James stared away for a long moment and took a deep breath before responding.

"I'm not that young anymore. I'd like to settle down, find someone to share my life with. Maybe have children. I brought as much gold with me as I could, so I have something to start a business with if necessary. The obvious answer would be to take advantage of my skills with ships. I'm willing to try anything."

As he was speaking he couldn't help noticing Sophie's eyes widen at his mention of settling down and having children, although she said nothing in response. James glanced at Fedon to gauge his reaction, but he gave no indication he had noticed her interest. Fedon sipped at his coffee and signaled to the servants to bring a round of cognac for all of them before responding.

"Well, God willing, we will prevail in this and

you will have the opportunity you seek."

James decided to turn the conversation to other topics.

"I know my life in the Navy sounds foreign to both of you. I confess the life you have here seems foreign to me. Julien, I know the events in St. Domingue inspired you. The thing I find so very strange about St. Domingue is the swamp of conflicting interests at play there. I don't think this is quite the same here, but I do see similarities. For example, how is it you seek freedom for all yet some people are still slaves? Forgive me if I am touching on a sensitive subject, but I don't understand how men of color can keep other men of color as slaves."

Fedon and Sophie looked at each other before he turned back to James and he sighed as he nodded agreement.

"You are right, as this is strange. The problem is money, of course. Please believe me we do in fact seek freedom for all. But the British are not going to go away just because we want them to. It has been a year since we began and, at least for now, there is no end in sight. Meanwhile, people have to be fed. Order has to be maintained to do that. While we know people should be free, what will replace the system of slavery in our economy? We haven't worked this out yet. Like myself, there are many who have worked hard for what they have. No one is interested in losing it. But everyone understands the first priority is to rid this island of the British. Once we have done that, our friends in Guadeloupe and St. Domingue will help us build something new

The Sugar Rebellion

and better."

"I don't know," said James. "St. Domingue I can understand, but Guadeloupe? Are the French truly friends?"

Sophie and Fedon looked at each other once again. This time it was Sophie who responded.

"You are very perceptive, James. Julien and I and the others have spoke of this on more than one occasion. Yes, the French in Guadeloupe have been in contact with us and provided support, at least to some extent."

Seeing a warning look on Fedon's face she quickly continued.

"Julien, I don't think I'm telling him a secret. Even if he is a spy, this must be obvious to everyone who knows anything about the situation here."

Fedon shrugged a moment later. "I suppose that is true. But you do not trust them, James?"

James shook his head. "I do not. I think they have their own interests in this and wouldn't trust them any more than I would the British. I know, some of the revolutionaries in France voice their support for freedom, but France is not speaking with one voice. I think they have the same problem of money and the same question of what the abolition of slavery means to the economy. So no, I don't trust them. I do trust you, though, and I understand I must earn your trust."

"Well, thank you. In truth, the French from Guadeloupe have shown us little more than words as support. Oh, they offer advice on our plans, but that is really all. We have been asking for

The Sugar Rebellion

something more tangible for a long time and keep getting promises. I am hoping that will change soon. I am expecting another visit from them any time now. I may introduce you to them."

"James," said Sophie. "Both Julien and I talk about this subject often. Humans have been enslaving other humans for centuries, all in the name of taking advantage of others in order to make money. It would be naive to think we could end this overnight and have a new system in place to solve all of our problems. But we will try our best."

James nodded. "I am certain you both will. You know, Royal Navy officers make much of the concept of honor and maintaining their integrity in all that they do. I think you both are doing a fair job of this too. I'd say I have come to the right place to make my new home."

Fedon and Sophie looked at each other before Fedon responded.

"Once again you are perceptive. We too have spoken of the need for honor and integrity in what we do. You need not say it, but I am certain this is important to you, too. You are welcome here, James. We have not had a conversation yet around your long-term role with us, but we will. I know you told Sophie you believe you can help deal with the British Navy, but I may have something else for you to do. We shall see, but this will be for another day."

Fedon raised his cognac glass in a toast and the three of them touched glasses before downing the remains of their drinks to signal an end to the meal. As one they rose from their places. Fedon gave

The Sugar Rebellion

Sophie a questioning look and was about to speak, but she forestalled him.

"Thank you for dinner, Julien. It was wonderful. I shall see you in the morning."

Fedon's face was frozen for a moment, but he finally nodded and bid them both good night. Once outside the room James and Sophie walked together up the staircase to the second floor where their rooms were. In the darkened hallway Sophie's face was in shadow as they stopped outside the door to her room. James took a deep breath and spoke.

"Perhaps it is just my imagination, but I think our host would have preferred you stay behind with him tonight. Not that this is any of my business, you understand."

A hint of amusement was in the tone of her voice as she replied.

"We've already noticed you are a perceptive man, so perhaps you are right. But you seem to be making it your business to notice my personal life."

James grinned in the darkness and he was sure she was smiling too.

"I like noticing beautiful women," said James. "Since you have denied our host the pleasure of your presence I'm hoping you perhaps have a different opportunity in mind?"

For her answer Sophie unexpectedly turned her face up and, hand on his shoulder holding him at a distance, gave James a long, electric kiss. The same burning quiver of energy he felt the first day they met came tenfold this time. Her scent enveloping him was like the sweetest honey he had ever tasted and the desire for her burned with a raging strength inside.

She stepped away and dropped her hand from his shoulder. Even in the darkened hallway James could see she was breathing hard.

"Perhaps, James. I like opportunities to know interesting men. We shall see what my future holds. Good night."

With that she opened the door to her room and left him alone in the hallway. James knew sleep would be hard to find once again tonight.

***

Baptiste saw James walking toward the nearby field where their dead drop was located, but as there were few people about he decided to risk a direct contact in case James had a message. Baptiste hailed him and James stopped to wait for him.

"Mr. Williams? I'm glad I found you. I was wondering if you like your room? Another has come available and I think it is better, so we could move you if you like?"

"No, I am happy where I am," said James, in a voice loud enough the few people nearby could hear him. "There is one thing you could do, though. Perhaps a bottle of rum could be sent to my room? I like to sit on my balcony and have a little drink before bed sometimes."

"Of course, sir. Is there anything else I can do for you?"

"No, that's fine, just deliver the rum."

James shook Baptiste's hand and made the surreptitious transfer of his second report to Evan.

"I will have your rum delivered within a day or two at most."

The Sugar Rebellion

As James turned and walked away Baptiste scanned their surroundings one more time to be satisfied no one nearby was paying them extra attention. He didn't see Sophie watching from the shadows of the balcony of her upper floor room.

The Sugar Rebellion

Chapter Eight
March 1796
Grenada

Over a full week passed before the raid was ready to be launched. James sensed an undercurrent running through all the planning sessions he attended, but deliberately brought no attention to it. On the surface it seemed odd the issue Fedon's commanders were facing was a lack of desire to join in the raid, but as James thought about the problem made sense. After a year of sporadic conflict the simple desire of the majority of the men serving under their banner was for the fighting to end so they could spend time with their families and get on with their new lives.

A large, solid core of men that had scores to settle with their British former masters remained though, and it took time to free them from whatever their duties were. James knew the real nugget of information Evan would want to hear of was the subtle tone of disaffection he could sense was in the front ranks of the rebel forces at being sent on yet another raid. The undercurrent was small, but it was there and would likely grow with time. The other news Evan would be happy to hear is how disorganized the rebels in truth were.

James noticed the disorganization right away during planning for and during the Gouyave action. He had not commented on this to Evan in his earlier report, but as he was now seeing a distinct pattern his next report would highlight the fact. Despite

The Sugar Rebellion

their enthusiasm and effort, it was now clear the rebel leadership were still the same plantation owners and shopkeepers they were before the fighting started. The same was true of the men they led, as most were slaves doing the mundane tasks of everyday life on plantations. The lack of professional military experience and skills hurt them more than they knew. James was one of the few in the room with such skills, but the many large egos around the planning table meant no one either thought to or wanted to ask his opinions.

At Fedon's request James joined his party to observe as the dawn attack was carried out. The first hint of light was appearing in the eastern sky as James and Fedon stood high on a nearby hill to watch. Screened by the heavy foliage around them they were certain no one would be able to pick them out from a distance. They, however, had a commanding view of the scene.

"The redoubt is as you described it, James. The gully has to be that little depression off on the left. The men should be on their way if they aren't already in place."

"I certainly hope so," said James. "That looks to be La Valette's main party massing out of sight in that clearing. He won't hold the attack back much longer."

The two men watched in silence and with the true dawn came the first signs of movement. A few minutes later the distant sound of sporadic musket fire broke the morning silence. Within moments the sound of weapons fire grew to a steady crackle without any break. From the height they were on

The Sugar Rebellion

James could see the red coats of Army regulars manning the walls of the redoubt. He also saw a group of men working to bring a small field cannon to bear.

"They'd better get that flank attack going soon or—there they go!" said James.

They could hear the howl of the attackers from the gully and watched as a mass of men appeared on the left, surging forward in a wave. These men were armed only with machetes and pikes because it would be impossible to load muskets in the low scrub brush they were forced to crawl through. The scene dissolved into chaos, making it difficult to determine what was happening, but James was certain several of the flanking attackers had indeed made their way over the walls and into the redoubt itself. La Valette's party making the demonstration on the redoubt's front screamed as they drove forward too, but a blast of canister from the field cannon ripped a huge swath through the wave of attackers.

"Good God," said James, awed at the destruction. "I think that cannon was double shotted. Has to be, from the damage it did."

Fedon glanced over at him, but said nothing. Confusion reigned as the battle continued to rage and it was impossible to tell whether it was succeeding. Several attackers were continuing to fire at the redoubt from cover, although from closer range. Other struggles continued along the left wall of the redoubt, where the flanking attack was still ongoing. A voice from behind made them turn their attention away.

The Sugar Rebellion

"Commander Fedon?" said a young black man, breathing heavily from the exertion of running from the front lines. "Commander La Valette desires to commit his reserves as the fight is in the balance and he believes he can inflict even worse losses on them. Your orders, sir?"

Both James and Fedon immediately turned back to stare hard at the scene before them. Fedon was the first to speak.

"God, James, what do you think?"

"Don't do it," said James, his voice firm. "Look over to the left, beyond the gully. I see movement through the tree cover. The British are bringing up reinforcements and I expect there are lots of them. I think you have achieved what you set out to do, given them a very bloody nose. Their soldiers are professionals and they will make you pay far more."

Fedon wasted no time, turning to the runner. "Request is denied as British reinforcements are coming. He is to retreat immediately."

Within minutes the attack was over. Fedon's forces pulled back and, as always, the British made no move to follow beyond their lines. James and Fedon made their way to the clearing where the survivors were regrouping. Fedon stopped to offer a word of encouragement and praise to several men as he made his way toward La Valette and his commanders.

"Report," said Fedon.

"I wish we could have continued on, Julien. We pushed them hard and we were making them pay dearly."

"I know. But as expected, we saw they were

The Sugar Rebellion

sending reinforcements. If we want to win this we must stick to our plans."

"Well, I remain worried they are just waiting us out and not the other way around. And my God, it would be wonderful to have some field cannon like they used on us. Did you see the carnage even one shot from that did? We are fortunate they had only one in this redoubt, as James predicted. But they did have more men than we thought, a lot more. This time we were fighting a mix of white soldiers and their black militia. Julien, if they get more reinforcements and, worse, more of these field cannon, we are going to be in trouble."

Julien nodded. "Yes, the time for the final push may be upon us soon. But for now we must gauge what we have achieved here today and give thought to next steps. How many men did we lose?"

"We lost almost a dozen for certain, with several wounded. We may lose a few more of them."

"And the British?"

"For once I think their losses have at least matched ours. The men that charged the redoubt from the flank made them pay. We need more outcomes like this."

"We do. And now I think I will make some personal visits to our wounded. La Valette, you and your men have done well today. I must ensure they know I am pleased."

***

This time it was Colonel Walter who was incensed.

"Well, I hope you two are happy," said the

The Sugar Rebellion

Colonel, his face suffused with anger. "The count is up to fifteen men I've lost from that raid because two more died in the night. Of the fifteen, nine of them were valuable white soldiers. As near as we could tell we inflicted roughly the same casualties on them. Governor, I must be blunt here. We can't afford to sustain those kinds of losses without something tangible to show for it."

"The measures we took to mitigate it failed us?" said the Governor.

"No, the double shotted cannon did its job, but if we had added a second field piece to the redoubt as I wanted they would have paid far more. The extra men we assigned to the redoubt acquitted themselves well, but the enemy brought up almost double the resources we thought they would. The pack of suicidal lunatics that attacked the flank didn't seem to care whether they lived or died. I suspect they may have been hand picked for the job because they already were that suicidal. So do we have anything to show for this?"

"I just returned from our dead drop and I've now got two more reports from Lieutenant Wilton. The first was from before this attack, while the second was after it happened. Their leadership continues to be nervous about our intentions. The Lieutenant has encountered some who are agitating for a full-scale onslaught against us, but no direct actions have been taken to make that happen as yet. Their strategy continues to be one of containment and hope we will be worn down and simply leave. But there are serious concerns we will be bringing in more resources before the beginning of hurricane

The Sugar Rebellion

season. The Lieutenant has not seen any French regular troops or direct support as yet. However, he reports hearing the bastard revolutionaries from Guadeloupe have been present on the island and offering advice prior to his arrival. They have apparently made promises of more tangible help, but little has been forthcoming to date. The Lieutenant was given a sense these same Frenchmen are due back soon. If they do come back they may have weapons for the rebels."

The Governor gave an inarticulate growl before he spoke. "Goddamn meddling frogs. I was afraid they would be involved in this mess. Is there anything else, Commander?"

"Yes. The Lieutenant reports there may be problems with morale. Limited, but he has hints of it. As he sees it, the issue is these people are not professional military, from leadership to their lower ranks. They are all civilians and, aside from some fanatics that Colonel Walter has encountered, by and large all they want to do is get on with their lives. Their economy is also rather muddled and they are having problems keeping people fed. So although he has nothing conclusive to prove it, his thinking is the rebels will in fact make a big push to drive us out some time before hurricane season. He cannot see the status quo as it is in their camp being maintained for another year."

"Good God, is this the best you bloody spies can do?" said Colonel Walter, his face contorted into a sneer. "Nothing you have said is really news, is it? We surmised most of that was the case already. Was there no word of something useful,

The Sugar Rebellion

like details of any further attacks planned?"

"With respect, Colonel," said Evan, his voice cold. "I disagree with your thinking, but you are entitled to your opinion. Simple confirmation of what we thought was the case is always going to be helpful, if only to ensure we are not caught with our pants down because our assumptions were wrong. And no, he made no mention of further attacks. He did say this man Fedon seems obsessed with knowing what the state of affairs is on our side of the lines. He wants to know if their strategy is working. We had word of a possible spy working in St. George's some time back, but have had no such signs recently. Their spy may reappear to gauge the impact of this latest raid. If so, we will be vigilant and will deal with him if at all possible."

"Bah," said the Colonel. "Governor, this skulking about is all nonsense. I have a better way for our Navy to support us, if that is truly what they are here to do. Since we don't have more Army resources coming our way just yet, give me men and equipment from the Navy. Commander Ross here has at least thirty men on that ship he prowls about with. HMS *Keene* has at least a hundred sailors on board her. I understand you have carronades, Commander Ross? If we took some of these and whatever smaller pieces we can get from the *Keene*, we could fit them with small carriages and put them to good use. In point of fact, we could carry the fight to the enemy for a change."

The Governor and Evan sat in silence for a moment and looked at each other. The Governor rubbed his chin in thought and spoke first.

The Sugar Rebellion

"Commander, what do you think?"

"Hmm. I allow there is possibility to provide the resources he wants here, but there are a lot of considerations. For starters, I cannot free up all of my men. Someone has to man the ship for us to pick up reports from my men behind the enemy lines and I am already quite lean in terms of men. I could give up maybe four or five, perhaps, but that would be it. I would be loath to provide my armament, as it would leave me defenseless. However, what no one knows is I have reserves in my hold. My cover has always been to look and behave like I'm a merchant, right? Having more than a few carronades in plain sight would give the game away, but the extra three carronades I have are for situations where I know I'm going to need more firepower. So, yes, I could countenance a loan of these if the Colonel thinks carriages can be made for them."

"That would be a welcome start," said the Colonel.

"As for the *Keene*, she has been seconded to Grenada to serve this island until the conflict is resolved, but I cannot speak for her commanding officer. He has proved willing to help already, so I see no reason to think he will balk at doing so again."

"Commander," said the Governor. "Were you in his shoes and assuming a will to help, what do you think he could provide?"

This time it was Evan's turn to rub his chin in thought.

"Were I him I would provide no more than twenty or so men. He would be left with bare bones to do his job, but as long as we are not threatened by sea it could be done for a while. As for armament I have no idea. His primary weapons are nine pounders, but I think he has a couple of six pounders fore and aft he might free up. He will also have plenty of swivels, which come to think of it, I have some extras of those, too. So, yes, once again I think it reasonable to say something could be done. However, I think the real question is to what end? Sailors are not used to land based fighting and I would be very careful about using them on any mission. On the other hand, the *Keene* has a complement of Marines who are used to that kind of fighting, but I have no idea how many the Captain would free up. They could be the best source of help."

"Well, I can set your mind at ease on at least one point, Commander Ross," said the Colonel, with a hint of sarcasm. "I wouldn't even think about using sailors for the kind of work I have in mind. They can replace some of my men at the front and just man the lines. I'll trust them to fire a cannon and use a cutlass to defend their position, but that would be all. The Marines I would absolutely welcome to do anything."

"Yes, well," said Evan, resisting the urge to scowl. "The question remains to what purpose is all this?"

"The purpose is to go out and hit them. Look, I don't know what fighting is like at sea, but on land if your opponent hits you, you bloody hit him back and make it harder than he hit you. This was a relatively big attack. If we don't respond appropriately to this goddamn raid, the rebels may get the idea we are weakening. I strongly recommend we give them some payback."

Once again Evan and the Governor remained silent, thinking about what the Colonel wanted. This time Evan looked at the Governor for a response.

The Governor grimaced. "There may be merit in what you say. I grow tired of this bloody stalemate too, Colonel. However, what you gentlemen don't know is the rebels have cause to fear we may indeed get more help coming our way. Nothing, and I repeat, nothing has been decided yet. However, discussions are underway to divert General Abercrombie here with enough troops to deal with this swiftly. Once this minor sideshow is over he could then get on with his real business elsewhere."

"Do you have any idea of timing, Governor?" said Evan.

The Governor shook his head. "Too early for that. But realistically, we all know the rebels are correct. The Army will have to get in and out before hurricane season. We can't have valuable troops sailing about in slow transports with the possibility of a major storm sinking them."

"So what does all this mean, Governor? What are your desires?" said Evan.

"Gentlemen, I am loath for the rebels to think we are weak, but I am also not interested in provoking them into a full scale assault, especially not before more help may be coming our way. Commander Ross, I desire you to contact the Captain of HMS *Keene* and brief him on this. Lets

The Sugar Rebellion

put in place what the Colonel desires as a precaution if possible. He may need the extra resources if the rebels are emboldened. Colonel Walter, you are authorized to *think* about how best to deploy the resources, but under no circumstances are you to go on the offensive unless you are specifically authorized to do so. I want regular reports on progress and I want to think more about it all. We will discuss this further. Gentlemen, have I made your orders clear?"

Evan and the Colonel rose from their seats, nodding agreement before leaving the room.

***

Fedon was closeted in a planning meeting most of the day and late into the evening with his brother and Besson, leaving James to his own devices. Feeling restless, James took a flask of water and went for a hike mid afternoon, climbing higher up the mountain past the endless rows of coffee plants. The slaves picking the ripe red berries looked at him with curiosity, but never stopped with their task. He found a path leading further up the mountain at the border of the plantation, although it didn't look well used.

The view from higher up the mountain was amazing, as he could see much further in a wide arc. The temperature was warm, but a gentle, steady breeze made it pleasant. He sat on a rocky outcrop and sipped at his water, resisting the urge to doze off. As he sat staring into the distance his mind wandered once again back to Sophie.

Thoughts of her were troubling him more and more. His last true lover was Manon Shannon. He

The Sugar Rebellion

had planned to marry her, but a French spy on St. Lucia brutally stabbed her almost four years ago. James paid him back by killing the man, but he couldn't save Manon. James had returned to his duties, but inside he was crushed. Time had healed over his inner wounds, but a part of him still felt lost. James had dallied with other women since then, but none came close to kindling the love and desire Manon had inspired.

Sophie was the exception. She was inspiring desire to a level he had not felt in a very long time. Whether this was love was another matter and only time could answer that. The cover story James gave Fedon over dinner contained large doses of truth, like all good cover stories. James was now in his early thirties and although much of his early life was spent at sea, for the last decade far more of his time was dedicated to shore-based missions. James knew of many men on warships who struggled to make the male friendships on board substitute somehow for the lack of female companionship. As strong as the bonds of friendship were, for most men they failed miserably at warding off the loneliness that was a daily knife to the heart.

The more he thought about it, James realized he had no interest in going back to a full time life at sea. Despite his love for the ocean, he liked the constant challenges and danger inherent in being a spy. But finding the simple love of a good woman and settling down to perhaps raise children some day seemed irresistible, too. The problem was finding a woman to fill the hole in his heart with Manon gone was easier said than done. James knew

The Sugar Rebellion

Sophie could well be this woman, but he rued his fortune she was on the wrong side of this conflict. James sighed, knowing at some point in the future he could be faced with a hard decision about her.

Even as the thought came his mind registered a flash of movement through the trees on the slope below him. He focused on the spot, which he knew was where the path to his location was. Another hint of movement further up the trail confirmed someone was coming, but the heavy tree cover meant he couldn't see whom it was. James was not concerned, as he was armed and knew he could deal with whoever was coming if necessary. He turned to face the spot where the person would break from cover and appear.

When Sophie walked into the clearing and moved to join him on the rock, James blazed with mixed emotions on the inside. He had a strange feeling that somehow all the turmoil he felt from thinking about her was naked and clear to her eyes and she would know everything there was to know about him. He shook his head to clear it as she walked up and stood beside him, putting a hand on his shoulder. A smile played across her face.

"What, are you so surprised to see me you can't believe your eyes, James?"

"I have a hard time believing my eyes every time I see you."

She laughed. "I like your thinking, Mr. Williams. You may continue flattering me."

"So, dare I ask, what brings you up here?"

Sophie shrugged. "I saw you leave for a walk and was watching when you left the plantation and kept going. I thought about it for a bit, finished what I was doing, and decided to give you some company. I haven't been up here for a while and it is a lovely day, so here I am, alone with you."

"Yes," said James, giving her a hopeful look. "Alone with me. Do many people come up here?"

"Rarely. In fact, we are quite alone and we should enjoy that fact. I think I will."

Taking her hand from his shoulder she used both hands to pull her shift up and over her head with one quick motion. She wore nothing underneath. The naked bounty of her full breasts and slim body covered with a light sheen of sweat from climbing the hill took James's breath away. Stepping over to stand directly in front of him, her dark brown nipples a bare few inches away from his face, she put a hand on each of James's shoulders and grinned.

"I enjoy the freedom of wearing nothing in the open air, don't you? Maybe you should take your clothes off, too."

James couldn't contain himself any longer. As he rose to his feet he ran his hands around her waist and crushed her to his body, molding the two of them together. The feel of her naked breasts mashed to his chest was maddening. Her found her mouth and pressed his own to hers in a long, slow kiss. When he ended it he stepped back long enough to shed his own clothes as fast as he could, while Sophie laughed.

"Why, James, I'd say that bulge in your pants needs some attention. Perhaps I could help?"

"My *God*, I want you so bad," said James,

freeing himself finally from the last of his clothes. "You can help with that bulge all you want."

Afterwards they lay on the makeshift bed of the clothes they had shed as their breathing returned to normal. Sophie turned and smiled at him.

"You know, if I didn't know better, I'd almost think you haven't had a woman for quite a while."

"I haven't had one like you in a very long time and, yes, it does get rather lonely on board a Royal Navy warship."

"But you have had one like me before?"

James took a long moment to think about how to respond.

"Yes, there was someone who I—desired as much as you once. Of course there have been others and some much more recently, but some women have something special. Her name was Manon, but she is no longer alive."

"I'm sorry, I didn't know. What happened?"

James pursed his lips as he thought about how to respond, before finally deciding to keep the story simple.

"She was murdered. It's a long story, but all you need to know is she was in the wrong place at the wrong time. I made sure her killer paid the price. He ended up with my knife in his heart."

Sophie nodded. "And now you have found me. You think I have something special, too?"

"I do," said James, as he turned to face her and stroked her arm.

"Well, I think you have something special about you. It's almost dinnertime, James. Let's go back to the plantation and have dinner. Fedon is

The Sugar Rebellion

busy today and we can have dinner all to ourselves. And when we are done I'd like to give you a tour of my room."

James grinned. He was glad he had slept well the night before, as he knew there would be little sleep tonight.

***

The next night it was the three of them for dinner again. Fedon was tied up with meeting people most of the day, but finally came to join them at the last minute. Within minutes, James was certain Fedon knew he had shared Sophie's bed. He had no idea how he knew it, but he did. But Fedon made no mention of the change in their relationship and the conversation focused on what James knew of general politics in the wider world. As they finished their dessert course and they all had their usual snifter of cognac before them, Fedon shifted the topic to James.

"So James, you may recall some time back I mentioned I might have a task for you? Well, I believe I do. I had to think about this for a while, but I have a mission that you are uniquely placed to perform. Others could perhaps do what I have in mind, but you have the knowledge that makes you the best choice. Are you interested?"

"Of course, Julien. I came to help and make a home here."

"Excellent," said Fedon. "Look, lets sit outside on the verandah tonight and finish this. I love to look at the stars."

Once they were all settled in Fedon returned to the topic.

The Sugar Rebellion

"So James, before we go further I need to know how well you were known in St. George's? Did you spend a lot of time on shore?"

"I'm not well known at all. I spent most of my time on the ship. Oh, the odd night I did go into town and have a few drinks. There was that one night in particular where I met those soldiers and gleaned the information I gave you about that redoubt, of course."

"I see. Well, this is going to sound unusual, but I want you to go back to St. George's and be a spy for us."

James couldn't help raising an eyebrow at the unexpected request. His mind raced through the ramifications of it, but he saw no way to avoid agreeing to what Fedon wanted. What neither James or Fedon saw was a momentary flash of surprise flit across Sophie's face before she mastered herself.

"Well, I have to say I wasn't expecting that kind of a task, but I am game for anything and if this is what you want then I shall do my best. How do you see this unfolding?"

"I am certain you will do well. Before we get to details, I need you to understand why it is necessary. We have been in this bloody stalemate for far too long. We have far more men than they do, but they have better arms and training. You know our strategy has been to wear them down. What I need to know is whether now is the time to make our all out push to wipe the British off this island. I need to know their morale and anything, anything you can get regarding whether or not reinforcements are on the way. Half of the

The Sugar Rebellion

commanders under me want to stay the course while the other half want to put it all on the line and hammer them now. I don't think it's a question of whether the final battle is coming, it is when."

"I understand, Julien. Look, while I am willing, there are many considerations. For starters, how do you propose to get me across their lines? Bear in mind if the Navy catches me I am a dead man."

Fedon grinned. "The Navy won't catch you if you disguise yourself a bit. You won't leave here for a few days because you need to grow your beard a little. We will find appropriate old clothes and I suggest wearing a floppy hat. The kind the slaves on fishing boats out in the sun all day long wear, right? You need to fit that part because we will arrange a meeting at sea with one of the fishing boats that leaves St. George's every day. You will become another of their crew. No one, and especially not the Navy, pays any attention to fishing boats."

James wanted to laugh at the irony, but couldn't. He and Evan had used fishing boats from the various islands throughout the Caribbean for years for exactly this kind of purpose. Fishing boat crews throughout the Caribbean were participating in smuggling as a side business on a broad scale. The crews weren't particular about what they smuggled, whether it was people, goods, or even information. The only requirement was to be paid. The even more amusing element was most Captains in the Royal Navy did indeed completely ignore fishermen. James and Evan were exceptions in their awareness of the true role the fishing boats played.

"I see," said James. "I guess that makes sense.

The Sugar Rebellion

What about when I am in St. George's?"

Fedon shrugged. "Money usually works for just about anything. I will ensure you have enough with you to buy information, if you can find a way to get it. Trawl the taverns where the Army drinks and see what news you can pick up. Stay in a brothel and talk to the women about whom they see and what they say. I don't want you to stay more than a couple of days. The longer you are there, the greater the possibility you will run into someone who knows you have deserted."

James nodded. "All right, I can do it. It is the least I can do."

"Excellent. We can talk more over the next few days. Stop shaving as of now. We will talk more of this over the next few days."

Fedon sat back and looked at his cognac glass, frowning at how little remained. He swirled the remainder for a moment, toying with his glass. When he looked up this time he turned to Sophie.

"As for you, I believe I have a task for you, too. You will be away for a time also. We will discuss this personally later. My friends, I sense matters may finally be coming closer to resolution here. Not tomorrow, but I think we will not be sitting here next year facing the same stalemate. If we have any fortune at all, this time next year we will be masters of our own republic. It is a dream worth chasing. To us!"

They all touched glasses and, following Fedon's lead, they all downed the remainder of their cognac. All three rose to their feet and Fedon gave Sophie a direct look, but said nothing.

The Sugar Rebellion

"Thank you, Julien, this has been another wonderful evening," said Sophie. "I am rather tired today, so I am going to my room. I look forward to whatever task you have for me."

Fedon gave them a slow nod and led them back into the dining room. He reached for the decanter of cognac and poured himself another small portion.

"I have been very busy the last few days and its time to treat myself. I'm going back out to look at the stars. Good night."

James waited until Fedon was out of earshot before he spoke.

"Is it just my imagination or does he not seem himself tonight?"

"I don't think it is your imagination. I don't know why, but I do know he is carrying a big burden on his shoulders. I will talk to him tomorrow and try to find out what is going on."

James grunted. "He almost seems—wistful or something. Well, please let me know if there is anything I can do to help."

They turned and left the dining room, once again stopping at Sophie's door. James gave her a questioning look in the darkness of the hallway, but she shook her head.

"Not tonight, James. Last night was wonderful, but I need a night on my own. I really am tired."

"Yes, last night was wonderful. I could get used to that," said James.

He ran a hand through her hair and gave her a long, slow kiss, before turning away to his own room.

The Sugar Rebellion

Chapter Nine
March 1796
Grenada

James was left on his own the next morning, as both Fedon and Sophie were in yet another meeting. James knew something was going on, but he had no details of what. With little he could do about it he focused on instead on thinking about what he would do once he was back in St. George's. The possibility Fedon had other sources in the town James knew nothing about was real, so contacting Evan wasn't going to be as easy as it might seem. He rubbed the unfamiliar, growing stubble on his face in absentminded thought.

His thoughts were interrupted as a slave appeared with a summons to join Fedon in their meeting room. When James walked in he found Fedon and Sophie sitting at the table, talking with two white men James had not seen before. As Fedon turned and saw James he stopped what he was saying in mid sentence.

"Yes, here he is. I haven't had a chance to tell you about James yet. James, this is—well, perhaps you have no need to know their names. These are French friends from Guadeloupe. They just arrived early this morning."

Fedon went on to explain whom James was and how he had provided the information leading to the successful defense of Gouyave and to the recent attack on St. George's. James watched the faces of the two men and saw the warning signs of muted

The Sugar Rebellion

alarm grow the longer Fedon spoke. When Fedon mentioned his plan to send James to St. George's as a spy, one of the men's eyes widened and he seemed no longer able to contain himself.

"Julien, you are mad. Are you telling me you trust him? How do you know he is not a British spy?"

Fedon saw the man's anger, but gave no sign of being cowed by it.

"Hubert, give us some credit, please. He has been with us for some time now and, as I just told you, he provided credible information that led to successes for us. He has military experience we lack and I am coming to value his opinion."

The Frenchman scowled and turned to glare directly at James. James locked eyes with him and gave a cold stare back.

"You know, I have heard a rumor there are British spies actively at work in the Caribbean. In fact, this same rumor holds that these spies are actually attached somehow to the Royal Navy. The really fanciful part is the vague story one of them might even be a black man. Like you. I don't suppose you'd know anything about this, would you?"

James shrugged. "Sounds like it would be a good story to read if it was true. I haven't heard anything about it, though."

"Of course not," said the Frenchman, as he turned back to Fedon and scowled again. "I think he is a spy and you should kill him, especially because he now knows my name, you fool."

"I am not going to kill him, Hubert. I fail to see

The Sugar Rebellion

how knowing your first name is a problem. Hubert is a common enough French name. You just need to trust that I have this under control. The reason I brought him into our meeting today is to demonstrate we are moving this forward, whether you believe it or not. The real problem here, Hubert, is your inability to deliver on what you promise. I have a feeling this stalemate isn't going to last much longer and that means I need two things. First, I need to know my enemy's mind. What are their intentions? What is their morale? Are they going to be reinforced and, if so, when? James here will try to answer all this for me. Secondly, I need better weapons. You have promised time and again to bring us field cannon to match the British, yet every time you appear you are empty handed. Oh, yes, you have brought another shipment of muskets and ammunition. This is welcome, but I saw the carnage from just one field cannon in our last attack. Hubert, you must do better and do it soon."

The Frenchman shook his head and spread his arms wide in frustration.

"Julien, must we talk of this again? I have told you we are doing the best we can. Field weapons are valuable and, to be blunt, the forges in France are working at capacity to make more. The problem is the need is greatest at home. Reactionaries that want to end what the revolution has started beset France on all sides. It will take time to get you what you want. In the meantime, you simply have to make do with what you have and we can find to bring. I believe another shipment of small arms is possible within the next month or two. Nonetheless,

The Sugar Rebellion

I will try for you."

"I see. Well, I fear there will be far more blood shed than I would desire."

"Julien, there is one other thing you should know," said the Frenchman, with a quick side glare at James. "There is a rumor out there the British are massing together a force for action. This is quite vague and recent. It comes from only one source and it may be questionable. We do not know what their intentions are if it is true. It may well be they will head straight for St. Domingue and have nothing to do with you. We are actively working on it and if I get word I will send it onward to you."

"Thank you for that, at least. Well, we shall see what James comes up with for us. As I said, I have a sense matters are progressing and the real question is who will make the first move, and when."

"You may well be right, Julien," said the Frenchman, before jerking a thumb in James's direction. "But as for this man, I still think your best course of action is to kill him."

***

Fedon and Sophie were finally alone together later that day, sitting on the verandah watching the sun cast rose pink hues on the few clouds about as it went down. Fedon poured them each a small glass of wine to enjoy. Sophie waited in silence for him to begin, knowing he needed to talk.

"I am sorry you have been out of the picture in what has been going on. Matters seem to be moving faster than usual and I simply haven't had time to talk to you, although God knows I wanted to. I know when I mentioned the raid my brother is

The Sugar Rebellion

planning to Montdenoix it was the first you had heard of this and I apologize for that. I have misgivings about it, but being a leader means being a politician, too. Besson has been pushing hard to keep the heat on the British, so I agreed. It was also a chance to show Montdenoix we are not waiting for him and to try goading him into action."

"They aren't going to do any more than they have already, Julien. I have given up on that. Oh, I still believe in our dream. Citizens, not slaves. It is a worthy dream and one worth fighting and dying for. If we have to make the dream come true with minimal help from them, then so be it."

"Well said, my love," said Julien, placing his hand on hers. "You noticed, of course, I did not mention the raid to James."

Sophie looked at Fedon with a raised eyebrow. "Yes, I did. Has your thinking changed?"

"Not really. Besson and my brother insisted they did not want him to be aware of the raid, as Besson still thinks he is a spy. It cannot hurt to keep him in the dark. What are your thoughts on this, Sophie? I know you have grown—closer to him. Is he indeed a spy?"

Sophie sighed. "Maybe. It is true, I have a much better sense of this man now. He is highly intelligent and, I sense, dangerous if you are opposing him. He is a man of action and not to be taken lightly. But most of all he truly is a man of honor. I'm sorry. I am no closer to an answer to your question than before. I need more time."

"Well," said Fedon, giving her hand a squeeze before removing it. "Words cannot adequately

The Sugar Rebellion

convey my appreciation for your efforts. I know you were surprised at the idea of sending him into St. George's, too. Once again I must apologize, as the plan came to me and I felt the need to just do it."

Sophie smiled and she took his hand back in hers. Fedon looked at his hand in hers and sighed in relief.

"Julien, you have no need to apologize. Nothing has changed between us. And I have no problem with you doing something without talking to me first. You are our leader, remember?"

"Indeed. Well, sending him into St. George's seemed a way to resolve a few things. I do think he likely is a spy, but I am not losing sleep over that. I don't see how his presence changes much of anything. So the plan is to send him in and see what he comes back with. If he isn't a spy then he may come back with something valuable. If he is, the results will be suspect. Your task is to go in a day before him. Having an eye on what he does as best you can will be how we determine whether to believe what he says. Of course, I need you to have your own eyes and ears open to learn what we need to know. I know it makes your life more difficult. He has no idea of your true role as my own spy, so you will have to be very careful."

Sophie looked at Fedon and nodded. "I will do my duty."

***

James was the first onto the dock from the small fishing boat, jumping the gap with ease as the other fishermen held the craft steady. Once James secured lines to the dock at either end he

The Sugar Rebellion

straightened up and looked around. No one appeared to take notice of the arrival of yet another nondescript fishing boat coming back at the end of the day, one among a large cluster in this part of the harbor. James made a show of working along with the others for a while to bring the catch ashore before as casually as possible slipping away with the small satchel of his belongings slung over his shoulder.

James made note of the *Alice*, berthed further along the Wharf Road docks, but he kept his hat low to remain unrecognized and walked right past it. He did the same to the *HMS Keene*, tied up not far away. He noticed with interest a large British frigate leaving port with the tide. Slipping into a side street away from the port he made his way to the brothel Fedon had suggested he use as a base. What he didn't know was Sophie's half sister lived right across the street from it and that Sophie herself had been watching his every move since he arrived.

After arranging for discreet accommodation in the brothel, James dined in a nearby tavern. He struck up several casual conversations and sipped at his ale. The food on offer was more limited than normal, but it was enough to attest Fedon's hope the British would starve was in vain. Somehow, rumors of a relief force had begun to circulate too. James nursed his drink to remain reasonably sober and, when he judged everyone in the tavern was too drunk to notice, he slipped away.

Despite the starlight of a cloudless night the harbor remained in semi darkness, lit only by the lanterns on the ships and in the homes around it.

The Sugar Rebellion

James made his way to the *Alice* watching for anyone taking notice of him. Judging no one had, James made as if to casually walk past the gangplank of the *Alice* before moving swiftly up and onto the deck. He failed to see Sophie tailing him, as she was wearing clothing dark enough to hug the walls of the buildings along the waterfront and meld with the shadows.

The watch on deck was taken by surprise as he appeared in their midst. Although the *Alice* was maintaining her disguise as a merchant ship, a surreptitious watch was always maintained. They overcame their surprise in an instant, reaching for weapons, but James forestalled them by quietly barking a command to hold fast and identifying himself. Within moments he was taken below to see Evan.

James couldn't help laughing as he saluted when he was ushered in to see Evan, knowing the picture he presented of a bearded, scruffy looking fisherman was the last thing Evan had expected to see that night. Evan's jaw fell open as James grinned.

"Aren't you going to welcome me back, sir? I thought I'd drop in for a late night drink and see if you think I look good with a little stubble on my face. I'm hoping the women will."

***

Two days later James made his way to the meeting Evan had arranged with the Governor at the fort. He had kept a low profile while trawling the taverns since his meeting with Evan, putting on a show of doing what he was in St. George's

The Sugar Rebellion

ostensibly to do. Meeting the Governor in Fort George was a step away from the role he was playing, so he took extra care as he zigzagged his way toward it. Sophie was tailing him without his knowledge again, but he lost her when he feinted looking at the wares in a shop window on the chance someone was indeed following him. James had no idea his maneuver forced her to step into an alley and by the time she peered around the corner he was gone into a side street, leaving her cursing to herself. The guards at the entrance to the Fort were briefed and watching for him. They whisked him out of sight the second he appeared. Minutes later he was once again seated at the Governor's meeting table with Evan and Colonel Walter.

James debriefed them on everything that had transpired since his infiltration into the rebel camp. All three of the men peppered him with questions. Evan wanted more details on the morale of the rebels and their organizational skills. The Colonel wanted information on the terrain Fedon's estate Belvedere was situated on, thinking ahead to a day when he might be attacking it.

His meeting with the two mysterious Frenchmen also got their attention. Evan was particularly interested in everything James could tell him of their opponents and the two of them had went over the details of the encounter at length before going to meet the Governor. Although it wasn't certain they were the foes waging secret war against them for so long now, the possibility seemed strong. James vowed to try and learn more.

The Governor scowled once again at mention

they were involved. He was also particularly concerned about the fate of the hostages, but James could offer little information other than to confirm they were still there and imprisoned on the estate. The Governor shook his head in dismay.

"My God, those poor people. It must be a living hell to be trapped in there after a year in that same place."

"Sir, I debated with myself several times about trying to get word to them of my presence and to ask how they are faring, but I felt it would not be right to offer them a hope of rescue that wasn't real."

"Yes, yes, quite right, Lieutenant," said the Governor. "I just wish we could do something."

Almost an hour later the questions slowed enough James decided it was time to turn their minds to next steps. He knew they were facing only one real question.

"Sirs, if I may suggest, I think the next question is whether I return to the rebels or not. May I also offer my thoughts on the answer to that?"

The other three men in the room all looked at each other before turning back to James.

"I think we would all welcome that, Lieutenant," said the Governor. "I confess I never thought for even a second the rebels might turn around and send you back here as a spy. It seems a possibility so remote I would have scoffed at someone suggesting it could happen. Until now, that is. And I guess we need to deal with that reality now."

"I need to go back, sirs. I don't think there is

any choice. I don't know what the consequences of not showing up could be, but it may cause them to make their move far sooner than we want. You will know the risk better than I. If I do go back I can feed them whatever story you wish. I can also send word if and when they do ready a major assault. They won't be able to hide that kind of preparation. Commander Ross, there is also the question of getting orders to Baptiste. He has done well and, as far as I know, has not experienced the same kind of suspicion I have, but I would like to see he gets out of this alive."

"I would like to see you get out of this alive, too, Lieutenant," said the Governor, before he turned to Evan and the Colonel. "Well? What do you think?"

"It is a risk for the Lieutenant, but I think the threat is unchanged from when he went to the rebels in the first place," said Evan.

"I agree, he should go back in," said the Colonel. "If you can get us warning of any plans of a major strike it would be invaluable."

"Indeed," said Evan. "Lieutenant, when you go back I think you should tell them we are in some disarray. Rumors of more troops coming seem to be just that, more rumors. In fact, see if you can slip in a hint that hopes are being dashed because it's starting to look like more help won't arrive until right after hurricane season. Tell them we are dispirited at how long this has gone on. Tell them some of the men have gotten sick because rations have been limited."

"Well, that's interesting," said James.

The Sugar Rebellion

"Everything you just said bears a striking resemblance to what Fedon wanted me to tell you if I was somehow captured as a spy. I was to say rumors of French field weapons coming are just rumors. Morale has sunk to rock bottom levels and defections from their units back to their home plantations are on the rise. The economy has become a disaster and food is in short supply, with people getting sick. Sirs, there are elements of truth to all of this, but I think he was trying to mislead us into thinking things are worse than they really are, just as you are doing."

Evan grunted. "This man Fedon isn't stupid, is he?"

"No, sir," said James. "In fact, I confess I like him. You may disagree with what he wants to do, but he has a vision and is trying to achieve it with honor."

"Honor?" said the Colonel, an incredulous look on his face. "What in God's name would someone like him know about honor?"

"With respect, sir, I've had a number of conversations with the man. I think I know what honor looks like when I see it. Sir."

"Lieutenant Wilton," said the Governor, after giving the Colonel a frosty look. "I believe I will take you at your word. What you don't know is matters have changed somewhat on our end. The Royal Navy has graciously once again stepped to our aid. The Colonel here now has an extra sixty Royal Marines on loan from the *HMS Keene* and one of her sister ships, *HMS Haven*. In addition, the Captain of the *Keene* and our friend Commander

The Sugar Rebellion

Ross here have between them freed up forty sailors from their ships to man the guns on our lines. Even better, all of them have seen fit to loan us cannons from their ships. None of them are bigger than a six pounder, although Commander Ross has freed up some spare carronades that will offer a punch the rebels won't be expecting. We are busy fitting all of these weapons to small field carriages. In short, we are sleeping in our beds a lot better at night thanks to their efforts."

"Lieutenant," said Evan. "What this all means is even if they decide to come after us with everything they have sooner than we think, we have enough fire power and men now that it may tip the balance. I think it could still be a close affair, too close perhaps, but I am confident."

The Colonel gave them a cold smile. "I, on the other hand, am fully confident. In fact, I would love to take the fight out to them now. I like these Marines. They know their business and will do well when the time comes. And, I grant, these sailors do know how to fire a cannon and swing a cutlass. Best of all is we have added another thirty or so highly mobile, small field artillery pieces to our defense. The rebels don't know this and are not going to like the pay back when it comes. If they want to come and be slaughtered by our guns, then let them."

"Yess, well," said the Governor. "I like your optimism, but I don't share it to the point we can risk big offensive raids just yet. The other factor is the decision to send a large force here to relieve us is hanging in the balance even as we speak. I have no doubt the time will come when we make these

The Sugar Rebellion

bloody rebels pay. It is not a question of *if* it will happen. So, Lieutenant, it seems we are agreed. The potential value of you being able to warn us of their attack, whenever it comes, is valuable enough to send you back in. We appreciate the risk you are taking."

The Governor nodded to everyone and rose, signaling an end to the meeting. James stood and saluted him, leaving with Evan and the Colonel. The thought came he had not told them of the other reason for being as willing to return as he was. James knew they might have thought differently had they known of Sophie and his desire to find a way to spirit her out when the fighting began.

***

Sophie was watching when James left the brothel early the next morning, knowing he had returned the night before. After having lost him during the day, she shadowed the owner of the fishing boat that would take James out on the return journey when the man returned at the end of his day, on the possibility James would appear to arrange his return. James did exactly that and then returned to the brothel after talking to the owner of the boat.

Seeing he carried his satchel she surmised at once he was leaving St. George's, but after following him to the port her suspicions were raised once again as he instead boarded the *Alice* and disappeared from her view. He remained on board less than fifteen minutes. After disembarking he went straight to the fishing boat and began helping the owner with his chores. After watching them cast

The Sugar Rebellion

off their lines and head to sea, Sophie emerged from hiding and turned her attention back to the *Alice*.

Sophie was puzzled by it all and knew Fedon would need to know more. She spent the rest of the day talking to people in the shops of the town looking for tidbits of information, but surreptitiously returning to watch the *Alice* every so often. The *Alice* provided little of interest. On the surface it was yet another nondescript merchant ship tied up along the docks. The only thing unusual about it was the lack of activity, as nothing was ever offloaded or brought on board. That no one seemed to know much about the *Alice* and what kind of cargos she bore was also odd.

By the end of the day she knew she could delay no longer. She made her way to the same dock James had departed from and met the fishing boat owner when he returned at sundown. After making arrangements to join him the next day for her own return journey she left and returned to her sister's home.

***

Alice joined Evan in their cabin on the ship late that evening and waited to make sure the door was closed before speaking.

"I have some news, lover man. I was out running errands today and when I came back a while ago I saw a woman loitering near the ship. She was watching us, Evan. I hung back to see what she would do. She waited till almost sundown and left. The interesting part is she went straight to a fishing boat owner and they talked for a while. I'm quite sure I saw her give him money and then she left. I followed her, so I know where she is staying. I hung around to see if she would leave again, but she didn't. The place is on the edge of the seedier part of town. What do you think, do we have a problem?"

Evan sat in silence as he considered the implications before finally responding.

"Well, I'm glad you finally showed up. I was going to start searching soon. And yes, it may be we have a problem. Have you seen her before?"

"No. I suppose I shouldn't tell you this, but she is likely about my age and quite a natural beauty. This woman is a mulatto like me and is just as pretty too, actually."

"Really? Well, I already have an armful with one beautiful mulatto woman. A pity James isn't here to chase her. But speaking of which, you say she went straight to a particular fishing boat? No hesitation?"

"Correct."

"Alice, I think we must consider the possibility it is the same man James is using. James was sent here to spy on us, so why wouldn't they have more than one spy using fishing boats? Were I them I would do it. Of course, I'm not the first person to use a woman as a spy either."

"Evan, how did she know to watch us? And what do you think she was doing with that fisherman? Is she maybe planning to escape to the other side using the same route?"

"All good questions, my love. I wonder if she is somehow connected to James? He never mentioned a woman, but then women find him like bees find

The Sugar Rebellion

flowers. If this woman is a spy maybe her job was to watch him and she saw him get on board the *Alice*. I don't know, this is stretching it and we have more questions than answers."

"Well, I'm not so sure it is a stretch. You remember when we first came here and I heard rumors of a beautiful mulatto asking questions around town, right? I am thinking this may be her."

"Yes, I forgot about that. Perhaps you are right."

So what do you want to do?"

Evan rubbed his chin. "Two choices. Grab her and make her talk. That could cause problems for James if she is indeed a spy and she doesn't return. Or, we watch and see what happens. If she leaves tomorrow morning on that fishing boat and doesn't come back at night, it will confirm our suspicions. But that might cause problems for James, too. Damn it, no good choices here."

"James can take care of himself, Evan. So why don't I just get up early tomorrow and watch to see what happens?"

After a moment Evan nodded. "Yes, please do. It's not likely she got information of any consequence while she was here and the *Alice* is hardly interesting on the surface. If pressed all James has to do is say he stopped to see an old friend while he was here. He can think on his feet and he'll figure it out. We can also have you keep an eye on this fisherman on a regular basis. This woman might just reappear some day."

***

"So it's settled then?" said Jean Fedon, looking

The Sugar Rebellion

at his brother Julien with a sidelong glance at Besson.

"It is," said Julien. "Tomorrow is the beginning of April. The attack will proceed within the next few days, at your discretion, when you believe you have the men ready."

"Julien, to be certain, you have made no mention of this to James?" said Besson.

"I have not and have no plans to do so. He has not returned as yet from St. George's anyway, although I expect he will be back soon."

"Excellent. I still do not trust this bastard, Julien. I feel better knowing he knows nothing."

With nothing left to discuss the three men rose from their chairs. Julien clapped Besson on the shoulder and grasped his brother's forearm with his own.

"Besson, my friend. Jean, my dear brother. God go with you. Come back safe."

The two men nodded and all three left the room. As silence descended Baptiste rose from his hiding place near the door in the anteroom where he had listened to their conversation. He was torn that Lieutenant Wilton was not there to guide him. Worse was the knowledge the Lieutenant had no idea another attack was being planned. As tempting as it was to simply wait for his return, Baptiste decided he too would be a man of action like his superiors. He went to his room to prepare a report with the details of what he had heard. Because time was short he would make his delivery to the drop location that same night.

***

The Sugar Rebellion

Evan frowned when he read Baptiste's report two days later as he was returning to St. George's from the drop location. He hadn't expected there would be a report, as James had only just left to return to the rebels. That the report was in Baptiste's handwriting was unusual, but not an impossible occurrence. They had foreseen the possibility Baptiste might have opportunity to learn something of consequence and report on his own.

What Evan wasn't sure about was the timing. The report gave all the necessary details, but did not clarify whether James knew of the raid or not. Evan knew James would have said something when he was in St. George's had he known. This combined with the fact the mystery woman watching the *Alice* had indeed not returned to St. George's after leaving on the fishing boat gave Evan pause. The difficult question facing him was whether the consequences of forewarning Colonel Walter of the attack would cause yet more problems for James.

Evan shook his head in dismay, knowing no easy answer was at hand, but he also knew what his duty was. Colonel Walter would be delighted to have his advance warning of the attack.

The Sugar Rebellion

Chapter Ten
April 1796
Grenada

The frozen faces of the men around the table were hard for James to read. He knew nothing he had told them was a surprise, but he kept to the story Evan had articulated for him to use.

Fedon was the first to speak. "Well, what do you all think? In particular, what about this vague rumor that troops might not be coming until after hurricane season? Does any of this change anything?"

Montdenoix had remained on the island for several days reviewing the rebel positions and offering advice. He was about to leave once again, but stayed one extra day for this meeting. He shrugged as he glared at James.

"This man has not given you anything tangible or really new. I cannot confirm or deny anything, including whether there will be a delay in getting troops. It certainly is possible as the British have their own share of problems, just like us. But I don't think this changes anything."

"That their morale is getting bad is useful to know, if true," said Jean Fedon. "It is also good to know there remains only one British warship on station, although the appearance and departure of this second frigate could mean anything."

"I think this is all shit," said Besson. "This is exactly the kind of information they would want to provide in order to make us think they are weak.

The Sugar Rebellion

They may not have the resources to come out, but I don't think they are in that bad a shape. So it means we should just kill this bastard now he has served your purpose and have done with the problem."

"I agree," said Montdenoix.

"Enough, please," said Fedon. "We will not be killing anyone today. I confess I had hoped for more, but I knew the possibility was good this is all I would get. I agree this changes nothing, so we will stay our course, gentlemen. James, thank you for seeing us before you had a chance to rest. I expect you are tired and want nothing more than to shave off that beard I made you grow. We will have a drink together later today. Good day, everyone."

***

Sophie returned late that afternoon and Fedon's summons for her to see him came right away.

"Report," said Fedon, as they sat across his desk from each other.

She first told him of what she had learned from trawling for information throughout St. Georges and confirmed there didn't seem to be any more troops in town than before, despite continued rumors more could be on the way. Fedon interrupted her and asked if she had heard any rumors there could be a delay until after hurricane season. She frowned and told him of hearing some mention of it, but more people seemed to favor the opposite possibility. She also told him of the new frigate which had come and gone. Then she told him of what James had done and of his visits to the mysterious ship. This time it was Fedon's turn to frown and he asked her opinion of what she thought it meant.

The Sugar Rebellion

"Julien, I truly cannot say whether he was doing something unusual or not in visiting this ship. It could mean nothing or everything. You will have to ask him. Of more concern is the day I lost him. All I can tell you is he was walking about on an erratic route and I couldn't determine why before I lost him. He was heading in the direction of the Fort, but once again that could mean nothing. In all other respects and, as near as I could tell, he did exactly what we expected him to do, work the taverns for information. I am sorry, I know you need better than this. I am willing to go back to St. George's again if you need me to."

Fedon rose from his chair and came around his desk to stand before her. He reached over and put a hand on her shoulder.

"Do not concern yourself, Sophie. I know you have done your best. Yes, I may need you to go back in again, but not right away. What you need to know is I had yet another session with Montdenoix before he left. Of interest he has had word he may finally be able to get us at least some field artillery. Notice I said may and not will. It is worth waiting just a little longer before we make our move. I will let you know when the time is right. On a more personal note, I have my own need to see you. It has been too long."

"Julien, I agree. The thing is James will be thinking the same thing tonight. What would you have me do? Is there still a need for me to go to his bed?"

Fedon groaned softly and closed his eyes for a moment.

The Sugar Rebellion

"God, there are days I ask myself what I have become. I find myself asking people to do things I never thought possible. I fear there may be more such days ahead. Sophie, I need you tonight. I beg you. It's that simple. I will keep him occupied drinking a bit tonight after dinner. You can join us, but tell him beforehand you are tired. Tomorrow I know you will do what you must, but right now I am not thinking that far ahead, as I don't want to know. I just want you now."

Sophie rose from her chair to give him a hug. "I will come to you tonight, Julien."

***

Fedon and James retired to the verandah with their cognac after dinner. James was disappointed Sophie begged off coming to his bed that night, but was satisfied knowing she had whispered a promise to make amends the next night.

Once again they had the benefit of a cloudless night and the stars were spectacular, seeming particularly bright. Another warm breeze made sitting outside pleasant. James thought Fedon seemed troubled and asked him about it.

"Troubled? Well, I guess that is as good a word as any. I grow weary of this task and the things I must do. I chose to accept it, but I don't have to like it. You know, to me being an honorable man means I must be honest, fair, and do everything possible to maintain my integrity at all times. And here I am, sending men to their deaths and asking people to do things they would not otherwise do. Tell me, men who claim honor while doing the same once surrounded you. Am I any different than they are?

The Sugar Rebellion

Do you think doing these things mean I am not a man of honor?"

"I think you are no different. I believe it possible to serve in the kind of role you have while still doing everything in your power to be an honorable man. Whether the outcomes of your actions are a problem is another matter. That is for God to decide."

"Indeed. So how did you reconcile your honor with your action in joining us?"

James took a moment to think before responding. "I was honest with myself about why I wanted to be here. I did my job well on the ship. I will do whatever you ask of me to the best of my ability. As for the outcome, that is for God."

"Fair enough. So, tell me James, are you a spy?"

"I thought we had already sorted that out."

"When you were in St. George's you stopped at a merchant ship twice. What were you doing on it?"

James kept a bland look on his face as he thought fast. "I went to see an old friend. The Captain of the ship used to be in the Navy, but he was badly injured and retired from the service. He couldn't stay away from the sea so he went into business as a merchant sailor. I recognized his ship right away and I decided to call on him in case I could glean some useful bits of information from him."

Fedon slowly nodded. "All right. I know, you are wondering how I know that. Yes, I have other people that spy for me, too. I'd be a fool not to have others, of course. Well, I think I believe you, but I

The Sugar Rebellion

can't say the same for everyone else. It is no matter. I think we are closer to the die being cast once and for all. We shall see."

James thought hard for a few long seconds before he spoke again.

"Julien, would you like my professional opinion?"

Fedon turned to look at James. "Yes."

"I think you have a problem. I know what I told you and the others, but you should not underestimate British resolve. The Army has at times not proved quite as resolute as the Royal Navy, but to be fair they will do what they must. If the British have done more to bolster their defenses without your knowledge, for example, you may find the path ahead is fraught with decisions you won't like."

Fedon looked at James for a long time with out saying anything, before finally responding.

"I won't ask what has moved you to say that, but I appreciate your honesty. I made my decision to do this and must live with the consequences. The opportunity to change any of it is likely long past. So you know, I am contemplating another role for you to help us with, if you are willing. I need to talk to others about it, so that is all I can tell you for now."

"I am willing to do whatever you want, Julien."

"Excellent. Then lets enjoy the rest of our drinks and the evening."

***

The attack was launched at a defensive position close to the shoreline. The fortifications took advantage of the thought the sand and water on the flank would slow advancing troops, discouraging any idea of using it altogether. The rebel plan was to send a host of men to the flank of the redoubt using small canoes and boats under cover of darkness. As the sun began touching the horizon a diversionary attack aiming for the other flank began, in the hope the defenders would fail to expect or see anyone coming from the sea.

Forewarned by Baptiste, the British struck when they had the maximum number of attackers in vulnerable positions caught in the open. A fusillade from six different field weapons smashed into both parties to devastating effect. Despite the horrific loss, the rebels struggled forward only to have even more die in a series of well-organized volleys from the soldier's muskets. When the British judged the maximum level of chaos was inflicted they left the safety of their redoubt, to the complete shock of the rebel commanders. Jean Fedon swore at the scene before him, but he committed his reserves to the battle. The attack became a muddled shambles as vicious hand-to-hand fights ensued all around the rebel leaders.

Seeing the rebels trying to shield Fedon's brother and Besson, the British redoubled their efforts and pushed hard to bring them down. Besson found himself fighting for his life alongside Fedon's brother and their reserves. The outcome hung in the balance, as neither side wanted to give ground. A young British officer wielding his sabre like it weighed a feather in his hand was not to be denied as he led his men forward and hammered at the now

The Sugar Rebellion

stunned rebels. Hacking two men out of his way with ease he went hard for Jean Fedon.

The one on one battle between the two men proved no contest. Although Fedon fought with energy and frantic desperation, he could not match the skills of a man trained from an early age to be a professional soldier. The young officer drove his sword hard into Fedon's belly, angling it upward and twisting his wrist on the withdrawal as he was trained to do. As their leader screamed and fell the men around Fedon turned and ran.

Besson was still fighting for his life a short distance away and could do nothing to stop the rout. A dark rage filled him and all he wanted to do was kill everyone in sight. He knew he would be the last man standing as they overwhelmed him. But even as the thought came distant horns sounded the British recall. The British troops instantly disengaged and within seconds they were streaming back to their lines, picking up their dead as they went. Besson howled with rage and waved his bloodied sword at the British.

"Come and fight me, you dogs!"

The young British officer was shepherding his men back to the redoubt and was now some distance away. He turned and gave Besson a grim smile as he replied, loud enough for all to hear.

"Not today, I'm afraid. But don't worry, I'll be back for you another day."

Besson shook with anger, but he knew the fight was over. Wiping his blade clean he put it in his scabbard as he strode over to where Jean Fedon lay. Besson sighed as he saw the glazed, unmoving eyes

The Sugar Rebellion

and knew he was gone. Lifting his head he looked around and took in the full scale of the carnage. The blazing, out of control anger he felt only moments before was slowly replaced by a deep, burning rage he knew would last all the way back to Fedon's estate. He bent down and lifted Fedon's dead brother, slinging him over his shoulder. Besson knew Julien would want the body.

He also knew there would have to be payback.
***

Fedon felt a grim foreboding of ill news as the bedraggled survivors began streaming back to the estate by late afternoon. He was on the verandah with Sophie awaiting word and he could tell by the looks on their faces it had not gone well. Besson appeared, leading a second horse behind him. When the two men saw each other Besson came straight over and dismounted in front of Fedon. He pointed at the body slung over the saddle of the mount.

"I'm sorry, Julien. Your brother Jean is dead. It was a rout."

"Oh, my God!" said Sophie, her hand over her mouth in horror.

Fedon felt wooden as he gestured to the body. "Bring him inside."

Sophie called for Baptiste and another servant to help. They laid him out on a table and Fedon stared unspeaking at his dead brother's face for a long time. A single tear coursed down his face as he finally spoke.

"What happened?"

Before Besson could speak James walked in and looked around.

The Sugar Rebellion

"I heard all this commotion. What is going—good God! What has happened?" said James.

Besson gave an inarticulate curse before speaking again. "As I said, it was a rout, Julien. I swear to God, it was a goddamn British trap. They were waiting for us and they killed us like we were insects."

"I don't understand," said James, a look of shock on his face. "Did they attack us? Where?"

"You lying bastard, I'm going to kill you where you stand," said Besson, drawing his knife from his belt. "You did this to us."

As Besson advanced James reached down in a swift move to draw out a small sheath knife hidden under his pants and strapped to his leg. The knife was far smaller than Besson's, but it was enough to give Besson pause. None of them noticed Baptiste's hand twitching at his side and the look of concern on his face.

"I don't know what the fuck you are talking about, but if you think you can get the better of me you are welcome to try," said James.

"Stop! Both of you!" said Fedon, the tone of command in his voice brooking no opposition. Fedon shook his head as the two men glared at each other, but held back.

"James, what do you know of this?"

"Julien, I have no idea what is going on. Obviously, from what he said, the British attacked us? The only other obvious fact is your brother was involved and is dead. You now know what I know."

Fedon nodded. "Besson, can you not see how puzzled he is? James, we are the ones that launched

The Sugar Rebellion

an attack."

"I see. Julien, I had no knowledge of it."

"Besson, I believe him. He was kept out of our counsels on this attack with great care and most of the time it was being planned he was in St. George's. But you say they were waiting for us?"

"Julien, let me give you the facts and you decide."

Besson took several minutes to describe the scene and what had happened. When he finished everyone fell silent, waiting for Fedon to respond.

"I see. Well. Baptiste, could I ask you to have the servants prepare my brother for burial and a plot dug for him in the graveyard out back, please? We must bury him soon. As for everyone else, please leave me. I must think about this."

"Julien," said Besson. "We cannot let this pass. We must pay them back!"

Fedon raised a hand to forestall him. "Besson, my friend, I completely agree with you. The question is not whether we should pay them back, it is how we shall do it and that is what I must give thought to. Send messages to the others to return for a council on this for two days from now. Now leave me, all of you. I must grieve for my brother."

Fedon dined alone that night, rebuffing even Sophie from joining him. The full bottle of cognac he took with him to the verandah after dinner was far from full by the time he fell asleep in his chair, his face wet from the many tears that had fallen.

***

Fedon seemed far more distant to everyone from that day on. Had he thought Fedon's attitude

The Sugar Rebellion

toward him was changed James would have been concerned, but it was obvious no one was exempt. A chill seemed to descend on everyone like a blanket when Fedon walked into a room. After a few days Fedon began inviting Sophie and James to dine with him again, but he remained detached.

James learned the reason for the detachment when they began building the scaffolds almost a week later. Soon enough it became clear the structure being built was enough to hang three people at a time. James was not invited to the planning meetings of the senior commanders, but the purpose of the scaffolds was obvious. The question was who was going to meet their end on them and James feared he knew the answer. His fears proved correct one night at dinner as Fedon casually told him what was happening.

"Yes, my commanders and I have agreed there must be a response to what happened. We also agreed the time has come to show the British how truly serious we are. We made several overtures to them about what could happen to our captives if they fail to cooperate and they were ignored. I always knew there would be some use for them and this will be it."

James digested this for a moment before nodding slowly. "Julien, I understand this is war. I also understand there are women and children in your makeshift jail. Are they all going to the scaffolds?"

Fedon gave no sign of showing compassion or having misgivings about what he was saying. His eyes and face were ice cold as he spoke.

The Sugar Rebellion

"My brother must be avenged. I loved my brother dearly and someone must pay. But we are not barbarians. The five children will be spared. The other forty-eight men and women will be the ones to pay. They will face their maker tomorrow morning."

James was silent on hearing this and he remained silent. Fedon remained silent too, but as the silence lingered on he finally sighed.

"James. What would you have me do? I chose to lead these people and they are unanimous there must be payback. We have few choices. My God, this was my brother! He was one of our leaders. Really, what would you have me do?"

"I see. And after that, what will be next?"

Fedon sighed and after a moment he shrugged.

"I need to replace my brother and then we shall see. I think the time is almost at hand to deal with this once and for all. I thought about using you as his replacement, given your military experience, but Besson and some of the others would never accept you. I will find another role for you."

"You know I am willing to help," said James.

The news Fedon shared cast a pall on the dinner. Both James and Sophie declined the offer of a cognac. Sophie also declined to stay with James, to his secret relief. The thought of what would happen the next day seemed an enormous, crushing failure. James lay awake for a long time, casting his mind back to when they had first become involved in Grenada and searching for whether or not he could have done something different to change the situation.

The Sugar Rebellion

Nothing came to him, except a dull, restless sleep.

***

James was standing beside Fedon on the verandah when it began and was horrified at the condition of the captives when they were led out. After over a year of living in the barn converted to serve as their jail, they were all in a pitiful state. One after another they shuffled out of their prison, blinking in the full daylight they had not enjoyed for so long. Their clothes were in tatters. Several were so weak they had to lean on others for help. James saw the guards wrinkling their noses at the stench of so many bodies that had not been washed in months.

As they were led into the clearing where the scaffolds were erected many cried out in shock and fell to their knees, the realization of what was about to happen striking like a lightning bolt. The women began crying and some begged their captors to free them to go back to their children. Their cries were ignored. This was not the first time James had attended an execution, but he fervently wished it would be his last. The one small mercy Fedon had granted was the children would be spared the horror of watching their parents be murdered, as the children were led away out of sight.

Governor Home was unable to walk on his own, so the guards dragged him to a spot right in front of the scaffolds and forced him to sit on a wooden chair to watch the proceedings. He railed at his captors for several minutes, calling them every pejorative name he could think of, but his protests and anger were ignored. In groups of three the captives were dragged to the scaffolds and dispatched with efficiency. After the third group was gone the Governor finally grew silent. Everyone knew he would be the last to hang.

The other mercy Fedon granted was to complete the task as fast as possible. Several slaves were dedicated to hustling new victims forward as the dead were removed and tossed without ceremony onto four carts sitting nearby. Some were even detailed to pull hard on the victim's feet as the support was kicked away, ensuring their necks were broken swiftly. Governor Home stood as straight as he could and cursed them all when his turn came, but his body soon joined the now heavily laden carts. James turned to Fedon with a questioning look.

"What will be done with the bodies?" said James, although he feared he knew the answer.

"They will be returned to the British. They need to see the consequences of their actions."

Fedon turned and walked away. James bowed his head and, although he had never been very religious, he offered a silent prayer for the victims.

***

The Sergeant in charge of the post held up his hand as a warning to his men to hold their fire as the rebel entered the clearing with a huge white flag of truce.

"I wonder what these buggers are up to now," he said, although he expected no response from the men around him. "Jenkins, go find the Lieutenant and bring him here. At the double."

The Sugar Rebellion

As he finished speaking he turned his attention back to the rebels and saw they were leading a team of horses pulling a cart into the clearing. Even as the first one was brought to a halt another appeared coming behind it. The Sergeant shifted his attention to the contents of the carts and immediately swore aloud. Moments later his commanding officer appeared at his side and spoke.

"Report, Sergeant."

"Trouble, sir. Big trouble."

***

Evan knew Governor Mackenzie was devastated.

"My God, I can't believe these animals did this. I cannot help but feel responsible. I never expected they would stoop to doing something so low."

"Governor," said Evan. "You had no choice. Official policy is we don't negotiate in situations like this unless someone far more senior than us says we do. I can't tell you what to think or feel, but I don't believe you shoulder any responsibility whatsoever."

"Commander Ross is correct, sir," said Colonel Walter. "And the only consideration now is how we make them pay for this atrocity."

Evan cleared his throat. "In this instance I agree with the Colonel, sir. The question is how and when. To me this is a sign the rebels are hardening their resolve. If we strike back immediately this could spiral into something much larger very quickly. On the other hand, when news of this reaches our respective masters I have a feeling it could tip the balance when deciding what to do with

The Sugar Rebellion

any available troops."

"Governor, although normally I would be more inclined to just go out and have at them in this kind of situation, I actually do agree with Commander Ross. I think we will get reinforcements."

The Governor sighed. "Yes. We are all in agreement and my inclination is to insist we get those extra troops. I will have a report with my request readied and sent before the day is out. We will know soon enough. So Colonel, we must prepare for all possibilities. Please work with the Commander here to put together a raid significant enough to make them pay dearly, in the event they do not send us help. I appreciate your sentiments, gentlemen, but I think the only way I am going to get any sleep at night in future is if we avenge these poor people. I will contact you as soon as I get word. Good day."

***

James and Baptiste were standing outside talking as Besson walked up to them and scowled at James.

"So Mr. big Navy man, I have just come from yet another conversation with Julien about you. Lucky for you, Julien still seems to think you had nothing to do with the British ambush of our men. That means I don't get to kill you yet, but I'm fairly sure that day will come. I'm here to tell you, if we have even one more incident like that I will kill you, regardless of what anyone says, and that includes Julien. In fact, you might be better off just leaving us. Sometimes bad things happen unexpectedly in the dark, you know."

The Sugar Rebellion

"As I told you before, if you have a problem with me you are welcome to try taking me on."

"Not today, Navy boy. Although I don't agree with Julien about you, he is my commander. But please do give me a reason to try in future."

Turning, Besson stalked away. Baptiste had hung back and said nothing as the two men sparred, but now he looked at James.

"Permission to kill him, sir? Please? He is a threat to you. I think he is going to make up some reason to try murdering you when there are no witnesses. If you are dead they might question whatever story he dreams up, but no one will be able to prove otherwise. Sir, he has no idea I am here in support."

James stood in silence thinking through the ramifications. Before he finished Baptiste spoke once again.

"Sir, I feel I am responsible for the bind you are in," said Baptiste, hanging his head in dismay and explaining he had passed information on the raid to Evan. "Lieutenant, if I had thought for even a moment that all of this would have come about I would have kept silent. I know, you weren't here to consult and I had to make a decision, but I am wishing I hadn't."

"Don't feel that way, Baptiste. I believe you made the right decision and I am quite certain Commander Ross will agree. As it happens, both of us subscribe to the thought action is better than indecision. As for dealing with our problem, are you certain you want to do this?"

"Sir, I am. I don't have the long experience you

The Sugar Rebellion

and Commander Ross have in this kind of thing, but I have been training with the men. And if you remember, this won't be the first time I have killed another man, either."

"Yes, I remember. If you have opportunity, then do it. It may only make things worse, but my position here is becoming untenable anyway. But you must be careful. If you are caught there will be nothing I can do. If it all goes wrong we may both have to make a run for it. If that happens wait for me at the drop location and we will go from there. If you cannot wait or you know I am done for, I order you to get out. You know where to go."

"Sir, I do. I appreciate your confidence in me. I will try to make sure I do it when you are with others, so you have an alibi."

"Very good. One last thing, I don't have a report ready to go for Evan and I'm not sure I have anything new to tell him he wouldn't already be aware of anyway. If you do this we will have to hold off on sending any reports for a while. Everyone will be under suspicion and it would be too risky for you to try slipping away."

"Leave it with me, sir," said Baptiste with a grin, before turning and walking away.

***

Baptiste was pleased there were high clouds to obscure the small sliver of moonlight on the landscape, as it was perfect for what he had in mind. Enough light was available to be sure of what he was doing, but only just. Baptiste made certain James was dining with Sophie and Fedon once again, still engaged with their meals, as he waited in

The Sugar Rebellion

hope for his prey to appear. Besson had not left to return to Gouyave and instead chose to stay and dine with his men. Baptiste knew this invariably involved heavy drinking, which in turn would sooner or later lead to a trip to the privy.

Baptiste waited in the dark shadows of a tree close to the path near the entrance to the privy. Three soldiers came and did their business, dashing his hopes each time. Baptiste knew he had only a small window of opportunity before he would have to abort the attempt for another night. But Besson finally came into view, weaving slightly as he made his way along the path. Baptiste smiled and gripped the wickedly sharp kitchen knife he had purloined for this exact purpose.

Besson strode past, intent only on relieving himself. Baptiste made certain no one was coming behind Besson before he struck. Clamping his hand on Besson's mouth from behind he plunged the knife into his back where he knew the heart would be. Besson stiffened as the life fled his body before finally going limp. Baptiste let the body deliberately fall forward to ensure little or no blood splattered on him. He felt for a pulse, but Besson was gone. He looked around and made certain no one was in the area.

Leaving the body with the knife still sticking in it, Baptiste swiftly pulled off his shirt because in the dim light he couldn't be certain it wasn't stained with any small drops of blood. He disposed of it in the privy and went back to the tree he had been hiding beside, pulling over his head the spare shirt he had secreted there. Moments later he was in

The Sugar Rebellion

hiding at a spot further up the short path to the privy, waiting for the next man to come along to relieve himself.

Baptiste considered dragging the body away and hiding it, but James needed an alibi and this meant the body had to be found sooner rather than later. Three minutes passed before the next man came by and Baptiste grinned again in the dark. The man soon sounded the alarm. Baptiste waited a few long moments before stepping back onto the path and making his way toward the privy again. As he walked up he called out to the soldier with a puzzled voice.

"What are you shouting about? I—oh, my God! What has happened here?"

"It is our commander Besson. Someone has murdered him!" said the soldier. "Go get help."

Within minutes the scene was bedlam. Fedon, Sophie, and James all set aside their desserts to come to the scene. Several of Besson's men also came and milled about in anger. A few of Besson's senior men pointed to James as the culprit without hesitation, but Fedon imposed order on the questioning and soon established they were wrong. Numerous witnesses had seen Besson alive not even twenty minutes before.

"Well, there you have it," said Fedon, glaring at Besson's men. "James has been with me for the last two hours having dinner. This is someone else's work."

Everyone was questioned as to where they were in the last hour. Baptiste responded truthfully he was in the kitchen and had returned to his room

The Sugar Rebellion

briefly before deciding to make for the privy, counting on the knowledge the kitchen slaves who had seen him would have not been paying attention to the time. Their testimony would have an element of vagueness to it, enough that if anyone asked it would be impossible to prove or disprove Baptiste's story.

Baptiste smiled to himself. Commander Ross and Lieutenant Wilton would be pleased. That was good, because he knew he rather enjoyed the danger of being a spy. He had found his true calling in life.

***

Four days later Fedon once again felt frustrated, wrestling with the need to replace yet another of his senior commanders at a point when he had a sense his opportunity to act and succeed was sliding from his grasp. Time had slipped away as it was now the end of April and events seemed to be moving faster ever since they had executed the hostages. The political need to consult his senior commanders on a replacement for Besson slowed everything to a crawl, as they all had to be brought together to discuss their options. James was not one of them, as Besson's senior men were adamant in wanting nothing to do with him despite the clear evidence he was not responsible for their leader's death.

After wrangling on the issue for hours a man was finally chosen, albeit grudgingly by some. As a concession to Fedon they agreed to have James help with the logistics behind the final attack. Staging areas would have to be identified, with stockpiles of weapons, ammunition, and supplies gathered to

The Sugar Rebellion

keep the men fed while they waited for the signal to begin. Although none of them liked it, they knew it was necessary and they agreed with Fedon that James would bring a degree of military discipline to the task that was desperately needed. Fedon gave a sigh of relief when they were done and ordered a glass of wine to be poured for each of the men in the room. When they each had their glass in hand Fedon began.

"Gentlemen, the time has now come. We can no longer wait and must act. We must make our great push and drive the British from this island once and for all. I know it will take time to get the men together and prepare. I desire to launch our effort by the end of May or early June at latest. I know our French friends have not come through as yet with everything we want, but the possibility still exists they could. Any help will be welcome. Gentlemen, are you with me on this?"

Everyone nodded and voiced their support. Fedon smiled and finally raised his glass in a toast. The rest of them did the same.

"Then this is a toast to success, my friends. There is no other option."

***

James and Fedon spent the next two days riding out to look at the forward lines. For James the task was to look at possible sites and weigh the options, a task made all the more difficult by the fact he had no idea of what the commanders were planning. But he made several choices and gleaned some sense from Fedon of the numbers of men he would need to plan for.

The Sugar Rebellion

Fedon went with him, in part to ensure no one challenged James on what he was doing and in part to simply show himself to the men. James soon realized the men standing guard on the front lines were the more fervent supporters of the rebellion and that Fedon was their hero. Many greeted him as a savior and he was cheered lustily at every stop. Fedon mingled with many, referring to the men as his free brothers and citizens. He promised them the time they all sought was coming soon.

***

Evan joined the Colonel and Governor Mackenzie in his office once again, closing the door as he came in and sat down. The Governor wasted no time, as he pointed to an opened letter sitting on the table before him.

"I have good news, gentlemen. They have seen fit to agree to our request for help. General Abercrombie is being diverted here to deal with the situation."

"Excellent!" said the Colonel. "When are we to expect them and what resources is he bringing?"

"No later than the middle of the month, sir. He is in Jamaica just now. The letter I have speaks of ten thousand troops, but they are not all coming here. It is the General's decision, but the thinking seems to be a minimum of two thousand men."

"Bloody wonderful!" said the Colonel, his fist clenched as he hammered the table. "Best news I've heard in months, sir."

"Sir?" said Evan. "Two thousand men are a lot. We will need to prepare for their arrival."

'Indeed. I will leave this to you gentlemen."

The Sugar Rebellion

"Sir? I propose to correspond with the general on this matter. We know there have been spies in St. George's and if we can find some way to keep their arrival secret as long as possible, it could only help our cause."

The Governor scratched his head and looked at the Colonel, who shrugged in response.

"More bloody skulking about, but whatever. I don't care if the General brings the men in disguised as a bunch of fairy princes. We won't be skulking around much longer."

The Governor looked at Evan. "If you think it will help, do it."

The Sugar Rebellion

Chapter Eleven
May 1796
Grenada

General Sir Ralph Abercrombie presented an imposing figure. In his early sixties, the Scottish General and politician had already seen more than his fair share of action during the Seven Years War that began in 1756 and in many subsequent actions since. His reputation for making strenuous efforts to ensure his men were healthy, properly resourced, and in good spirits was well deserved. In recognition of his service he was knighted in 1795. Evan sensed right away the man was radiating a degree of competence and skill few could match. Evan had conversed enough with senior diplomats to know many people fervently wished there were more such officers in the British Army. Governor Mackenzie made it clear he was a part of this group after introductions were made and a glass of wine was poured for each of his visitors.

"General Abercrombie, you have no idea how good it is to see you here and to know your capable help is on the way. This bloody stalemate here has gone on for far too long."

The General nodded, smiling as he looked at the men around the table. Colonel Walter was the only other person in the room with them.

"Yes, gentlemen, it seems our masters agree with you," said the General. "This appalling murder of innocents seems to have been the last straw. They wanted our men for other tasks, but those will have

The Sugar Rebellion

to wait. So, I came on ahead of those slow troop transports because I need to know more of the tactical situation and a little extra time to prepare is never a bad thing. We have time to get into details later as we don't need to waste the Governor's time on these, but perhaps I could have you two give me a general briefing? Colonel Walter, lets start with you."

The Colonel droned on for almost ten minutes before the General finally cut him off, having heard enough, and turned to Evan. His report was much shorter. The General sat back in his chair, digesting all he had heard and softly drumming his fingers on the table, deep in absentminded thought. To Evan's surprise the General turned and stared directly at him for several long seconds before finally addressing him first when he spoke.

"Commander Ross, I've heard of you. You have a reputation for being very good at what you do. You come through when it counts."

"Sir. Thank you, sir. My colleagues and I try."

"Not everyone succeeds consistently when they try, but you seem to. So you have concerns about the rebels having plants here in St. George's and spying on us?"

"Sir, we believe there may be a few people out there that are at least sympathetic to the rebel cause, although not active. They aren't the concern. The one definitely active spy I mentioned a moment ago is a woman. We have not caught her, but we know what she looks like and we know the method she has used to enter and exit St. George's. Because Colonel Walter and his men have a very tight

The Sugar Rebellion

defensive ring around us, in hindsight it is no surprise they resorted to paying their way onto the daily fishing boats that come and go from the harbor. Since we identified the method we have been watching all of the fishing boats like hawks. We are satisfied no other spies have come in via this route. Our various sources around town have not given any indication of other dubious sorts about asking the kind of questions that would raise suspicion. The woman has not come back, but we think it only a matter of time. The rebels do not know we have identified the woman and her route. If and when she returns we will have a decision to either simply restrain her or, if possible, feed her some misinformation and send her back."

The General rubbed his chin in thought. "I see. The letter you sent me suggested you would like to keep the arrival of my troops as low key as possible, to ensure possible spies do not get confirmation we are reinforcing the defenses. I believe I know your answer, but tell me what your purpose is behind this."

"Sir, you are correct we think keeping them in the dark as long as possible could help ensure they do not attack before we are ready for them. Rumors have abounded for weeks this might happen, but news it really is proceeding, along with intelligence of how large a force arrives, will be like gold to the rebels. If they get wind of this, they may strike before we are ready."

"So what exactly do you have in mind?"

"I took the liberty of assuming you might be interested, so I drafted some plans for your

The Sugar Rebellion

consideration. First, I would like to bring the transports into the harbor in stages over a few days and do it at night with the help of local pilots. Once offloaded the transports would stand out to sea and either wait or sail empty to another harbor until needed. This avoids having an all too obvious flotilla in harbor that gives the game away. Once the men land we shepherd them immediately to a variety of temporary accommodations. Governor Mackenzie has been most helpful in identifying a number of nondescript local warehouses we can assign to the men as their quarters until needed. The Governor also has some room at the Fort itself. We are confident we have the space needed overall. I've inspected all of the locations and they are clean and spacious. The logistics of keeping the men all organized may be a bit more challenging, but we anticipate it won't be long before the need for secrecy is behind us, so once again we believe it can be done. We'd like to keep most of them off the streets, at least until we have done with this spy or you are ready to move."

    The General sat staring for an instant before his broad Scottish accent came out and he chuckled at Evan.

    "Well, lad. You really do have a devious turn of mind, don't you?"

    Evan smiled. "Part of my job, sir."

    "General," said Colonel Walter. "With respect, is all of this really necessary, sir? I'd rather make a show of force. Let the rebels see we mean business. I think they will be shaking in their boots at the sight of more redcoats they know will soon be

The Sugar Rebellion

coming after them. In fact, if your men can replace the forces I've had on the lines, I would be more than happy to lead my men out on offensive raids. The men would love to see an end to waiting for them to come to us. Take the fight to them sooner rather than later, as it were. Sir."

The General stiffened slightly and frowned before he responded.

"I appreciate your willingness to have at them, sir, but that will be all in good time. I don't think I need tell you what voyages of even a few days in close quarters on troop transports can do to the health of soldiers. The sooner I get them off those ships and give them some rest, the better. Even more important is to get them some decent fresh food and clean quarters to bunk in. The basic rations we have to feed them on board don't help. The last thing we need is for them to get sick. If one gets something, they will all get it. So the logical desire of Commander Ross to keep our arrival low key dovetails nicely with my own desire to keep the men fit. If they are at their fighting peak they will account for themselves well against the foe."

"I see, sir," said the Colonel. "Sir, are you bringing field weapons with you?"

The General raised an eyebrow. "Of course. I have a number of four and six pound field cannons on each of the transports. That is another reason why I like Commander Ross's thinking. If we can make them think you have not been reinforced yet and they launch their attack, we will make them pay far more than they want. And that will be before we even set a foot beyond your defenses."

The Sugar Rebellion

Seeing the Colonel had nothing more to say the General looked around the table at the men and continued.

"One last question for you. Food supplies?"

"Commander Ross and I went over that detail, sir," said the Governor. "Rationing of some items is a necessity to a certain extent, but we have been getting supplies by sea and there is always the bounty of the ocean. We will dip into reserves to keep your men fed, but knowing that there will be resolution to this soon enough changes the situation. Once this is all over I expect we may need to keep rationing in place until we get matters under control, but that is for later. So yes, there is no problem."

"Excellent," said the General. "Governor, we have taken enough of your valuable time. Commander Ross, Colonel Walter, let us retire elsewhere to go over details. I would like to discuss exact timing of the arrivals and other considerations with you first, Commander. I need to get messages by that packet ship I came in on out to the transports as soon as possible. The Colonel and I will need more time on our own to have a look at maps and detail some plans. Shall we, gentlemen?"

All four of the men rose as the Governor raised his glass in a final toast they all matched before they left.

"To success."

***

As she had every night for several weeks now, Alice sat at her usual table nursing her glass of wine. She was happy to have found the little inn

The Sugar Rebellion

with its small terrace overlooking the harbor. The terrace had room for only three tables and was a pleasant retreat from the bustle to be found dockside. The perimeter was lined with flowering plants, some hanging in baskets from the ceiling, with scents far more agreeable than what was in the air around the fishing boats she was watching.

The innkeeper was curious enough to gently quiz her about what she was doing after it became obvious she would be there regularly, but she kept her responses vague and made it clear she wasn't going to satisfy his curiosity. Why this beautiful woman kept appearing every evening at the same time remained a puzzle, but the man was all too happy to ask no questions when he saw how generously she tipped him.

The innkeeper served dinner, too, and on a few occasions a one armed man had joined the woman to sample his wares. Being as close as he was to the fishing boats his dinners invariably consisted of the best of the catch that day, brought to his kitchen straight from the boat. The woman and her one armed man seemed to enjoy the creativity he put into enhancing the flavors of the different fish with local spices, sometimes adding a delicate bread crust or simply serving it all in a fresh stew. But the two mysterious patrons kept to themselves as they enjoyed the pleasant scene of the fishing boats coming in at the end of the day to their part of the port with their catches.

By now Alice knew exactly how many fishing boats came and went every day, along with how many men were on each and what they looked like.

The Sugar Rebellion

The woman she sought had not reappeared and Alice was satisfied no one else had come to take her place. Alice rather enjoyed sitting there each evening, despite the lack of action. The smooth, rich French wine the innkeeper had somehow acquired and served on a regular basis made the vigil all the more palatable. Alice knew from the price the man charged he had undoubtedly arranged for his own private stock to be smuggled in from God knew where, thus avoiding British duties. Alice didn't care, as she was there to catch a far bigger fish than the innkeeper.

If the innkeeper had been watching Alice this particular night he would have seen the moment she sat bolt upright in her chair, staring intently down at the port. She remained in this position for a minute before standing up and throwing enough coins on the table to pay for her wine. She caught his attention and pointed to the coins lying in sight by her unfinished wine as she dashed out, leaving the man stunned.

She made it down to the fishing boats in time to watch Sophie once again slip away in the bustle of the men unloading their catches. Alice followed at a discreet distance, close enough she felt confident she would not lose her. Sophie made a point of slowing her pace significantly as she walked past the *Alice*, still moored in exactly the same location as it was the last time she was in St. George's. Alice smiled as she saw Sophie turn and take one last look at the ship with a puzzled frown, before finally continuing on her way.

Alice was certain the woman was heading for

The Sugar Rebellion

the same place she had stayed in the last time she was in St. George's and she was proved correct. After knocking she was ushered into the residence and the door closed behind her, but only before the woman took a careful look about to see if she was being watched. Alice was expecting the maneuver and was already hiding in shadows dark enough she knew she could not be seen.

Alice crossed the street and went into a tavern with windows open to the street. She selected a table with a clear view of the building her quarry had disappeared into and ordered a drink, settling in to wait once again. Although it was still early in the evening the bar had a few patrons already well into their cups. Alice knew it wouldn't be long before the lure of a beautiful woman seemingly alone would draw attention and within a few minutes it happened. He was a big sailor Alice had seen around before, off one of the merchant ships that came and went on a regular basis. The man slurred his speech as he slid into the seat across from her, almost spilling his drink as he slumped into the booth with a grin.

"Damn, I haven't seen anyone as pretty as you in this place before. And here you are, all alone. I think you need some company, girl."

Alice smiled. "I think not. Piss off."

"Oh, come on, don't be that way. Listen, this isn't a very nice place," he said, waving his free hand at the tavern around them before putting his hand palm down on the table. "You need someone like me to protect you."

Alice slipped out the wickedly sharp sheath

knife she had strapped to her arm underneath the long sleeves of her dress and in one swift, practiced motion stabbed the knife down hard on the table. Her target was the man's hand splayed out on the table. Alice's strike was perfectly aimed at the space on the table between his thumb and forefinger. She had not intended to cut him, but he began to move in surprise and she caught a little bit of the webbing between the fingers.

"Goddamn, you—" said the drunk, pulling his hand away and staring at the stream of blood that appeared. "You cut me, you bitch!"

"Well, that's because you moved your hand, you arsehole. I practice using this all the time and I don't miss my targets. I have another even bigger knife on me, too. So since I don't need your protection, you really should piss off."

The drunk scowled at Alice and looked angry enough to strike her, but Alice held the bloodied knife up once again.

"You want some more of this, you fool? Listen, keep it up and I'll cut you in places you won't want to be cut. And when my husband shows up, he'll just carve your balls off and feed them to you. So for the last time, piss off."

The drunk had seen enough and, taking his drink, slipped out of the booth without a word. Throughout all of it Alice had flicked her eyes periodically to the building she was watching for brief moments, so she was certain her quarry had not slipped away. The rest of the men standing around the bar were watching it all and laughed at the failure of the man she had cut, but none of them came to try their luck. An hour later Evan slipped into the booth across from her, after reading the quality of the patrons staring at him with curiosity. Evan had arranged long before that if Alice had not returned to the ship by a certain time then he would seek her in the tavern.

"Well, isn't this a pleasant place? Such interesting customers, too. Come here often, good looking?"

"Only when I want to meet men like you."

Evan laughed and jerked a thumb over his shoulder at the crowd around the bar. "I assume you had to explain to them you wanted to wait for me?"

"They got the message. Our bird has arrived and, as we expected, unless she somehow slipped out back, she has remained inside."

"Well done, my love. Well, let's have a drink and enjoy the atmosphere for a bit to be sure. Don't think I want to try dining in this place, so it'll be a late dinner tonight."

"So we stick with the plan for the morning, Evan?"

"We do. The timing on this couldn't be better. The first of the transports are coming in tomorrow night, so our spy has nothing of consequence to see."

"Evan? Since we have a little time to ourselves while we wait and you are sitting down, I have some news. I'm past due my time this month."

Evan's eyes widened and he reached across the table to grip the hand she offered. He smiled and squeezed her hand hard. Alice knew the words coming to her mind were inadequate for how she

The Sugar Rebellion

felt and, without asking, that it was the same for Evan, but he finally broke the silence.

"My love."

***

Alice was waiting in the shadows early the next morning as Sophie walked out the door of her half sister's home and came up the street toward her, oblivious to Alice's presence. Alice had brought two of the sailors from the Alice with her and she gave them the prearranged signal before stepping into the street herself. Alice timed it so her quarry would think she was another pedestrian until the last moment when she stopped directly in front of Sophie and faced her. As Sophie stopped in obvious surprise and confusion, any opportunity to escape disappeared as the two big sailors appeared on either side of her.

"Good morning," said Alice, with a wide smile on her face. "There is a lovely little place not far from here down by the docks where we can stop and have a coffee before you leave. I'd like to have a brief chat with you."

Sophie was silent as she turned her head to look at each man in turn.

"Oh, don't concern yourself with them," said Alice, still smiling. "They are just good friends of mine who are tagging along. Your conversation is just with me."

"I see," said Sophie, making an obvious effort to pull herself together. "And why should I do this?"

"You know why. We think you are here to spy on us, but I'm afraid that isn't going to happen. Follow me."

The Sugar Rebellion

Minutes later they were sitting across a table from each other at a waterfront tavern that at any other time of the day sold ale and not coffee. The two sailors sat at a separate table not far away, but out of earshot. No one else was in the tavern, making it perfect for what Alice wanted. Alice waited until the coffee appeared and the server left before beginning the conversation. Sophie forestalled her and spoke first, going on the offensive.

"You think I am a spy. I'm afraid I don't know what you are talking about. I resent being taken here as if I'm a prisoner."

Alice smiled and shrugged. "Well, you are a prisoner, although not for long. You can stop pretending. You were observed the last time you were here behaving in a highly suspicious manner. You were asking questions of people all over town. You left disguised as a fisherman and haven't returned until now. And what a surprise, you came back disguised as a fisherman. I suppose if you insist we could toss you in some stinking jail and leave you to rot there. Even worse, we could leave you for the inmates to amuse themselves with."

"I see. And why exactly are you telling me this? Actually, why are you not tossing me in this jail?"

Alice shrugged again. "You know, you really are a beautiful woman and, let's face it, so am I. I'm not bragging, but it's not often I meet someone who can rival me. It's a fact this is just the way God made me and I can't control that any more than you. How we look is both a blessing and a curse, as I'm

The Sugar Rebellion

sure you know. Men are attracted and sometimes you get used and discarded all too easily. I've never been in a jail, but from other past experiences I can well imagine what it might be like to be trapped in one with a bunch of animals. So no, I won't be having you tossed in jail."

Sophie was silent, obviously digesting all she had heard. She finally offered Alice a brief, tiny smile for the first time as she responded.

"Yes, I think we understand each other on that point. I suspect we have more in common than just our looks, so thank you for not doing that. But again, why are we having this conversation? What do you gain by doing so?"

"Not much really, other than to have you go back and tell your masters how effectively we stopped your business. We will not quit watching all possible ways in, of course. There is little point in keeping you around. Oh, we could use some unpleasant methods to make you talk, but we don't think you would have a lot that we don't already know after all this time. It's rather doubtful the rebel leaders would send a spy here that could confess anything truly critical, don't you think?"

Sophie nodded slowly. "Well, that all makes sense. And I do appreciate you are not torturing me, either. But look, you are like me, are you not? You are a mulatto. Why do you serve the people that enslave us? We are trying to free everyone. Do you not see this is a worthy goal?"

"Yes, we do have some things in common, don't we? However, it is not as simple as you portray it. As far as I'm concerned your goal is a

The Sugar Rebellion

worthy one, no question. The problem is there are plenty of people on your side, mulattos, just like you and I, that will be all too willing to find a way to keep enslaving people. You know you can't deny it. Maybe they will put a different story or face to it, but they will. We have lots of those people on our side, too. And then there are the French. I'm not certain their fine words will translate into reality. The problem is, as always, money and greed."

Sophie hung her head for a moment. "No, I cannot deny what you say. But we have to try. This rebellion against the greed and evil sugar has brought to our island is the only hope we have."

"It's not the only hope. You may not believe this, but I know of men on our side who quietly do what they can every day to try and change things, like my husband for example. Yes, he is a white man. He is also a man of honor and he abhors slavery. I was a slave in a rather bad situation and he saved me. Anything I am or I have today is entirely due to his kindness in freeing me. There are people in England working hard to abolish slavery, too, just as hard as the French, except they aren't going about with guillotines chopping people's heads off."

"A man of honor, you say? Is he by chance in the Royal Navy?"

Alice's guard came up instantly as she thought fast about how to respond. The question seemed far too close to home and she racked her brain for reasons the question would arise. In a flash of insight the answer appeared. The only possible explanation was this woman had somehow

The Sugar Rebellion

interacted with James. As that thought came she also knew with virtual certainty James and this woman had become lovers. Alice felt unexpected warmth toward her captive and she smiled as she responded.

"I confess I've met a few Royal Navy officers over the years and, in my experience, they are all very much men of honor."

"I see. Well, if you are sending me back you had better get me to the boat soon. They leave early every day."

Alice looked at their now empty coffee cups and smiled again.

"They do, but you need not worry. Your fisherman knows he isn't going anywhere until you show up. And I do agree it is time you left. But you know what? I think I wish it could be otherwise."

Sophie raised an eyebrow to let the question show on her face, but she remained silent as Alice continued.

"I think we really do have things in common and, were this mess not in the way, you and I could find ourselves being friends. Perhaps I am wrong."

Sophie studied Alice's face for a moment and, for the first time, let her own brilliant smile crease her face. Alice matched it.

"You are not wrong. I was a slave when I was very young. I can only imagine my life would have been filled with the kind of abuse my mother endured had my father not freed me. Perhaps the same kind of abuse I think you may have suffered. He didn't have the resources to do so right away, but he kept his word to my mother. He was a kind man,

The Sugar Rebellion

too. You know, friends know each other's names. Mine is Sophie."

Alice stared into Sophie's eyes and realized it was as if she were staring into a mirror that reflected not her face, but her own soul. Alice had many female friends and some, like Manon Shannon, became as close as a twin sister. But to find a friend like this, only to instantly lose her, seemed a bittersweet irony. Alice bit her lip in frustration.

"Mine is Alice. And it really is time to go."

They both rose from their chairs and as she stood Alice extended a hand. Sophie grasped it and they shook hands.

"Perhaps we will meet some day when this is all over and it will be different," said Alice. "I would like that."

"I would, too," said Sophie.

***

The troops came in over the course of the next three nights, with two transports coming in each night. The big frigates escorting them stood guard at sea over the horizon and bore away to leave the transports on their own as soon as the glow of light from St. George's could be seen in the distance. Evan was tired, having lost sleep each night as he stayed up to ensure the plan was working, but the time put into planning it all paid off as everything went smoothly.

The arrival of the troops was not his only concern. No messages were waiting at the drop from either James or Baptiste for far too long now. Evan had taken to checking it much more often,

The Sugar Rebellion

sailing out every day to check it. On the third day of the transports arrivals he even had a surreptitious look at the spot they had hidden the small cutter, in case James and Baptiste had somehow found cause to use it, but everything was undisturbed and still in place.

Because he loitered longer that day it was close to dusk when Evan was finally on the return journey home. He was preoccupied with worry at the silence of his men, but the lookout's hail from the masthead drove it from his mind.

"Deck there! One sail due west off the starboard side—no, two sails! I think second sail is in chase!"

Evan swore to himself, training his glass to the west while he gave orders to stay their course out of the side of his mouth. The growing darkness made it difficult to see anything from the deck, so he sent a man aloft to learn more. Minutes later he returned.

"Sir," said the sailor, breathing hard. "The lookout and I both agree, this is a chase, but it won't last long. We are fairly certain the lead ship is French, based on the shape of her sails. The chase is definitely one of our frigates and I would put money on it being that other frigate *HMS Haven* that was in St. George's to drop off the Marines a while back. He isn't going to catch the Frenchie. It's too dark."

Even as he finished speaking the masthead lookout hailed once again.

"Deck! Chase is bearing off and discontinuing!"

Evan thanked the man and moved to the weather side of the quarterdeck to think. The worry

The Sugar Rebellion

was whether the mystery ship was indeed French. If so, and if they saw the transports and recognized what they were, the rebels might be forewarned of what was happening. Evan shook his head in dismay, as he had little he could do about it now beyond adding this to the list of his worries. Evan rubbed his forehead with absentminded concern. His plan had always relied on James and Baptiste both being able to support each other in case of trouble. The flaw in this thinking was a situation where either one or both were taken, or where one was under too much suspicion to change the situation. The possibilities were endless.

He shrugged and turned his thoughts to the next day, knowing the only thing he could do was to await developments and bury himself in his duties to keep himself sane. The General was pleased to learn they had found and stopped the spy from learning anything of significance. Once the last group of soldiers was offloaded and their immediate needs met, the General would be turning his full attention to the coming battle. While it wasn't properly Evan's domain, the General had asked Evan to attend the various planning sessions taking place and Evan was expecting another summons to attend a meeting likely the next day. The General was all too happy to let his soldiers rest and was in no rush to attack anyone, but he was highly disciplined and eager to focus on planning the details to ensure their success.

As they tacked in toward the port and the glowing lights of the town Evan's mind drifted once again to what Alice had told him of the woman

Sophie. Evan had long since learned to trust Alice's intuition and judgment, which meant he accepted Alice was correct that James was having a relationship with the woman. The problem was Evan wasn't certain whether this was good or bad or somehow even a little of both. He shook his head to clear it one last time. He would find out what it really was sooner or later.

***

Fedon was disappointed to learn the reason for Sophie's quick return from St. George's. Both Fedon and Sophie agonized over whether she had been betrayed and, if so, by whom, but they agreed they had no evidence for this. In the end they had to attribute the British spotting her to no more than sheer bad luck. He had badly wanted some sense of how the executions affected British morale, but it was not to be. The only intelligence she brought was what the taciturn fisherman and her half sister could offer, and it was nothing new. The British had been outraged and rumors still flew of the possibility of more troops.

Her lack of success was driven from his mind when Montdenoix and Linger reappeared again two days later. As they were ushered into a meeting with him Fedon prayed once again the French would finally deliver something truly useful. To his surprise, Montdenoix was smiling broadly when he walked in.

"Julien, I am pleased to bring some better news for you. Yes, we have the usual additional small arms to add to your stockpile, but this time we bring more than that. Perhaps not as much as you want, but we were able to secure a dozen field artillery pieces for you. They are a little older vintage, but all have been well maintained and are quite serviceable. We will remain a little longer to train your men on their use, but we cannot stay long."

"Hubert, this is the best news I have heard in a long while. It may be too little and too late, but we will take everything we can get. The time is upon us to make our move."

As Fedon briefed Montdenoix on everything happening since he was last on the island the Frenchman's face grew long and he rubbed his chin in thought.

"That might explain matters. I wish we had been here to offer you counsel on dealing with the hostages. I respect your decision, but I'm not sure the executions were a good idea. This may have goaded the British into moving now, before hurricane season. I had hoped we had more time, as it is possible I could get you even more field artillery perhaps by July. But that could indeed be too late."

Fedon felt a sense of foreboding as he responded. "What do you mean?"

"We were chased by a British frigate as we came into your waters. Fortunately it was toward dusk and they broke off their pursuit. The problem is when we came upon them there were actually two frigates and they appeared to be guarding what looked very much like two troop transports heading into St. George's. I'm sure you understand we didn't have time to stick around and take a closer look. The right decision was to run and deliver the

The Sugar Rebellion

weapons you so desperately want."

"Of course. When exactly was this?"

"Why, last night."

"And there were only two transports?"

"That's it. Why do you ask?"

Fedon explained what had happened with Sophie and that she had seen no sign of extra troops or transport ships in the harbor.

"Montdenoix, do you think there could have been more transports about? Perhaps some that slipped into St. George's earlier?"

The Frenchman shrugged. "It is possible. Two frigates would seem to be overkill to protect just two troop ships, but who knows?"

"How many men does a troop transport bear?"

"Depends on the size of the ship and other factors. From what I saw I'd estimate somewhere between three to four hundred troops per ship, if that indeed is what they were."

Fedon was silent, digesting everything he had heard for several seconds.

"Well, it seems we now face more enemies, but we at least have some better weapons to help us kill them with. In other words, the situation is unchanged except for the fact it is time to stir ourselves and take the battle to them."

***

Sophie was troubled, lying alone in bed and struggling to sleep. Something ill defined was nagging at her ever since her return from St. George's, but she hadn't been able to grasp what it was. She felt it was something she had missed, yet was important enough she had to find it.

The Sugar Rebellion

Being torn between two lovers was the bigger problem. Every time she was in the presence of Julien she knew he embodied everything she could want in a man. That he was doing his utmost to lead a cause so close to her heart made him irresistible. The problem was the intangible, raw thrill she experienced the first time she met James was still there in each and every subsequent meeting, and when they were alone all thought of anyone else disappeared.

Sophie had found ways to divide her nights between the two men several times since the day on the mountain with James, but she found herself growing increasingly torn between them. Both men knew this, but they had nothing they could do. She was the one facing a decision. Since her return from St. George's she had made excuses to both men, knowing the situation couldn't go on. Remaining alone seemed the only way to delay making a decision she didn't want to make.

Her conversation with Alice had affected her too, more than she had realized at first. Having looked into the eyes of her enemy and found instead a friend with the potential to be as close as a twin sister was disconcerting. Alice's comments about mulattos being willing to keep slavery alive and her distrust of the French were the unspoken fears of Sophie herself. To find people on the opposite side with strong values and who cared about honor as much as she did was unsettling, too.

As the thought of honor crossed her mind a sudden flash of insight striking enough to make her sit bolt upright in bed came. She groaned softly,

The Sugar Rebellion

shaking her head at how something so simple had eluded her for so long. The mysterious merchant ship James had visited twice when he was in St. George's was named Alice and the question was whether it was a coincidence her captor bore the same name. Coincidence or not, the connection was made in her mind and the conviction grew that James was somehow connected to the woman who had captured her.

Even as this thought came a flare of jealousy blossomed inside and Sophie wondered if this Alice and James were lovers. Then she remembered Alice had said her husband was a white man and Sophie marveled at how easily the jealousy had overcome her. Looking into her heart she knew the reason was in truth she both wanted and needed James tonight. Whether it would be the same tomorrow was another matter.

She knew James was in all likelihood a British spy and she was now closer to confirming this than ever before. The question was whether any of it mattered now. Sophie knew a battle was coming and the outcome was out of her hands. She also knew it was unlikely anything James could pass to the other side at this point would be enough to change whatever the outcome was to be. She wasn't even certain whether she cared if James was a spy anymore.

With a sense fate had taken a firm hand on the whole situation she slipped out of bed naked and pulled on a large robe. She quietly left the room, making her way down the darkened hallway to his door. The door was unlocked and she slipped inside.

The Sugar Rebellion

Moonlight coming in the open window lit the room. She sensed him rustle and give a small start, coming awake as she came to his bedside.

"I—oh, it's you. I wasn't expecting you tonight."

Sophie pulled the mosquito net aside and reached out to touch his face.

"You really are a man of honor, aren't you, James?"

James was silent for a second. "Yes. Yes, I am. You know that."

Sophie pulled off her robe and slipped into bed to lie on top of him in the moonlight. As James enfolded her in his arms she stared into his eyes.

"I need a man of honor tonight."

The Sugar Rebellion

Chapter Twelve
June 1796
Grenada

Fedon's meeting room was packed with people. Senior commanders and their immediate juniors from all over the island were present. Most of the junior commanders were standing and holding their drinks as nowhere was left for them to sit. A huge hand drawn map of St. George's and the area around it was spread on the table.

James was in the room at the start of the meeting. He had done as asked, making arrangements for food and weapons to be stockpiled in the three different locations Fedon had designated as forward supply depots for use when the men were finally gathered. James had arranged to stockpile the weapons first and perishable food as close as possible to the day it would be needed. The problem was some of the commanders still had no trust for him and weren't prepared to tell him when it was. James spread his arms wide in frustration as he finished speaking.

"I'm sorry, but you are asking the impossible. I can't make arrangements for perishable food to be delivered by a specific date if you aren't prepared to tell me what that date is. Julien, perhaps you should have someone else finish this part of the task."

Fedon was frustrated and nodded his head in agreement with James, but he knew he couldn't simply make an arbitrary decision on the matter at this stage.

The Sugar Rebellion

"James, thank you for your effort on this. I know you understand the problem. I must ask you to leave the room while we sort this out and make other decisions."

Once James was gone Fedon sighed. "Well?"

"Julien," said La Valette. "I know it frustrates you some of us still don't trust this man. I give him credit, he has done a good job of organizing our supply depots and making sure what we need is either there or about to be. He has made good choices for their locations, too. But I am volunteering a man to take care of the remaining details. Let us move on."

"Very good," said Fedon. "And the field cannons, Ventour? Have arrangements been made to bring them up?"

"Yes. For those of you concerned about it, we are fairly certain we have been successful in keeping knowledge of them from this man James. Also, the men are all now as proficient as they ever will be at using them. All that remains is to decide where to site them and how they will be used."

Fedon sighed once again. "The time is upon us to make a decision once and for all. I know everyone has thoughts, but we have been debating this for far too long. I am going to suggest we narrow this to the two best options that I happen to like. I think La Valette and Ventour both have plans that have merits for different reasons. And if we can't make up our minds, why don't we try to marry the two together? Take the best elements of each plan and discard those that aren't so good."

Both La Valette and Ventour slowly turned to

The Sugar Rebellion

look at each other as they considered the idea. As the inspiration took hold they began going back and forth over different possibilities. Thirty minutes later Fedon's suggestion proved the catalyst they needed and a plan was in place. The overall plan was for coordinated attacks on the entire front, with attempts to bring flanking actions into play at every opportunity. For maximum effect three of the mobile field cannon would be deployed in a spot they thought would be best to try luring the British out of their defenses. A squad of volunteers would make a demonstration before finally appearing to retreat in disorder. Once the British came after them a vicious cross fire from the cannons would decimate them. Another four of the pieces were concentrated in another location where they felt they would have most impact. The remainder was spread out across the broad front.

Fedon sat in silence contemplating the plan they had wrought and, after several moments, he realized they were waiting for the final word from him. They had assured him at least eight thousand men and possibly much more would be there for the attack and Fedon was reassured by the knowledge. But the number of field artillery pieces seemed woefully insufficient, with large gaps in their deployment against the many British defensive positions. Well, thought Fedon, they would soon find out if it was enough. He looked at the waiting faces and rose from his seat to give them a grim smile.

"The attack begins at dawn on the third morning from now," said Fedon, raising his glass.

The Sugar Rebellion

"To success."

The men echoed his toast and downed the remainder of their drinks. The meeting broke into myriad different conversations, as they knew this to be the signal it was over. Senior commanders began issuing a stream of orders to their men and several left the room to begin. Fedon remained long enough to answer a few questions before slipping away and returning to his office, where he sent a servant to find James. When he came in Fedon sat forward to lean on his desk and signaled for him to sit.

"James, I am sorry for this. Maybe you are a spy, maybe you are not, but as far as I am concerned you have been helpful to us. The problem is I can try to influence my commanders, but I cannot tell them what to think. Another man will come to see you and will ask for a briefing on what you have done to date. He will finish the job you began."

"Julien, I completely understand and it is not a problem."

"So now that the work you have been doing is ending, you are likely wondering what you are to do next, correct?"

"Actually, yes."

"I would like you to be with me when the time comes. I would like your experience to help guide me and tell me what I am seeing. Are you willing to do that?"

"Julien, I would like that very much."
***

With the estate a hive of buzzing activity in preparation for the assault the opportunity for

The Sugar Rebellion

Baptiste and James to meet without being noticed was far easier. The two men had kept their meetings limited and furtive after the death of Besson out of necessity. James knew the lack of reports would be worrying to Evan, but without a firm date he had little to report Evan would not already know. James knew the attack was coming soon and he wanted Baptiste to be safe. He was also certain his own escape would be easier if he didn't have to be concerned about Baptiste too, so as soon as they were sure they were alone he told Baptiste it was time for him to leave.

"Lieutenant?" said Baptiste. "With respect, I don't want to leave you here without help. I can take care of myself."

"I respect that, Baptiste, but I don't know when this is all going to happen, let alone what the outcome will be. So I'm going to make this an order. Commander Ross will be happy to have you on hand to question. He may have things he wants to know we are not aware of, so the time has come."

"Sir, I still don't like leaving you, but I will go tonight as you wish and hopefully the Commander will pick me up at the drop tomorrow. But you say you don't know when the attack is coming? It is the third morning from now. I overheard some of them talking about it."

James was surprised as Baptiste's face fell, as if a sudden realization had come to him.

"Sir," said Baptiste, his voice excited. "If you didn't know the date perhaps they have not told you of the field cannons they now have?"

"Cannons? Good God, no. I have been under

The Sugar Rebellion

suspicion. What do you know?"

"Not much else, sir. They only just got them recently. I don't believe they have many. I don't know what they plan to do with them. The French brought them on their last trip here."

"That settles it. Baptiste, you leave tonight. Commander Ross absolutely needs this information. Make up some story that you have a sister who is dying and you must go to her. Make up whatever you think will work. Just put someone else in charge and go. This place is so crazy busy right now no one will think twice."

"Sir, if I may? Why don't you come with me? Staying longer puts you more at risk with every day that passes."

James was silent for a moment before he responded. "It does, but this is my job. If I disappear they may think something is up and change their plans. I need to stay. Do not concern yourself for me."

"I understand, sir. Good luck."

James shook hands with Baptiste. Once again, he wondered if the reason he offered had made sense or whether it was all too transparent the real reason he was staying was Sophie.

As the two men disappeared from sight Sophie stepped out of the shadow she had remained in when she came upon them in time to see the handshake. Her small frown showing her puzzlement remained on her face for some time.

***

Evan brought Baptiste to the meeting with the General, the Governor, and Colonel Walter. The

The Sugar Rebellion

questions had come fast and the General in particular was relentless in drilling into as much detail as possible. When the questions finally dried up an hour later the General broke the ensuing silence as they digested what they had heard.

"Well, gentlemen, we have a date. Let's be on our guard in case something changes, but I don't think it will. Our forward observation posts have seen a lot of activity they normally don't see, so I believe this man has accurate information. That they have some field cannon is useful to know. Were I them I would try luring us out and putting the cannon to use. I will have to dream something up to counter that possibility. In any case, we are as ready as we are going to be for them. Commander Ross, I congratulate you and your men. Your reputation is well deserved."

Evan responded as the General rose to signal an end to the meeting.

"Thank you, sir. If there is anything we can do to help let us know."

"Actually, I may have a small role for the Navy to play. I will be in touch."

Evan saluted. "Very good, sir."

As he left with Baptiste in tow Evan's thoughts turned to James. On the surface the explanation for his decision to remain behind made sense, but Evan had a nagging feeling something more was happening. That he was likely involved with a woman on the rebel side complicated matters. Evan knew it was the one weakness James had, but he understood. He shared the weakness.

***

The Sugar Rebellion

That night the three of them made an effort to share dinner together, knowing it was unlikely another opportunity would present itself before the attack. The unspoken sense this could be the last time they did so hung in the air. The conversation was light, as the coming battle dominated everyone's thoughts and there was little else to say that had not already been said.

Sophie knew whether she would stay with one of the men this night and who it would be was the only immediate topic on the minds of the two men. She answered it as she turned to look at Fedon while she finished her dessert.

"Julien, I was thinking you might like some company looking at the stars tonight. Perhaps I could join you?"

"Yes, I would like that," said Fedon, giving her a slow smile, understanding her meaning. But he turned to James to play the proper host.

"James, would you like to join us for a cognac while we enjoy the stars?"

As Sophie anticipated, James appeared to have taken note she had not included him in her request to join Fedon.

"Thank you, but no, I am a little tired tonight," said James, wiping his lips with his napkin and rising from his chair. "Another fine meal, Julien. Thank you both for the wonderful company."

Sophie watched him bid them both good night and leave. She knew James was likely crushed, but she had little she could do to prevent it. Fedon reached over and put his hand on hers while pouring her a glass of cognac with the other. They both remained silent for several long seconds.

"I know you have chosen to stay and drink with me, but I confess I'm not sure what this means. I still fear I have lost you. I rue every day that I asked you to do what you did with this man and I understand why you have grown attached to him. To be fair I think he is as worthy of you as I. But the sad part is I don't know if I would change anything I have done. I am sorry if this has hurt you, though."

Sophie looked at Fedon, her face a mask. "Thank you for that, but you do not need to apologize. Everything I have done has been of my own free will. I don't know why I am cursed to be in love with two such deserving men, but I am. The problem is I am too weak to deal with it, although I know I must."

She paused a moment before gripping his hand and squeezing it for emphasis.

"The only thing I do know for certain is we should go enjoy the stars for a little bit and have our drinks. And after that, tonight I stay with you."

Fedon smiled and they both rose, heading for the verandah. As she followed him outside a small voice inside her asked whether now was the time to tell Fedon of her growing certainty James was a British spy. But even as the thought came she dismissed it, without being certain as to why. Somehow, it simply didn't seem important anymore.

***

"Etienne, I need your advice, my brother," said Sophie.

The two of them were alone at Sophie's request

The Sugar Rebellion

the next day. The harried look on his face showed the strain he was under, about to leave the estate to assume command of his portion of the front lines, but he saw the troubled look on his sister's face and made time for her.

"Sophie, I have but a little time. What is wrong?"

"I know, and I am sorry. I am troubled and I don't know what to do."

Sophie quickly told him of having fallen in love with the two men and of feeling torn, unable to make a decision. Her brother frowned at mention of James.

"Sophie, you know some believe he is a British spy. Personally, I am willing to keep an open mind about him and I am not at all certain he is trouble, but many others disagree with me."

"I know, Etienne. He may well be a spy, but I have come to know him and I believe him to be a good man. Equal in all respects to Julien, and this is my problem. How do I decide?"

"My dear sister, I am not sure what to tell you. I have had my own troubles with affairs of the heart and, if I have learned anything at all, it is answers never come easily."

Sophie bowed her head. "I know, Etienne, but you are my older brother. You are the one that kept me from harm and picked me up when I scraped my knees and cried when I was young. I need your wisdom."

He put his hands on her shoulders. "Sophie, we have started something important here we must see through to success. Julien is a fine man and I consider him my brother. I trust you when you say this man James is his equal, although I find it hard to believe, as Julien has done so much for us. But I think all you can do is listen to your heart and trust it in this matter. If you do that and you can remain true to what we have started here, then I think you will have found your answer. And now I simply must go, I have so much yet to do."

He gave her a hug for several long seconds before finally disengaging himself and leaving the room. Sophie called her thanks to him as he left and sat down as he closed the door. She remained sitting with her hands in her lap and staring into space for a long time.

***

The day before the battle was cloudless and the weather stayed this way as the sun went down, leaving the night sky lit with an endless array of stars. The night was so clear even features on the face of the quarter moon seemed visible, which gave an illusion the orb was larger than normal. Other than being grateful for the dim light to see by, however, no one was stopping to enjoy the scene.

The rough semi circle of the defenses around St. George's presented a host of choices to launch the main thrust of their attack, but some locations had distinct advantages. One with no advantages at all was within range of the cannons on Fort Frederick. The French had built this fort over twenty years before. The French had attacked from the landward side of St. George's to take the island from the British and on succeeding they promptly built Fort Frederick, with its guns facing inland, to

The Sugar Rebellion

prevent the British from doing the exact same thing. With its location almost due east of St. George's, this left a choice of either the northern or southern sectors of the semi circle to choose from. Because they wanted to reach the seat of power in Fort George as fast as possible the logical choice was the northern sector, which was closer than the southern positions defending the harbor.

James found little sleep and knew he was far from alone. All around him in the darkness men were on the move, heading for their assigned positions. He knew the dawn would not be far off. Before being assigned to work with Evan he had risen to greet the dawn in the ritual of standing to their weapons on warships every day for years. The custom was out of necessity, for one never knew if the morning light would reveal a foe nearby. This seemed different only in the fact he was not at sea.

Fedon and his commanders chose to establish their command post on the slope of a small mountain facing St. George's. The only one of Fedon's senior men with him was Etienne Ventour. The others were further in the field with the men, although they had left a few of their junior lieutenants with Fedon. James approved of their choice as he was aware of it from an earlier visit and the sweeping view the mountain afforded was perfect for their needs.

Sophie was standing beside her brother as they all clustered about Fedon. She had seemed distant from him since the night she remained behind with Fedon, but from what he could tell she seemed the same way with his rival. James sighed and knew all

The Sugar Rebellion

he could do was hope her decision would be to choose him.

Time seemed to crawl. Men fidgeted around James, moving about with restless energy for the sole purpose of finding release. James remained impassive, standing with arms folded and awaiting the dawn, as he was more used to what was happening. As the first hint of the transition brought by the coming light showed on the hills and mountains of the eastern skyline stillness finally fell over the watchers, knowing the wait was over.

In the half-light of the false dawn James struggled to make out where the rebel forces were located and whether they were ready. But as he looked to the southwest toward St. George's he saw something on the periphery of his vision that made him instantly turn his attention to it. His mouth fell open and he turned fast to stride over to where Julien was standing. The urgent tone in his voice interrupting Fedon brought everyone's attention to him.

"Julien, your men on the right flank are in grave danger. You need to get them to pull back and redeploy now!"

"What? Why?" said Fedon.

Fedon was unable to hide the look of naked alarm as James pointed out to sea. Anchored offshore and presenting her starboard side to the land was *HMS Haven*.

"Julien, I don't know if this is deliberate or not, but if they are even remotely awake on that ship, your men are within their line of fire and they will pay in blood. You see this small ridge over here?

The Sugar Rebellion

Their guns can reach that far. You do not want to watch what a broadside of grapeshot or canister from that ship can do."

"Can it be so bad?" said one of the junior field commanders. "It is only one ship."

"Trust me. Your men will be food for the scavenger birds if you do not act now."

"Why is the ship waiting there anyway?" said another of the junior commanders, wearing a look of suspicion. "I wonder if someone has warned them?"

"I can't imagine why they would anchor offshore when St. George's harbor is nearby, so I can only assume they are waiting for exactly what is happening right now," said James. "As for being warned, who knows? We all know the British are expecting an assault. It may be they decided to have this ship station herself in this spot every night as a precaution."

"I think you are a liar," said the commander, stepping closer to James and shoving him hard on his chest. As James fell backwards, struggling to stay on his feet, the man followed and tried throwing a punch.

Although he was caught off guard, James was a veteran of countless brawls. On regaining his balance he easily sidestepped the punch, hammering his own into his opponents midriff. The man gasped at the unexpected blow and doubled over, crumpling to the ground. As others came forward in support Fedon put a stop to it all.

"Enough! I am in charge here. If I see a problem I will deal with it, you fools," said Fedon,

The Sugar Rebellion

turning to one of the junior commanders. "Those are your commander's men on that flank. Send a fast runner to him at once to have him pull back and redeploy in support of La Valette."

A runner was quickly dispatched, but James was watching the eastern horizon and wasn't certain he would make it in time. The line of hills and mountains in the distance were tinged with glowing light and he knew the sun would break free in less than a minute. The rest of the people in the command post knew it too and they all fell silent, waiting for the dawn to break. As the rim of the sun finally crested the horizon the first crackle of sporadic small arms fire came in the distance at the location La Valette was leading the attack. James watched, sensing everyone seemed to let out a sigh of relief the wait was finally over.

The sound of weapons firing in La Valette's sector was the signal to the rest of the waiting rebel forces and the popping sounds of muskets firing became widespread and continuous. No one had deployed the field artillery yet and the ship was still silent, but James knew it wouldn't be long. The details of what was happening on the ground were impossible to see everywhere, but the first few minutes of the fighting appeared to be going as expected. The rebels were surging forward along the broad front while the British lines were holding.

The change came less than five minutes later, as with a flurry of sudden movement they saw the rebels pulling back along the right flank. A signal rocket flared into the sky on the British side of the lines and seconds later the warship responded.

The Sugar Rebellion

James was certain the massive broadside was an avalanche of grapeshot, judging from the damage done as it ripped into the disorganized and retreating rebel forces. The report of the guns echoed around the hills and several of the people in the command post put their hands up to cover their ears. Many had never heard anything as loud.

"Good God," said Fedon, shaken at the carnage on the ground. A huge swath of destruction was ripped through the men and numerous, unmoving bodies strewn haphazardly about could be seen.

"The survivors would do well to keep moving," said James, moving to stand beside Fedon. "There will be another broadside in less than three minutes, perhaps even only two."

Fedon remained silent, continuing to watch the scene unfold. James looked around and saw everyone else in the command post was intent on the scene before them, with no one else close enough to overhear anything he said to Fedon.

"Julien, there is something I feel I need to tell you. If things do not go well here, as I suspect may be the case, I want you to know I have a way to help you and Sophie get away. The two of you deserve my help. It is up to you whether to accept the offer."

Fedon was silent for several long seconds, still watching the battle, before he turned to look James in the eyes.

"Is that a confession, James?"

"I'll let you decide what it is, Julien."

"I see," said Fedon, nodding his head. "Did you know the ship was going to be there?"

"No, Julien, I did not. But now I see it, I am not

The Sugar Rebellion

surprised at the tactic they are using. To be honest, the possibility should have occurred to me."

Once again Fedon gave a brief nod. "Once again, I believe you. Thank you for your offer. I will give it thought if need be. I am not concerned for myself, but I would not wish to see harm come to Sophie. I think we both want to see that."

"Yes, we are agreed on that."

The two men continued to stare at each other in silence before Fedon offered his hand. James took it and they shook hands, but as they did the sound of field artillery coming into play at last drew their attention back to the battle.

In every location along the lines the small field cannons of the British were at last being unleashed in a cacophony of blasts coming at an alarming rate. Small puffs of smoke from the weapons told of their locations and with only a light breeze to blow it away a dirty, growing haze soon began drifting about the battlefield. Although they couldn't see what was happening further to the south and east around Fort Frederick, the distant pounding of field guns could be heard and a similar murky haze grew there too.

The warship made its presence felt with another three broadsides before finally falling silent, as another flare from the British lines signaled a halt to their action. James sighed, knowing what this would mean. From what he could see, Fedon's men had pulled back either far enough away or out of sight of the warship to escape its wrath. The British would not wait long to exploit the gap. An out of breath messenger came staggering into the

The Sugar Rebellion

command post, having left his mount at the base of the hill and run upwards to make his report. What remained of the men on the right flank was now positioned in the first of their fall back defensive lines, although there were gaps as some of these were exposed to the warship and there was little point in being decimated further. A number of the survivors were now supporting La Valette's attack as ordered.

Two relay messengers from the attacking forces to the south staggered into the command post only a minute apart. Both reported heavy resistance and losses, but the attack was still proceeding.

Despite the setback on the right flank, James knew the real action was in front of them where La Valette's men were sticking to their plan to lure the British out, but the ruse wasn't working. The British remained behind their lines, maneuvering the field guns they had as needed to fire at whatever targets presented. James frowned, realizing the British seemed to have more field guns than he had anticipated. The sector of the British lines La Valette was attacking had three different redoubts sited close enough to each other that in principle the flank of each could provide support for the other. However, the gap between the one in the middle and the one to the west was just a bit too large.

"They are not coming out after us. Why is it not working, James?"

Even as he spoke Etienne Ventour came to join them, a worried look on his face. He nodded agreement.

"It looks to me like the British have more field

The Sugar Rebellion

guns than anticipated," said James. "If so, there is little reason to come out until they can be assured of success. All they have to do is keep killing men until they believe you are sufficiently weakened. It's what I would do. Look, La Valette appears to be trying the strategy one more time."

As they watched a brave group of rebels tried skirting away from the killing zones the field guns had already established and rushing forward, but James knew it would soon be countered. The minutes passed, but nothing changed.

"Julien, if I may suggest?"

Fedon didn't turn to look at him, but he replied nonetheless. "Please do."

James pointed to the gap and explained its significance to Fedon and Ventour.

"If you have La Valette shift all of his field guns to target the flanks of those two redoubts and reduce them to rubble, you may be able to punch a hole through their lines. It will take the British time to counter it by shifting their field pieces, but if he pushes hard and fast they won't have time. Once you breach the line you can send enough men into the hole to turn the tide. But you need to do this now, before any more men are lost. Also, your men over on the right flank are going to face trouble soon. I think the British will be coming out to do exactly what I am proposing you do very soon. I suggest send a message to those men that they need to defend the fall back positions, no matter the cost. If the British flank La Valette, the game will be over."

Fedon was silent for only a second as he

The Sugar Rebellion

thought through what James was saying. He turned to Ventour and raised an eyebrow in question.

After taking his own moment to think, Ventour nodded agreement. "He is right, Julien. We must try it."

Stirring himself, Fedon called the men serving as messengers over and rapped out a series of orders to two of them. Ventour volunteered to join the man going to La Valette to help. Within seconds they were all on their way and Fedon came back over to where James was standing with arms folded, impassively watching the attack unfold.

"Thank you for that. Those are good suggestions and I agree with your analysis. If they cannot hold the flank and La Valette fails, it will be all over."

More long minutes passed before James pointed to the British lines on the right flank. A sudden flash of movement and color had appeared. Several men wearing the unmistakable, bright red Army uniforms stepped into the open. As they did the field weapons the British had shifted and brought forward in their sector to hammer new targets spoke as one. They couldn't see the impact, but the soldiers began moving forward the second the guns finished. What was of interest was the sheer number of soldiers still coming and, as he watched, James knew the rebel defenders would soon be hard pressed.

More time passed and the red coats slowly moved forward to establish a new forward perimeter. The British were paying for their advance, obvious from the number that fell and

The Sugar Rebellion

didn't get up as they went. The steady crackle of musket fire punctuated by the periodic full volley from the British companies grew.

More time passed before the fruit of James's suggestion was realized. The sudden concussion of several field artillery pieces firing as one brought their attention back to La Valette's sector. James estimated they had combined over half of their field pieces to concentrate on the spots he had pointed out. As he focused on the area a second round of shots ripped into the same redoubts to devastating effect. The guns continued to hammer the area around the position for almost ten minutes before a final fusillade echoed around the hills. As it died down a huge mass of rebel soldiers moved forward to take advantage.

"Come on, please," said Fedon, a worried look on his face.

The sheer number of rebel soldiers who fell as they advanced showed the British were responding and reinforcing the beleaguered section of their defenses. The huge mass of men was too large to stop, however. The wave of attackers crested the redoubts and carried on out of sight. Masses of red-coated soldiers stood to the defenses and mingled with the rebels. The heart of the battle became a heaving mass of struggling men in vicious hand-to-hand combat.

The minutes passed and more sweating messengers stumbled into the command post and this time they were calling for reinforcements. Two of the men were once again from the sectors to the south and west, and both reported heavy losses. The

The Sugar Rebellion

men were holding, but only barely, and the commanders sought help to turn the tide on the desperate stalemate they were facing.

The third messenger was from the commander on the right flank whose troops were decimated by the warship and his was not a message of stalemate. The man warned of imminent collapse if help was not sent right away.

Fedon looked at James, who knew he had to offer yet more advice. James was torn, knowing his words could result in even more British deaths. But he felt no choice was left and he knew men would die regardless of anything he said. He would tell Fedon no more than facts anyone could see.

"Julien, you have a thousand men in reserve exactly for reasons like this. I think you must use them to best effect. The men elsewhere are simply going to have to hold on and you should tell them so. I recommend send five hundred to shore up the right flank. The other five hundred send to La Valette. The battle is hottest there and I think he can use all the help he can get. If the fight is lost in either of these spots, everything will be lost."

Fedon didn't even nod his head this time. Rapping out a series of orders he committed to the course James outlined.

The morning wore on and the day grew warmer. James knew from experience the combatants on both sides would be growing tired and thirsty. Something would give, sooner or later.

The pall of haze hanging over the battlefield made it difficult to see, but when the end came it was all too plain. Having secured a tenuous hold on

The Sugar Rebellion

the redoubts they had assaulted, the momentum stalled when the rebels tried to carry on to the next one and punch further beyond the lines. By this time the British had committed their own reinforcements and with them came even more artillery. With great effort the British seized a small hill overlooking the main battlefield. After slashing enough trees and brush down to establish a clear field of fire on an outcrop, teams of sweating men had hauled three small field pieces into positions which could sweep the entire combat zone. Swaths of rebels assaulting the British lines were cut down every time one of the cannon fired.

At first it was only a few, but the few turned into a growing stream running from the fight and the commanders could not stop it. Many bravely carried on with the battle, but when the outcome became clear James knew one of the commanders must have sounded the retreat. As one, the rebels began falling back. Some units tried maintaining order in a fighting retreat, but over half of the men simply ran away.

Fedon hung his head in dismay even as more messengers came staggering into the command post. The news was universally bad. Fedon looked up at James, the obvious unspoken question framed on his face. James could only shake his head and remain silent. Fedon nodded and, with a sigh, began issuing orders for a general retreat to the agreed fall back position. Everyone knew where to go. They would meet at an abandoned plantation at the nearby foot of one of the highest peaks on Grenada, Mount Qua Qua, because the battle was lost.

The Sugar Rebellion

Chapter Thirteen
June 1796
Grenada

Stragglers made their way to the rendezvous from the battleground over the course of the rest of the day, coming in small groups of weary, disheartened men. A few larger groups maintained discipline enough to remain together. To those already there the constant stream of so many disheveled, tired, and footsore men shuffling into the camp was like a crushing weight on their spirits that only got heavier by the second.

Many bore small injuries from the shrapnel of the British weapons, with dirty, blood stained rags tied over their wounds. James knew the ones with far worse wounds were likely still lying where they fell and most would not survive the night. The remnants of the rebel army seemed pitifully few. The largest group to march into the camp toward the end of the day was led by Ventour and La Valette. James estimated the survivors numbered no more than two thousand men at most. From an attacking force of close to five times this number, it was a horrific loss. James suspected many ignored the order to retreat to Mount Qua Qua and simply went into hiding.

Ventour was uninjured, although he appeared weary to his core. La Valette was not so fortunate, limping into camp on the arm of Ventour. A vicious cut to his thigh was wrapped with a rag oozing blood. James doubted he would survive the wound.

The Sugar Rebellion

One of the junior commanders came after James the second he arrived in camp and saw him. The man had a knife and was about to drive it into James's back when Sophie shouted a warning. James couldn't see what was coming, but he ducked aside in time for the blow to miss. His attacker attempted a backhand slash and succeeded in grazing James's forearm, enough to draw blood. Angered, James stepped inside the man's guard and kicked him hard in the groin. The man screamed and dropped the knife, rolling into a ball of pain. Once again, Fedon appeared and shouted at everyone in sight to stop the fighting. The other men following their commander in support hesitated and stopped. With dark side looks at James they nodded to Fedon and backed away as they slowly complied.

After his outburst Julien went back to sitting on a chair on the verandah of the old plantation, wanting to be visible and receive reports as they came in. He remained there all day, ever since arriving at the rendezvous. James knew he was crushed by the defeat and was trying to keep a brave face for his men, but every so often he would slump forward, holding his head in his hands. Ventour came over to Julien after ensuring La Valette was given a place to lie down and made as comfortable as possible.

"Julien, I am sorry to tell you this," said Ventour. "The British had scouts following us. Their main forces did not come with them, but I fear it won't be long before they are on the move. It is almost dark and I doubt they will attack tonight.

The Sugar Rebellion

But come the morning, I fear they will be upon us at dawn. I may be wrong."

James came over to join them in time to hear Ventour. A bloodstained rag was now wrapped tight around his forearm where the knife had slashed him.

"You are not wrong," said James. "Julien, if they know where you are, they will not stop. They do not want you to regroup."

Julien lifted his head for a brief moment when Ventour started talking, but let it droop and kept it this way on hearing the news.

"I am so sorry, I have failed everyone. It is a disaster. I don't know what to do."

"Julien, we must be strong for the men," said Ventour.

"I know. I will try," said Julien, standing and turning away to receive yet another report from one of the junior commanders who had just arrived in camp.

Ventour and James stood looking at him for a moment before they turned to face each other. James motioned in silence to Ventour to join him out of earshot of Fedon and Ventour followed him. When certain no one else could hear them James spoke.

"I have a way to get both him and your sister away from here. I know of a small boat they can use to sail for Martinique or Guadeloupe. There is no guarantee the British will not catch them, but there is a good chance of success. I told him of it, but I fear he is crushed with this defeat. You are, of course, wondering why I am offering this and the

The Sugar Rebellion

answer is I like both of them. They are both good people and I would not have them end their days rotting in a British prison or swinging at the end of a rope."

Ventour kept his face a mask and remained silent for a long time, arms folded as he stood before James. But James saw the moment he made an inner decision and Ventour gave a small sigh as he responded.

"I see. And what of you?"

"I will obviously have to go also, to show them where it is. I will not be joining them on the journey. I can take care of myself."

Ventour nodded. "And if my sister chooses to stay with you, what will you do?"

"She has told you, I see. I have my doubts she will, but if she does I will ensure no harm comes to her and I will be the best I can be for her."

"Good enough, I believe you. So what now?"

"We need to quietly leave here, right now. We will have to walk through the night. If we wait for dawn it will be too late, because the British will be moving into position. There will be patrols everywhere. They are likely bringing the men up and building a plan even as we speak. I am not certain if Julien and your sister will agree to this, but if the suggestion comes from you I think it will carry more weight."

James paused a second before continuing. "You should know this is a small boat, but it could hold the three of you, if you desire to go with them."

"I will not leave my men," said Ventour. "But I thank you for the offer. I agree Julien and Sophie

The Sugar Rebellion

may be willing to do it if I push them. I will go talk to them now. And James, if that is your real name? You are, of course, a British spy, but my sister has high standards when it comes to men. I am sure at heart you are a good man, too. The two of them would not have befriended you were it otherwise. I wish we had met under other circumstances."

Ventour turned and went to find his sister, who was busy tending to some of the wounded men. He brought her back with him to join Fedon and James could see the three of them were soon engaged in an intense discussion. James was beginning to doubt Ventour would succeed, but five minutes later he turned to look directly at James and he nodded firmly once. James sighed with relief and went to join them for a moment.

"We need supplies," said James. "I will go deal with this. You wait here."

Thirty minutes later he returned from having raided the small supply of stores Fedon had secreted in the old plantation in the event they would be needed. The three small packs held enough basic food and flagons of water to see them through a few days. After ensuring Fedon had enough gold on him to see him settled on a new island, James signaled it was time to leave. The dim light of late evening was about to be replaced by full night, but once again stars and the moon were there to light their way. Ventour gave his sister a crushing hug before they parted. Sophie was so overcome with crying she could only whisper her love for her brother in his ear.

James led the way as the three of them slipped

The Sugar Rebellion

away unnoticed from the camp.
***

Ventour knew he could not rest now Julien was gone. La Valette was too badly wounded to help and none of the other senior commanders were left alive to help. Ventour called the remaining junior commanders to join him around a fire they had built. The men before him were disheveled and downcast. Ventour wished he had a better message for them as he began talking.

"I am speaking on behalf of Julien. He is not well. We all know the battle is lost and all that remains is how to deal with the aftermath. Each of us has a choice to make. The decision is to remain here and fight the British in the morning or to simply run away. If we stay they will kill you or, at the least, throw you in prison. If you run they will hunt us down. You may have a chance to survive, but I suspect they will treat every one of us as slaves, whether we were before this started or not. Because they see you as a slave, they will undoubtedly beat you severely. You will survive, but you will be a slave. You can try arguing the point and I suspect you may even be able to prove you were not a slave before this started, but I don't think they are going to be in a mood to listen. So does anyone disagree with anything I have said?"

Some of the men turned to look at each other, but no one spoke. Many simply nodded their heads, acknowledging their agreement with his words.

"With this as the choice I do not believe it right for us to make the decision for the men we command. My choice is to stay and fight. They will

The Sugar Rebellion

kill me, but I will die as a man and not a slave. I desire all of you to communicate this message to the men with us. You must also make your own personal decision as to what you will do. I strongly suggest to any who wish to run away they do so as soon as possible, for I fear the British will be upon us by morning. So please go do this now. Those of you choosing to remain with me come back here within thirty minutes."

The men rose as one from their seats around the fire and dispersed without speaking. For a time Ventour feared he would be left alone at the fire, but a gradual trickle of men returning to their seats grew. When no more men had returned for some time Ventour stood and was gratified to see the vast majority had come back.

"Thank you," said Ventour. "And the men?"

One of the commanders looked around and spoke up. "Perhaps one man in ten has left. The rest chose to remain with us."

"Very good. I have a plan."

***

Once again Ventour stood watching in the still dim, but growing light, waiting for the coming of the full dawn. He had always enjoyed hiking and had climbed the steep slopes of Mount Qua Qua many times in past, so he knew its paths well. Many of the men with him were also familiar with it and together they were determined to make the British pay for every step they took along those paths.

The men needed rest, so all of them were first given two hours to do so. On rising in the middle of the night the entire camp went on the move and

The Sugar Rebellion

began climbing the mountain. Each man carried what he could for food and water, along with whatever small arms and weapons they could find. They had little enough to fight with, but fight they would.

Ventour knew the British had established pickets around their camp in the night. His own guards had clashed with some of them, but the British had no intention of forcing the issue in the middle of the night. He knew the enemy might be surprised when daylight revealed an empty camp, but they would realize where they had gone soon enough.

Perched on a ledge a thousand feet up the mountain, Ventour had a commanding view of what the dawn revealed when it finally came. His heart fell when he saw how many red-coated men were gathered at the base of the mountain. He had hoped it would not be this bad, but it was. He could see light reflect off several telescopes the officers had brought with them as the lenses were trained on the mountain and he knew they could not hide. The British had brought field guns with them, too, enough to be a problem he had hoped not to face.

Ventour's hope faded as he could see soon enough there would be no escape from the guns. The British took their time building makeshift platforms and using whatever terrain features they could to elevate the weapons to a point the shots could be brought to bear higher up the mountain. They had no need to rush, knowing the rebels weren't going anywhere. Although the remaining rebels could hide behind rocks to escape a bombardment, the real purpose was to keep them pinned down while the British soldiers were climbing the mountain. Over an hour later the barrage finally began and, as it did, the first of the soldiers began picking their way up the paths and steep slopes.

Ventour sighed and turned to La Valette. His friend had rallied after resting and, although weakened, he had somehow found the sheer will power to drag himself up the mountain. On reaching the ledge he simply collapsed to rest where he lay. Ventour reached over and touched his shoulder.

"They are coming, my friend."

La Valette opened his eyes and looked at Ventour, reaching a hand out for help to stand. Ventour marveled at the sudden display of inner strength as his friend stood and took in the scene below them. More of the British field guns began pounding the slopes. Although most of the shots fell below their position, a few were high enough to make them the men around them duck for cover and cringe. Ventour knew the British would work hard to improve the range and their targeting.

The battle raged over the next four hours, without quarter asked or given by either side. By the time the soldiers were in range and the field guns had to stop, they had already accounted for the death of several rebels. Screaming rebel soldiers hurled rocks down the slopes at the masses of soldiers making their way up foot by foot and using every scrap of cover they could find. Musket fire crackled all over the slopes and men screamed as they were struck, lost their balance, and fell tumbling down the steep slopes. But the determined British were not to be denied as they continued winning the one on one fights everywhere.

When the end came four men in red coats had surrounded the first of the rebels to choose an alternative. Facing certain death, the rebel soldier decided to make it happen himself. Stepping to the nearby edge of the ridge he was on, he simply walked out into empty space. Ventour watched as the man fell straight down almost two hundred feet before striking the rocks and tumbling down the slope. Within a minute more of the rebels did the same and soon there were too many flinging themselves down the slopes to count.

Having run out of ammunition and left with only a machete to fight with, Ventour looked around and saw the red-coated solders were now closing in on the two of them. He turned with a grim face and looked at La Valette.

"It is over, my brother," said Ventour, putting his hand on La Valette's shoulder.

La Valette did the same. "It is. We tried, Etienne. But we will die for a noble cause and we will die as free men."

Ventour nodded and with their arms still on each other's shoulders the two men flung themselves down the mountain.

***

All three of them were tired and on edge by the time dawn broke. James made them move with caution throughout the night, desperate to avoid danger while ensuring they remained on the course he set for them. He remained ten paces in the lead

The Sugar Rebellion

the whole time, staying alert for British patrols. Three times they encountered what he was certain were indeed patrols and they were forced to remain silent in hiding until they passed. They also came across a patrol camped right on their path for the night, forcing them to backtrack a considerable distance. As dawn broke James was able to get a clearer picture of where they were and as his certainty grew he knew he had succeeded, as they were close to where the boat was hidden. He prayed it was still there.

The problem was the location where the boat was concealed relied on a cliff to hide the small cove behind it. What they had not realized when they chose the location was a road not visible from the water ran along the shoreline directly behind it. This meant they had to expose themselves on the road itself in order to climb around the rock face and down the slope to the water where the boat was. James looked up and down the road, but could see nothing either way. He frowned, but they had no way around it. They would have to risk being on the road for at least three or four minutes before they could get out of sight. Julien and Sophie both looked awful from lack of sleep, but James tried to rally them.

"The boat is just over there, behind that rock face. We are almost there. We must risk the road, though. Let's go, as fast as we can, please."

Both gave him tired smiles, but they nodded agreement. They were almost at the point James had decided to duck into the roadside brush to fight their way down to the water when a distant, faint cry came from behind them. James groaned as he turned and saw a flash of red in the distance at the far end of the road.

James swore and turned to his two companions. "Run for it!"

They followed him as he ducked into the brush at full speed, being forced to slow down within seconds for fear of tripping and landing on his face. They picked their way steadily downhill and around the rock face as James stayed alert looking for the spot. Although it was several weeks since he was there last, James recognized some of the terrain features he had memorized and he knew he was in the right place.

"Thank heaven it is still here," said James, relieved when he finally saw the mast still where it should be, masked by the surrounding trees.

As they reached the boat James threw his pack into it, before grabbing the packs his companions wore off their backs and doing the same with these. He signaled for Julien to help him raise the sails and soon the boat was rocking with the wind and straining against the lines tethering it. James jumped off to the shore and began untying the lines. When he had only one left the faint sound of several voices came in the distance and James knew the patrol had found their way to the spot they had entered the trees. He turned to face Sophie, who was standing there looking at him.

For a long moment they looked at each other and for one brief second of the moment James dared to let a tiny flame of hope flare in his heart, but she snuffed it out.

The Sugar Rebellion

"I have been blessed to find not one, but two men to love. I must choose, though, and I choose to go with Julien. I love you, but I could not live in a British world and be something I am not."

She flung herself into his arms and gave him one final, torrid kiss before turning and jumping into the boat. James did not hesitate as he untied the final line and gave the boat a hard shove to send it into the channel. Fedon worked the tiller to catch the wind with the sails and in seconds they were on their way. James could not bring himself to wave goodbye, but he remained standing there looking out to sea. Fedon was already away from the confines of the small cove and well on his way in open water by the time the patrol found James, still standing in silence on the shore. The sergeant leading the patrol strode to the fore as James raised his arms in surrender.

"What is going on here? Who are those people in that boat?"

"Rebels. They are escaping. I am British Royal Navy. My name is Lieutenant James Wilton."

The Sergeant eyed him with suspicion. "Navy? Good Christ, I don't believe you. That has to be the biggest tale of shit I've heard in a long time and I've heard plenty. Wilkins, try a shot at that boat—no, never mind, he has to be out of range now. Well, at least we have this bastard."

"I tell you, I am a Navy officer. They had me at gunpoint and I couldn't stop them from escaping."

The Sergeant, a craggy faced veteran, eyed James with suspicion.

"And why exactly did they have you in the first

The Sugar Rebellion

place?"

"I was on a secret mission from Governor Mackenzie. The boat was my means to escape if I had to. They were going to kill me if I didn't find a way to help them escape. So here I am."

The Sergeant stared hard at James, before finally shaking his head.

"I still think you are a liar, but we can let them sort you out in St. George's. Keep an eye on him and let's get out of here."

***

Colonel Walter was tired and more than ready for his day to end with a glass of brandy, but yet another of his Lieutenants appeared at his door hoping for attention. The General had assigned Colonel Walter the impossible task of ensuring a defensive perimeter was maintained in case the rebels had held back an unknown force to attack the undefended rear. He was also given the job of sending patrols out to areas further afield from the combat zones to scout for trouble and deal with fleeing rebels. As a result his day became an endless stream of decisions over deployment of patrols and listening to reports coming in from the field to Fort George as he tried to keep a finger on the pulse of what was happening. The Lieutenant standing patiently at attention in front of the Colonel's desk was unwelcome, but he knew he had to deal with him.

"Right, then, what is it now?" said the Colonel, sighing aloud. "Out with it."

"Sir, one of the patrols along the western coast road has just returned. They came across something unusual."

"Well? Go on."

"Sir, they found a black fellow who claims to be a Royal Navy officer named Lieutenant James Wilton. His story is he was on some secret mission for the Governor. He was on shore watching a small sailboat leave with two other people on board. He claims they were rebels holding him at gunpoint and he was forced to show them where his boat was hidden or they would kill him. The Sergeant that found him doesn't believe a word of it. This Lieutenant was in fact armed with not one, but two knives strapped to his body. When the patrol first spotted the three of them they all ran for it. This Lieutenant, if that is really what he is, had opportunity to escape in a different direction at this point. I have to agree with the Sergeant, something is odd here."

Colonel Walter scowled as he thought about it. Too many elements in what he had heard didn't add up and he didn't like it.

"I agree with you. As it happens, I am aware of—a mission involving this man, but something does seem odd here. Where is he now?"

"Sir, we have him on his own in a holding cell below. If he is indeed an officer I can go release him at once."

"No, this doesn't feel right. If he has done something suspicious better to let his commanding officer sort him out. Leave him where he is and I will send a message to Commander Ross about it. Send my clerk in on your way out."

"Thank you, sir," said the Lieutenant as he

saluted and left.

***

The one advantage the prison held was the temperature, which was pleasantly cool. Being dug into the bedrock below Fort George meant the heat of a warm June day in Grenada had no way to penetrate to the cells. The air was stifling, as the only way for it to get in were a number of windows cut into the walls of the jail near the ceiling. Heavy metal bars cemented into place to block the windows discouraged any thought of escape by them. That they were almost twenty feet above the floor was also an impediment.

James grew discouraged as the night wore on, resigning himself to spending the whole night there and possibly longer. He had done all he could to request a message be sent to Evan, but his jailers weren't interested in what a man under suspicion wanted. He was tired and all he wanted was to get out of his grubby, sweat stained clothes to clean up, but it was not to be.

James had seen far worse jails, though. This one was relatively clean compared to others of his experience. The pails provided for prisoner excrement radiated the usual disgusting stench, but James was in a cell on his own with walls along either side, so it was bearable. From what he had seen when they brought him in the other cells were packed with prisoners, so it was something at least they kept him on his own. With little else to do James lay on the sleeping pallet and tried to go to sleep.

He had lain awake for a long time, though.

The Sugar Rebellion

With Sophie now gone from his life the same emptiness in his heart he had felt years before when Manon Shannon was murdered reappeared full force. He had somehow found two women he wanted to share his life with and lost them both. Where or even if he would find a third was a crushing thought. When sleep finally came was fitful.

He knew it was morning as the light slowly grew in the windows and became steadily brighter. With nothing else to do he willed himself to stay asleep, but after an hour it was impossible. In the cells around him other prisoners were awake and stirring, talking and making too much noise. He got up and, after relieving himself in the pail, he went back to sit on the bed and wait. He knew at the least they would bring food for the prisoners, bringing a welcome break from his thoughts.

The sound of a door opening came from where James knew the entrance to the jail was and he assumed they were coming at last to feed the prisoners. The sound of boots on the stone floor came closer and as James looked up he saw Evan appear on the other side of the bars with a jailer in tow. The jailer pulled out a ring of keys and after selecting one he fitted it into the lock and opened the door. Evan flung the door open and looked at James.

"Let's go," said Evan, standing stiff beside the jailer as he jerked a thumb in the direction of the door. "We'll talk outside."

James was shocked, having never seen Evan this angry. James knew the subtle signs of Evan's

The Sugar Rebellion

wrath, having seen it directed at other people before. Wondering if he was in for a major dressing down, he followed Evan out of the jail and outside into the light. When they got to the inner courtyard of the Fort Evan looked around and signaled to James to follow him to a spot where they could talk without being heard by others. James could stand it no longer and forestalled Evan by speaking first.

"Sir, I am sorry if I have failed you somehow. I—"

"Failed me?" said Evan, with his eyes bulging wide. "Good God, no, no, no. Yes, I am seriously pissed off, as I expect is obvious, but it is not at you. Far from it. It's that son of a bitch Colonel Walter I am angry with. I only got word about this an hour ago. When I found out how long they've had you in there I went straight to his office and had it out with him. I expect the entire Fort knows we had a shouting match. I swear to God, I came within an inch of calling the bastard out for this. I told him if he wanted to learn out how well a one armed sailor wields a sword he was welcome to find out. And then I came straight here. Bloody arsehole."

"They didn't tell you last night? I wondered what the hell was going on."

Evan took a deep breath, visibly trying to calm down before he continued.

"The story is they were suspicious of what you told them. He decided to let me sort it out, but instead of freeing you and sending you off with orders to find me, as he should have, he instead passes a message to his clerk to track me down. Well, his clerk is as useless a fool as his master and

The Sugar Rebellion

I didn't get the message till now. My God, if I ever found reason to throw an Army officer into the hold of the *Alice* and leave him there to rot, the shit flying over it would be endless. I don't know what this idiot was thinking."

"I am sorry to be the cause of this. They told you what I told them?"

"They did. They told me why they were suspicious, too. You didn't try to escape when you had a chance and you were still armed. So what did happen?"

"Well, I suppose they are right to be suspicious. Evan, you may well want to throw me in jail. The real story is I helped Fedon and his woman escape in the boat we left hidden for me."

"Helped them escape? Why?"

"I spent a lot of time with him and, I know this may sound crazy, but I liked him. Yes, it was my job to bring him to account, but I am certain he will make himself pay inside for the rest of his life for what has happened. He was a good man forced into a role I don't think he wanted to have, but he took it on because he believed freeing the people was a worthy cause. God knows we have encountered more than our share of people all too willing to say one thing and do something completely different at the expense of others, but I believe this man really intended to do what he said he would. I was skeptical at first, but I came to believe in him. He was a man of integrity and, I think, honor."

"Honor, you say. Truly?"

"Honor. I do not use the word lightly."

Evan stared at James for a few long moments

The Sugar Rebellion

before speaking again.

"The troops thought they saw a woman with the two of you. Alice tells me the spy they sent into St. George's was named Sophie. Is this the woman that left with him?"

"Yes."

"Alice also tells me she thinks you and this woman got to know each other rather well. Not sure how she knows that, but I don't question my wife when it comes to her intuition. Is she right?"

"Yes," said James, pausing for a brief second. "She was like Manon, Evan. I couldn't help it."

Evan nodded. "I see. And she chose to leave with this Fedon. I'm sorry, James. You deserve better."

James was silent, knowing he had nothing else he could say or would need to. Evan took a deep breath and spoke again.

"You have the rest of the day off. Go back to the ship, get yourself cleaned up, and get fed. Pour yourself a large drink. I would like to hear more of these people and what happened. I will invite Baptiste and Alice to join us for dinner and you can tell your story. After all this, we deserve a nice dinner. Tomorrow we will sail for home with the morning tide."

James saluted and turned to go, but Evan stopped him. Evan put his hand on James's shoulder and smiled

"This is a job well done, Lieutenant."

***

Governor Mackenzie poured a small glass of wine each for Evan and himself before speaking.

The Sugar Rebellion

The two men were alone in the Governor's office.

"I am sorry to hear what happened with Lieutenant Wilton, Commander. If I had known I would certainly have done something to free him. The Colonel is obviously a complete buffoon. The General was not happy to hear of it either."

"The General already knows, sir?"

"Oh, yes. My boy, *everyone* knew of it. I must say, I wouldn't want to be on the wrong side of you when you are in a bad mood," said the Governor with a chuckle. "I had long since made my thoughts known about the man to the General. This incident just lends weight to it. I daresay the Colonel will be enduring another unpleasant conversation when the General has a free moment."

"I see. Well, so you know, I have debriefed the Lieutenant and I am satisfied his conduct was beyond reproach."

"Commander Ross, I never had any doubt. I will be filing a report to both my superiors and yours commending the efforts of you and your people in the highest possible terms. The General has also assured me he will be doing the same. I will ensure the First Lord of the Navy knows of your efforts and our gratitude as well."

"Thank you, Governor. I shall make certain my people know."

Draining his glass, Evan stood up and shook hands with the Governor.

"We will be leaving with the tide first thing tomorrow, sir. I like Grenada, but Antigua has become my home. It will be good to be back."

The Sugar Rebellion

The End

Author Notes

Far better authors than my humble self have suggested prostitution is likely the oldest profession in the world, followed closely by people making a career of spying on others. I expect there are few out there who will disagree with this premise. I like to think I am the first to suggest there is a third occupation deserving to be included in this mix, though, that of enslaving other people for the purpose of personal gain. The enslavement of Africans brought to the new world of the Americas is only the most recent significant example. The enormous scale of the slave trade and the vast profits made from enslaving Africans stand out, but the practice of making other humans into slaves has been around for centuries.

The common denominators with all three occupations are large sums of money, plenty of greed, and power over others, which is perhaps why slavery continues to exist in today's world. They may not be prostitutes, slave owners, or spies in the exact same way as in past centuries, but I submit all three occupations exist to varying degrees in today's world. With this said I expect you may be thinking I am a cynic about the future of humans, but in truth I am an optimist. Men and women of honor are out there, too, just as they were in the world of 1796.

As always, I tried to remain true to the historical framework of the story while working my

The Sugar Rebellion

fictional characters into it and every effort was made to ensure I have my facts straight. This proved a bit more of a challenge with this particular story because there is relatively little about these events in the history books and references available to me. Some of the references conflict, which makes it rather difficult to gain a clear picture of the people and events. But if there are any major elements in this story that do not align with the reality of what happened, any fault will still be mine.

Little known Fedon's Rebellion was real, as are most of the basic elements and events in this book. Besson, La Valette, and Ventour were all real supporters of Fedon, although everything about them beyond the fact they did not have military backgrounds has come from my imagination. Governor Mackenzie was real, but he was replaced before the end of 1795 and for simplicity I kept him to the end. Victor Hugues was indeed based out of Guadeloupe and making the British merchant shippers lives miserable with his privateers, as well as having an active hand in St. Domingue.

Governor Ninian Home was also real, as was his capture. He was hung along with the other forty-seven captives, although whether he was forced to watch them all die first is unknown. I would not be surprised if it did happen this way, as it seems the French mulattos leading the rebellion particularly disliked him. His murder was sparked by the death of Julien Fedon's brother at the hands of the British.

Julien Fedon was real. He was married, but for the purpose of injecting a little romance into this narrative I made him single and part of the love

The Sugar Rebellion

triangle with my two fictional characters. His ultimate fate is unknown, but the popular theory is he escaped in a canoe and drowned. His rebellion, of course, suffered the same fate as that of my story. This is really no surprise as the leaders of the rebellion were plantation owners and businessmen, not professionally trained soldiers.

General Abercrombie and his well-trained men were real, although some historical references suggest he brought far more men to Grenada than I have portrayed. Other references suggest the British may have been more aggressive in launching raids beyond their lines than I have them doing. The final confrontation was in fact on the steep slopes of Mount Qua Qua, where many of the rebels did fling themselves to their death.

What I found compelling about these events when I read about them in the history books was the contrast between this situation and what was happening in St. Domingue, or Haiti, as the country is known today. The first slave revolution occurred there and Fedon cited it as inspiration to make Grenada a black republic, just like St. Domingue. The difference is St. Domingue, as you will learn in the next book in this series, was a total quagmire of several competing interests.

Grenada, as near as I can tell, was much more straightforward. This actually appears to have been a locally led uprising with relatively minimal direct outside influence. The principle of freedom for all citizens, as espoused by some of the French revolutionaries of the period, seems to have been the ultimate goal. Ninian Home designed policies

The Sugar Rebellion

intended to drive everyone with any hint of French blood in them off the island. This persecution combined with the idea of freedom for all spurred the desire to act.

Having said that, I think it reasonable to question whether the local free mulattos like Fedon were truly serious about ending the institution of slavery or whether the French on Guadeloupe were in truth seeking this goal, too. I'm sure the French in Guadeloupe were all too happy to have a local uprising making British lives miserable, but they had far bigger issues at hand with St. Domingue and it seems to me their support was about as tepid as portrayed in the book. In St. Domingue, it would definitely be valid to question what French leaders really thought, along with what the 'gens de coleur' or 'men of color' mulatto slave owners wanted. I scratch my head at the mental gyrations necessary for any free person of color to justify ownership of black slaves, while at the same time supporting the concept of freedom for all.

I may be wrong in my assessment of all of this, but I like to think most of the rebellion's leaders meant what they were saying. The history books suggest over half of the 28,000 slaves on Grenada believed in the rebellion and joined the fight to become citizens. This must have been a hard, hard decision on their part, for many of them would have known no other life than that of a slave. Of those joining the rebellion, the estimate is over 7,000 died for it.

The fight against persecution and the desire to bring freedom for all was the inspiration to portray

The Sugar Rebellion

Fedon as a man of honor and principle. Most of the references I found led me in this direction, but I did find hints of another man, one that revealed a leader who was the most bloodthirsty of the lot. Perhaps the character of the real Julien Fedon was somewhere in between.

Honor was not a concept confined to the military or the upper classes in many societies, and it has been around for centuries, like slavery. We don't talk much about honor in today's world, perhaps because it somehow seems an old fashioned concept. That it does still exist and we maybe call it other names is a good thing. We need people with honor in this world, more than ever before, and I for one have no problem calling it what it is.

The fifth book in this series, *The Sugar Inferno*, is set in St. Domingue, where nothing will be as clear or simple as this. Our French spies, Montdenoix and Linger, will be back to make Evan's life more complicated than he wants.

The bad news, for anyone who is enjoying this series, is there will be only one more book after *The Sugar Inferno*. As much as I continue to love writing these books, one has to know when to fold the tent and move on to somewhere or something different. I have other projects percolating in my mind and the first tentative steps to make them reality are taking shape on my computer screen.

The good news is this series is not done with Horatio Nelson yet. For those of you Nelson fans out there wondering whether I was ever going to bring him back into the picture, fear not. If you are at all familiar with his history, you can without doubt put it all together as to how he will reappear as a major character in the sixth and final book of this series. If you aren't familiar with him, then please trust me on one point. When he does reappear, no one should be surprised to find the action is hot, furious, and non-stop. With Horatio Nelson in the story, how could it be otherwise?

I do hope you have enjoyed *The Sugar Rebellion*. Please watch for *The Sugar Inferno* to appear, coming soon.

Made in the USA
Columbia, SC
23 May 2018